The Prototype

A Novel by
Sam Mitani

Published by Waldorf Publishing
2140 Hall Johnson Road
#102-345
Grapevine, Texas 76051
www.WaldorfPublishing.com

The Prototype
It was never meant to exist,
But now the world's fate
Depended on its survival

ISBN: 978-1-64136-976-3
Library of Congress Control Number: 2018933200

prototype, noun, \ˈprō-tə-ˌtīp\
— a first full-scale and usually functional example that is used as a model for what comes later.

Chapter 1

The shiny black Jaguar XF came seemingly out of no-where. Cruising in the fast lane at an even seventy-five miles per hour, Stockton Clay noticed the oversize British luxury sedan just in time, as it cut across two traffic lanes, heading straight for his beloved Nismo 370Z.

Clay leaned on the horn, swerved his Z into the car-pool lane and, at the same time, slammed the brakes, letting the Jag cut right in front of him, missing his car's front bumper by inches. Once he straightened his car out, Clay moved it back into the fast lane and got back on the gas pedal, pulling up beside the Jaguar. He gave the driver as hard a stare as his twenty-five-year-old baby face could muster, but he wasn't sure if his anger was effectively conveyed through the XF's tinted passenger-side window. Then the window slowly lowered, and from within the darkened interior, the long barrel of a revolver emerged.

Instinctively, Clay got back on the brakes, invoking the Nissan's anti-lock braking system, letting the Jag shoot forward. The day was still young, and the U.S. 101 freeway was relatively empty, dotted with a few compact pickups and mid-size sedans, so he yanked hard on the steering wheel, forcing his car across the width of the freeway until it danced on the outside edge of the slow lane. After grabbing the next gear on the six-speed manual transmission, Clay mashed the throttle, unleashing all of the Nismo's three-hundred-and-fifty horsepower onto the rough tarmac.

The gun could be a fake, he thought, but because drive-by shootings were all too common in the Los Angeles area, he wasn't about to take any chances. Clay took the first exit onto Ventura Blvd. and glanced into his rearview mirror. The Jag was following him. *Shit.*

Clay sped up and took a left onto Topanga Canyon Blvd. When he checked his rearview mirror again, he saw that the XF had made the same turn, running a red light in the process. A chill ran up his spine. Reaching for his smart phone from the passenger seat, Clay changed lanes with one hand on the wheel, and with the other, punched nine, one, one on the phone's touchscreen.

"Nine-One-One," a female voice answered. "What is your emergency?"

"There's a guy chasing me. I have no idea who it is, but I think he's got a serious case of road rage. And, he has a gun," Clay said.

"Please state your location," the operator said calmly.

"I'm heading south on Topanga Canyon Blvd., near the 101."

"Can you describe the car chasing you?"

"Yeah, it looks like a brand-new Jaguar XF, no plates, and he's catching up. I'm in a silver Nismo 370Z."

"Okay, don't hang up. I'll get the police to your location," the operator said.

After tossing the smart phone back on the passenger seat, Clay decided to outrun his pursuer. A few cars occupied the four-lane side street, leaving plenty of space for maneuvering. As he worked the gearbox and steering wheel, a late-model Dodge Charger approached at high speed in the opposite lane with its headlights flashing. Clay kept his right foot to the floor, but then the Charger changed its heading and drove into his lane.

Clay steered his car out of the way, as the Charger sped right past him, before screeching to a stop, blocking the path of the pursuing Jaguar.

The XF did a one-eighty, coming to a halt just short of hitting the black Dodge sedan. Clay was tempted to stop and see the aftermath of the near head-on collision, but he thought better of it and kept on going, taking the first corner he came upon and quickly making his way back onto the freeway.

Once clear of the danger, he reached for the cell phone in the passenger seat. "Are you still there?" he asked into the handset.

"Yes, we're sending someone out there now," the operator said.

"No need, one of your unmarked police cars saved the day. I didn't realize that they were painted matte black. And, thank you for the quick response."

"Sir, none of the law enforcement agencies report they have a vehicle in the area. Are you sure it was a police car?"

"I don't know. Well, whoever it was just saved my neck back there. Thanks for your assistance." Clay abruptly ended the call. If some kind of gang war was going down, he didn't want to be involved in any way. It was the first time a real gun had been pointed at him, and the thought of possibly being shot horrified him, but at the same time, the notion of escaping death gave him a rush that he had never before experienced.

He recalled a quote from Winston Churchill that he had once read online: "Nothing in life is so exhilarating than being shot at with no result." Little did Clay know then that it would be a sensation that he would soon become accustomed to.

Chapter 2

With old-school punk rock band Agent Orange blaring on his custom audio system, Clay pulled up to the Automobile Digest magazine offices with his nerves relatively calmed. This place was home for him as he spent nearly all his waking hours here. The three-story glass-and-concrete building was perched on a small hilltop in the ritzy neighborhood of Malibu, California, about a mile from the ocean. Built in the nineteen sixties to specifically serve the purposes of an automobile publication, it was the ideal location for a car magazine, as the Pacific Ocean sparkled in a majestic blue hue on one side and a series of twisty canyon roads decorated the other. Automobile Digest's editors had immediate access to a variety of the area's winding roads to evaluate their test cars, and the photographers never had to stray far to get the perfect shot. And the Malibu zip code gave the publication a high level of pedigree.

As was the custom, Clay entered through the front doors at 8:30 a.m. sharp, before most of the other staffers sauntered in. He made a quick greeting to the security guard and took the elevator to the second floor where he stopped at the vending machine for his usual can of Red Bull before heading into his office—a small square room he shared with another employee, the most junior member of the staff, Peter Lee, who was not at his desk.

Clay sighed when he saw his own workstation, cluttered with enough paper and empty Red Bull cans to completely hide the desk's wooden surface. Lee's, on the other hand, was impeccably neat, graced with only an Apple laptop and a wireless speakerphone. Tidiness was never one of Clay's strong suits, and his attire said as much—he almost always wore faded Levi jeans and a wrinkled polo shirt that fit loosely on his lean five-foot, ten-inch body, which he kept in shape with daily exercise. His cheeks were usually covered with uneven patches of stubble and his black hair was always unkempt. Because of his somewhat grubby appearance, no one really noticed his large hazel eyes, milk-tea complexion, and reasonably handsome face.

As he sat in his chair and powered up his computer, Craig Riley, one of a few people he considered a close friend, walked up to the doorway pushing his mail cart. "You look pale, bro, something wrong?" Riley asked as he leaned against the door frame.

"You won't believe this, but some road rage guy pulled a gun on me on the way into work today. I barely got away," Clay said as he tapped in his password on the keyboard.

"Holy shit. What did you do to piss him off?"

Clay shrugged. "Nothing, at least not that I know of."

Riley reached into his cart and pulled out a shiny gold envelope. "Well, this may cheer you up. It came for you via special delivery. Looks pretty important because it's like the fanciest envelope I've ever seen, and you're the only one who got one."

Taking the piece of mail from Riley, Clay looked at the oversized envelope and saw his name handwritten on it in exquisite calligraphy; the return address at the top left corner read Kamita Motors. He carefully opened the package using a letter opener and pulled out a single card. On it were the words:

Kamita Motors, Ltd. is pleased to invite Stockton Clay to be part of an historic event on September 20, personally hosted by our President and CEO, Tetsuro Kanda.

RSVP to the Kamita Motors Public Relations Staff to organize your travel.

He held his breath and read it again. "This event is at the end of this week. You sure no one else got one?" he asked.

"Just you bro. All the mail goes through me here, you know that."

Clay reread the contents on the card a third time. "But I'm low-man on the totem pole. Why did I get this?"

"Don't ask me. By the way, some of my mechanic friends are throwing a small party downtown next weekend. You should come," Craig said as he tossed a couple of envelopes on Lee's desk, none of them golden.

"Nah, I won't know anyone there, and I'll just end up standing in a corner looking stupid…like I always do."

"There'll be a few cute girls there. You really should come and just hang out."

Clay shook his head. "Thanks, but no thanks."

"You really need to get out and break out of your shell. Will you be on Combat Shooter tonight?"

"For sure."

"Then I'll see you online, and be prepared to get schooled." Craig turned around and pushed his mail cart to the next office.

Clay held up the invitation card and examined it under

the fluorescent ceiling light. He knew full well of Kamita's reputation for spending gobs of money on its media guests—flying them first-class to exotic destinations, putting them up in five-star hotels, hiring the best chefs in the world to prepare the most scrumptious cuisine, and sending each one of them home with a generous "press gift." And these events often included a private performance by a well-known musician or band. Clay heard that at the last Kamita press junket, held at the Ritz-Carlton in Half Moon Bay located just outside of San Francisco, the company's public relations department handed out Apple MacBooks to its five dozen media guests. Of course, they were specially-made with the Kamita logo etched into them, and you had the option of having Bruce Springsteen, the celebrity performer on that particular event, sign the cover. Automobile Digest had a policy that forbade its editors to accept any gift that was too extravagant, which usually meant anything worth more than a hundred bucks. Clay had no problem with that rule, even though he thought having an Apple MacBook signed by the Boss would have been really cool.

He delicately rubbed the edges of the invitation card, feeling the high quality of the paper. His hands shook at the thought of what the small square piece of cardboard repre-sented: it was the break he had long been waiting for; the as-signment that would put him on the map. He had just scored the Golden Ticket to the Chocolate Factory.

Chapter 3

The short walk down the hall to the editor-in chief's office was like running a gauntlet into the depths of the inferno. Clay approached the extra-large corner office slowly. Jeremy Simmons, who had taken the editor-in-chief position only a half-year ago, already had his favorites on staff, and Clay was sure he wasn't one of them for he was rarely included in impromptu staff meetings that Simmons occasionally held during lunchtime nor was he ever assigned to any international press trips. Clay had all but given up climbing the editorial ladder at Automobile Digest, but the letter he held gave him new hope.

After weeks of self-doubt and slight fits of depression, the small, shiny envelope put Clay spiritually back on track. For as long as he could remember, he wanted nothing more than to be accepted and admired by others. He had been abandoned by his biological parents at birth, discarded like an unwanted piece of garbage for someone else to deal with. Despite being adopted by loving parents, he never felt he belonged with them, or with anyone else for that matter. His inherently low sense of self-worth produced in him a strong desire to prove himself to be worthy of this world, to be someone whose accomplishments made a difference. However, he found, as most everyone does, that the road to enlightenment is filled with obstacles, and a stroke of bad luck could set a person back indefinitely. In the past year, he had two of them: one was when Simmons was named the editor-in-chief; the other was when Peter Lee was hired.

Still, Clay was never one to give up easily. And on top of that, there was something inside of him encouraging him to stay the course, at least until they showed him out the door.

Clay walked up to the executive secretary, Lorraine, seated outside the editor-in-chief's office. Her graying short hairdo, wrinkled cheeks and blouse with flower printing made her seem like she was on her way to Woodstock fifty years late. She looked at Clay over her reading glasses with a half spaced out look and smiled. "He's in there with Peter. He left the door open, so I don't think it's anything important. Go on in."

Clay nodded and quietly stepped into the doorway of Simmons' office. He knocked softly on the open door.

Simmons stood at the far corner of the room, carefully placing an ornate bottle of Glenfiddich on a side table. He flashed a disgruntled look when he turned and saw Clay. Simmons, who emigrated from England during his college days, stood about six-feet tall, with narrow shoulders and skinny legs that accentuated a bulging potbelly, the result of a fondness for beer and whiskey. His wardrobe always seemed as if they were stripped off the mannequins at Sears—on this day, they consisted of a plain short-sleeve pink dress shirt, gray nylon slacks, and slip-on loafers. His clean-shaven face, plastic-framed spectacles and balding head made him look like your typical high school chemistry teacher and much older than his actual age of forty-one years.

As was expected, Lee was there too, dressed in creased khakis and a blue button-down shirt that fit loosely on his chubby five-foot-six-inch frame. Sitting in one of two Barcelona leather chairs in front of Simmons' grand walnut desk, he greeted Clay with an equally sour look on his round Asian face, which was half-covered by large spectacles and topped with thin stringy black hair. Lee was what one would call an Asian mutt, consisting of Japanese, Korean, and Thai ethnicities, with a pinch of German thrown in for good measure.

"I'm sorry to bother you Jeremy, but do you have a second? I think it's important," Clay said.

Simmons didn't turn his way, but let out a sigh. "Sure, come in," he said in his watered-down English accent.

Lee, realizing that it was his cue to leave, stood up and headed for the door.

Simmons called out to him. "Peter, don't forget to ask the travel agent to confirm our flights to Tokyo next week," he said. He then pointed to the bottle of liquor on the side table. "And please, thank your parents for the generous gift."

Lee beamed. "Yes sir."

As Lee walked out the door, Clay took a seat in the other Barcelona chair, deliberately avoiding the one that his colleague had just occupied. It bothered him to no end that his less-experienced—and in his mind, less-talented—colleague received all the plush assignments over the rest of the Automobile Digest staffers, not because he was a better writer or car evaluator, but because he constantly showered the boss with compliments and gifts generously supplied by his wealthy father. And the fact that Lee named his firstborn after Simmons didn't hurt his cause either.

"What do you want, Stockton?" Simmons asked as he

dropped into his brown leather office chair behind his desk.

Clay cleared his throat and said in a shaky voice, "I received this invite from Kamita Motors. It seems like a pretty big deal."

"Let me see that." Simmons reached across the desk and thrust out an open right hand.

Clay leaned forward and held out the envelope, which Simmons swiped clean and held under his desk light, carefully studying every angle. He took out the invitation card and examined that with equal attention.

Clay felt a warm fluid sensation on his upper lip. His hand instinctively went to his nose, and he saw that his fingertips were covered in blood.

"Jeremy, may I have a tissue?" he asked with his head tilted back, his left index finger pressing his bleeding nostril shut.

Simmons sat upright in his chair, and he hurriedly pulled a box of tissues out of his desk drawer, handing it to Clay. "You all right?"

"Yeah, I've been getting these a lot lately."

Clay wiped his nose clean and jammed a small rolled-up piece of tissue paper into his nostril.

"You should get that checked out by a doctor. The last thing I need is a dead staffer in my office."

"Thanks for the concern, Jeremy. If I do croak here, I'll try not to dirty the carpet."

Simmons frowned at the remark and held up the invite. "So, this trip, it's to the South of France. Pretty fancy."

"I have a hunch it's for that supercar they're supposedly

working on. I've been monitoring it on all the forums."

Simmons scoffed. "Trust me, Kamita Motors is not working on a supercar. What I don't understand is why you got this invite and not me?"

"Maybe they liked the online story I wrote on the KamitaJet last month."

"Not likely. In any case, I don't like car companies dictating who I can and can't send on press trips, so leave this here while I make a few calls."

Clay leaned forward in his chair. "You mean I can't go?"

"We should probably send someone with a bit more seniority, don't you think?"

"Like who, Peter?"

The words weren't supposed to come out, but they did. And they hung in the air like a mushroom cloud. Clay would have given his soul to take them back.

Simmons took off his glasses, revealing his beady gray eyes. "I was thinking of going on this myself. When you're in charge around here, you can go on any trip you want, but for now, you do as I say. Got it?"

Clay shrank in his chair. "Yes, of course."

"And do me a favor and get the Z4 test car gassed and washed. That will be all."

With his shoulders slouched and his gaze fixed on the floor, Clay rose slowly from his chair and walked out of the office without saying another word. He dragged his feet into the bathroom to wash off the blood that dried on his fingers and placed a fresh tissue into his nose, before making his way back to his own office. The feeling of elation he had just experienced was wiped clean in a blink of an eye. He picked up his wallet from his desk and grabbed the Z4 keys from a hook on the wall, not bothering to look over at Lee, who was watching a YouTube video with his headphones on. Washing and gassing test cars were traditionally the jobs of the newest staff members, but he couldn't remember the last time Lee had performed those duties.

Clay dragged his feet to the elevator, and, as he was about to push the down button, Lorraine called out to him from the other end of the hallway. "Stockton, Jeremy wants to see you right away."

"He wants to see me? Why?" he asked.

Lorraine held up her hands. "Beats me."

Clay paused for a moment. Then, after nervously rubbing his forehead, he followed Lorraine to the corner office. When he got there, he saw Simmons in his chair facing the door.

"Come in and sit down," Simmons ordered.

Clay took a seat in the same chair as before. "You wanted to see me?" he asked, thinking perhaps his previous outburst had cost him his job.

"What's the connection with you and Mr. Kanda?" Simmons asked, his gaze fixed intently on Clay.

"The president of Kamita Motors? I've never met him before in my life, why do you ask?"

"He's the most reclusive man in the industry. He avoids the media like the plague, yet when I called the PR department at Kamita Motors, they said that Mr. Kanda insisted on seeing you, just you. They said he handpicked you to attend this reveal. So what I want to know is why?"

Clay held up his hands. "Jeremy, really, I have no idea. I can't believe he knows I even exist."

Simmons gazed at him through the corner of his eyes. "I don't know what you're up to, but if you're trying to pull a fast one here, I will get to the bottom of it, and you will be held accountable."

"Honest, Jeremy, I have no idea."

"Well, we can't afford to miss this opportunity, so I don't seem to have a choice. You're going to France." Simmons tossed the invitation back to Stockton.

Clay caught the envelope in mid-air. "Thank you, Jeremy. You won't regret this. I'll do my best."

"Make sure you get the Z4 gassed and washed before you go. That'll be all."

Clay sprang up from his seat and while delicately holding the envelope, he made a beeline for the elevator, doing a couple of fist pumps along the way. The doors slid open and inside the elevator carriage stood Tiffany Velasquez, holding a bundle of files in her arms. She worked as a secretary for the advertising department on the third floor, and in Clay's eyes, she was the most attractive girl in the building, perhaps the city. Her long black hair always seemed to have an impeccable shine to it, and her office suits hugged the right parts of her curvaceous figure.

"Hi Tiffany. How are you?" Clay asked.

She forced a smile. "Good. Thank you."

Clay pushed the elevator button marked "P" and stepped to the back of the tight square carriage, being careful not to invade Tiffany's private space. At that moment, his entire body overflowed with confidence and self-assurance that made him feel as indestructible as one of the video game characters he often played.

"You know, I'm leaving for the South of France in a few days. I'm working on the next cover story," he said, although Simmons had said nothing about his assignment being a cover story.

"That's nice," Tiffany replied, looking at him for the first time since he walked into the elevator. "What's that in your nose?"

"Oh this. I had a slight accident." Clay pulled out the tissue paper out of his nostril, partly brown with dried blood, and shoved it into his pocket.

Tiffany winced and turned her head away.

Clay straightened his posture. "I was wondering, you know, if I can bring you back some perfume or something. The south of France is famous for its…"

"I'm sorry, I have a boyfriend," she cut him off.

"No, no, I know that. I was just thinking, you know…"

"I'm sorry, Stockton. I'm not interested. My boyfriend owns his own business, and he can buy me any perfume I want. But thanks for the thought."

The elevator jolted to a stop at the ground floor. The doors slid open, and Tiffany stepped out, walking briskly down the hall without looking back. Clay quietly watched her as the doors closed shut.

Ten minutes later, driving along Pacific Coast Highway with the top of the BMW Z4 down, he played out the scene in the elevator over and over in his mind. He shifted uneasily in the seat each time he remembered the look of disgust on Tiffany's face. He knew he had no chance with her from the get go. *What the hell was I thinking?*

As Clay attempted to turn his thoughts to more pleasant things—such as what kind of luxurious hotel he would be staying at on his upcoming trip—he didn't notice a matte black Dodge Charger, with tinted windows, following him in the adjacent lane three car lengths back.

Chapter 4

Stockton Clay looked out of the airplane window and envisioned himself sunbathing with topless women on the pristine beaches of the French Riviera as the Airbus A320 made its final approach into the Cote D'Azur Airport.

The Cote D'Azur Airport in Nice, France, was an unassuming facility, much smaller in scale than the likes of Charles de Gaulle in Paris or London's Heathrow; in fact, the main and only terminal looked more like a train station when seen from the runway for the first time. It served as the gateway to the legendary South of France, where successful businessmen and glamorous celebrities passed through on their way to exotic destinations that included Cannes, St. Tropez, and Monte Carlo; therefore, the first-time visitor usually expected something a bit more grandiose, but Clay knew better for he had flown into and out of this place numerous times on his computer's flight simulator.

After a smooth landing, Clay went straight for the exit, while the other passengers from his flight strolled to the luggage carousel. He followed the advice of Automobile Digest's senior editor, Ray Hymson, who told him to never check bags: "If the airlines don't lose it, which they will, yours will be the last one to come off the plane." So everything Clay brought on the trip was crammed into a small Samsonite roller suitcase and an oversize Oakley backpack.

The arrivals terminal was sparsely crowded as tourist season officially ended a month before, with most of the French Riviera visitors long gone. Clay scanned the faces of those gathered to greet the recent arrivers, some holding flowers, others waving signs and placards. Most of them looked like locals—middle-aged men wearing cargo shorts and golf hats, accompanied by slightly younger women dressed in light printed flower dresses. There were a few hippy-like backpackers, who lounged around the power outlets recharging their smart phones. Clay's eyes stopped on a large white sign with his name on it, held up by a strikingly tall blonde woman wearing tight-fitting white jeans and a blue polo shirt with the Kamita logo embroidered on the chest.

Clay quickly walked up to the hostess. She stood about six-feet tall, and her emerald-green eyes accentuated her blonde hair. Her build was thin, but not overly skinny. She looked to be in her early twenties. The nametag pinned to her shirt read Anika.

"Hi, I'm Stockton Clay," he said as he pointed to his name on the placard.

Anika smiled. She looked down at her wooden clipboard and checked off Clay's name with a ballpoint pen. "Welcome to Nice, Mr. Clay. May I help you with your luggage?" she asked in a Scandinavian accent.

"No, no, I'm good," Clay answered, trying to keep from staring below her neckline.

She turned around and stepped toward the only escalator in the building. Clay waited for an explanation regarding their destination, but none was forthcoming, so he followed her without uttering another word.

After going up one level, Anika walked down a small empty hallway that led away from the main hub of the airport. She stopped at the only door on the floor.

"We are here, Mr. Clay," she said as she opened a wooden office door that led to a small waiting area. The sign on the wall read Vitesse Hélicoptère. "Please wait here until the helicopter is ready."

Helicopter? No one said anything about helicopters.

Clay stepped into a small room furnished with two large sofas and a small bar, complete with bartender. A small side table near the entrance held cookies and several flavors of Fanta sodas.

After Anika excused herself and left the room, Clay grabbed a Grape Fanta can from the table, popped the tab and took a big gulp.

"Close the damned door," a squealy male voice shouted from the middle of the room.

Clay stretched his neck to see where it had come from. Sitting on a sofa, typing away on his laptop was a man in his mid-thirties with a cropped haircut, buzzed at the sides, thick rimless spectacles, a scrawny build, and bad complexion. He wore a white short-sleeve golf shirt buttoned all the way to the top.

"Sorry," Clay said as he closed the door softly. He then felt a gentle tap on his shoulder.

"Hey, you must be Stockton Clay from Automobile Digest."

Clay turned around and saw a man in his early-forties, slightly taller than himself, but with the same lean build. He had wavy brown hair and a nice tan, though his skin looked a bit weathered. He had a coffee cup in his hand and a big smile on his face.

"I'm Mark Tyler from Car News Weekly. It's good to meet you. I've seen your name in the magazine many times," the man said with his right hand extended.

"Thank you. It's good to meet you, too. Do you know what this trip is about?" Clay asked as he shook Tyler's hand.

"No idea, but it's big, whatever it is. I've never heard of Mr. Kanda attending one of these junkets before. The guy almost never makes a public appearance. Something major is definitely going down."

"I can't believe we're riding helicopters to our hotel. How cool is that?"

Tyler chuckled. "Don't tell me that you've never been on a Kamita press trip before."

Clay shook his head.

"Well you're in for a treat. These cats go all out, from the food to the accommodations to the hostesses. No expense is spared. None."

"Hostesses?" Clay asked.

"Yeah, that girl who greeted you just now, she's probably a high-end fashion model. Kamita flies them in from all over the world, and I'm sure they pay top dollar for their services. They hire the best-looking women—the hostesses, the waitresses, even the maids, all of them perfect tens."

"Wow. I never heard about that."

Clay and Tyler's conversation was interrupted by the man on the sofa. "Hey, will you guys keep it down. Some of us are actually here to work."

"Take it easy Shane, this is a waiting room, not a library

for Christ's sake," Tyler said.

When Clay heard the man's name, he immediately recognized it. "That's Shane Boyle from Wheel and Engine magazine, right? I read his articles all the time. I've always wanted to meet him."

"Don't waste your time. He's not what you'd call a very social person. In fact, he's pretty much an asshole," Tyler said in a voice just low enough so Boyle couldn't hear.

Anika returned to the room through the front door, instantly commanding the attention of all three men. "The helicopter is ready. Please follow me," she said.

A couple of luggage handlers, built like football players, came in through another door. They grabbed the three automotive journalists' luggage and carried them through a sliding glass door that led out to the landing pad. Anika gestured to her three guests to follow them out. A few yards away from the building, sitting on the tarmac was a Sikorsky S-76C helicopter; its long thin propellers slowly rotating like a giant windmill.

Anika walked up to the copter and opened the rear door for her guests. Tyler lifted himself into the far rear seat, and Clay followed, offering to sit in the middle. But Boyle had other plans. He walked to the front of the chopper and presumptuously climbed in next to the pilot, a thirty-something dark-haired man with a stubby beard and a gray baseball cap. The pilot stared at his unexpected copilot with a look of disgust. Clay could have sworn he saw him mouth the word "Americans" under his breath as he turned his attention back to the helicopter controls.

The pilot pointed to his ear, gesturing to his three passengers to put on their headsets. Anika closed the door and stepped away from the helicopter as the rotor blades began spinning faster and faster. Clay was a bit disappointed that she wasn't joining them. A few seconds later, the S-76C was airborne.

For the next thirty minutes, Clay was treated to a bird's eye view of Provence. The green hills that linked the sea to the Alps were dotted with old rustic buildings with sloping vineyards and small farms squeezed in between. When the helicopter touched down on a landing circle within the hotel grounds, Clay tapped the pilot on the shoulder and gave him a thumbs-up sign. The pilot nodded and pulled out a box of Gauloises cigarettes.

As he turned in his seat to offer his guest a cigarette, his leather jacket slightly opened, revealing the butt of a handgun in a shoulder holster. The sight of the gun made Clay freeze, but only for a moment, as he quickly recomposed himself, smiled, and held up a hand.

"No thanks. I don't smoke," he shouted over the sound of the helicopter engine powering down.

As the three journalists stepped out of the chopper, Clay tapped Tyler on the back and asked: "Is it normal for the hired help to carry guns on these events?"

Tyler flashed him a confused look. "What are you talking about?"

"Our pilot had a pistol stashed under his jacket."

"You must've been seeing things, my man. Never heard of such a thing."

"I saw it as plain as day."

"Well, what does it matter now?" Tyler said. "We're here at the hotel, safe and sound."

Clay nodded. "Yeah, I suppose you're right."

As they stepped off the helipad, Clay, Tyler, and Boyle were greeted by an Asian woman wearing a form-fitting tweed Chanel blazer, knee-long skirt, and gloss black Valentino heels. She was average height, about five-feet-six, but her near perfect face, curvaceous build and flawless proportions suggested she was anything but average. Her shiny black hair was tied in a librarian bun at the back of her head. She looked to be in her mid-twenties, but Clay would later discover that she was actually a couple years north of thirty.

Any concerns Clay previously had about the armed helicopter pilot were completely wiped away at the mere sight of her.

"How was your flight?" she asked in perfect English.

"It was fine, thanks," Tyler answered.

Boyle put his hands on his hips. "I don't know why we didn't just drive here. The helicopter was a complete waste, and when those things go down, you can kiss your ass goodbye."

"I'm truly sorry about that," the woman said. "My name is Maki Takano, I'm the new public relations director for Kamita Motors. Welcome to Paul Ricard racetrack and Hotel du Var." She shook all three of the journalists' hands. "Now if you could follow me to the hotel lobby, I will give you the keys to your rooms."

She walked toward a large rustic one-story stone building with large sliding glass doors.

"See? What did I tell ya," Tyler whispered to Clay as they watched Maki from behind. "All tens."

Chapter 5

As Maki Takano led the four men through the hotel grounds, Clay couldn't keep his eyes off of her, hardly paying attention to the pristine entranceway of the hotel.

The Hotel du Var, a luxury five-star hotel in the heart of Provence, sat atop a cliff overlooking a wide valley and the Mediterranean Sea. Visitors who didn't fly in drove up to the property on a grand tree-lined driveway that led to a large brick building, which served as the main lobby. An over-sized fountain graced the circular driveway immediately in front of the main building, with most of the rooms spread across the grounds in separate wings ensuring privacy for its usually wealthy clientele. The hotel was open only during the early spring and late summer months, and it was primarily known for accommodating famous race drivers who came to test their machines at the nearby racetrack, Circuit Paul Ricard.

Maki entered the main lobby through large ornate double doors, followed by the three journalists. In contrast to the traditional nature of the building's exterior, the lobby was a study in modern interior design, with shiny marble floors, black leather furniture and a stainless-steel check-in counter. The place was empty, save for a young woman behind the counter.

"Where is everybody?" Clay asked.

"Kamita probably booked out the entire hotel. That's usually how they roll," Tyler said.

Maki walked over to the check-in counter, said a few

things in French to the receptionist and returned with three card keys in her hand.

"Here are your keys gentlemen," she said as she handed each person a card key. She pointed to three golf carts waiting outside, occupied by staff drivers. "These men will take you to your rooms. Please get some rest, and we will meet in the restaurant for our grand announcement at eight sharp. Your luggage should already be in your room."

The golf-cart ride from the lobby to his room provided a chance for Clay to see how grand and well-kept the hotel grounds were. There were a couple of spas here, a six-hole golf course, and a large swimming pool that overlooked the sea. His driver, a young man with a boyish face named Daniel, pulled the golf cart to a stop in front of a room that hung on a steep cliff. Daniel opened the hotel door and stood next to the doorway, waiting for Stockton to enter before he spoke.

"This is one of the five new suites here at the hotel," he explained with a French accent. "The bedroom is over there, and the bathroom is on the right, and the television remote is on the shelf. If you need any assistance with anything, please dial zero on the telephone."

He placed the key on the mantle.

Clay pulled his wallet out and realized he forgot to exchange money at the airport. "I'm sorry, I don't have any Euros. Will American dollars be okay?" he asked.

Daniel held up his hand. "All tips have been taken care of by Kamita Motors." He left without saying another word.

Clay walked into the bedroom and noticed that his small

Samsonite suitcase was already sitting on top of the luggage rack next to a king-sized bed with a Napoleonic wooden headboard. On top of the bed was a small gift box, wrapped in colorful paper, and a pink ribbon. Clay ripped the wrapping paper off and removed the lid of a white cardboard box underneath. Inside was the latest tablet from Dengaku Electronics, a subsidiary of Kamita Motors, with a card that read, "Compliments of Tetsuro Kanda and Kamita Motors."

Clay held up the tablet and inspected it carefully. It was the top-of-the-line model and one of the most desired electronic gadgets in the world, easily worth more than half his paycheck.

Damn, they do spare no expense.

He then noticed a small piece of notebook paper folded at the base of the box. Clay pulled it out and unfolded it. Scribbled in red ink were the words: "Watch your back. There are people here who want you dead."

He crinkled the paper into a ball, tossed it into the wastebasket, and thought nothing more of it. He'd be damned if he was going let some lame gag spoil this once-in-a-lifetime experience of being part of the biggest automotive event of the year.

Chapter 6

Clay wondered if he had accidentally walked in on a secret meeting of organized crime bosses when he entered the main dining room of Le Restaurant Dantès. He arrived twenty minutes early, but the place was already bustling with people, most of them dressed in shiny suits and sporting giant Swiss watches. The air reeked of cigar smoke. He was relieved that he made the effort to dress up; his wardrobe for the evening consisting of a navy blazer that was one size too big, slightly wrinkled khakis and black Nike cross-trainers.

Le Restaurant Dantès was located on the grounds of Hotel du Var, a short walk on a gravel pathway from the main lobby. Although it was housed in a simple one-story clay building with extra-large black wooden doors, the restaurant had garnered a reputation for being one of the best in the region. Getting a table at Dantès was more difficult than securing a tee time at Cypress Pointe because the restaurant was only open during the spring and fall, with bookings made a year in advance. It had been awarded at least two Michelin stars every year since it was founded in the late nineteen eighties; it specialized in Provencal cuisine, using only ingredients that originated in the area, including its most highly prized product, truffles.

A sign at the entrance read, "No photography allowed," and a woman in a Kamita windbreaker at the door placed small black decals over the camera lens on everyone's smart phones. About two dozen men and women were gathered at the main bar, gleefully conversing amongst each other as they knocked back their favorite cocktails. Others were seated at their tables, sipping the complimentary glass of champagne placed in front of every seat. It was obvious to Clay that the entire restaurant had been booked out because the dining room no longer looked like a place where one went to enjoy a quiet meal; it had been rearranged to resemble what could best be described as a mini circus arena. A large round open section dominated the middle of the room, with ten or so dining tables placed in a semi-circle around it. In the middle of the open space was an object hidden under an electric blue veil, guarded by velvet ropes on all four sides and two burly men in tight black short-sleeve T-shirts. The veil was suspended by thin metallic wires that descended from the ceiling forming a square box, completely concealing the size and shape of whatever hid underneath, making him wonder if what lurked beneath the veil was the rumored super sports car that he had read about on the various automotive black sites.

Name cards were placed near the place settings at every table, so he set about looking for his assigned seat, deciding to start from the outside and work his way in.

"Hey Stockton, over here," Tyler called out from one of the tables in front.

Clay made his way to where Tyler casually sipped a martini while surfing the web on his new Dengaku tablet. Clay carefully checked each name card, not expecting to find his at the head table, but to his astonishment, there it was, a few seats away from where Tyler sat. In fact, it was the best seat in the house, for not only did it face the center of the room, the chair next to his was reserved for none other than Mr. Kanda himself. Either someone had made a big mistake or the seating assignments were randomly arranged. He considered switching name cards with someone else's, not wanting to deal with the pressure of having to converse with one of the most important men in the industry, but changed his mind when he considered that he had been presented with a once-in-a-lifetime opportunity. As soon as he sat down, a waiter walked up to him and stood in attention, a napkin draped over a forearm and a bottle of red wine in his hand.

"May I bring you something to drink, sir?" he asked with a French accent. "Perhaps some red wine?"

Clay contemplated having a try at the wine, when Tyler interjected. "Their martinis are the best. I would highly recommend one," he said as he popped an olive into his mouth.

"Sounds tempting, but I think I'll just stick with orange juice for now," Clay said to the waiter. He enjoyed a drink now and then, but he wanted to have all his senses at full capacity for the event.

The waiter bowed his head and briskly walked away.

Shane Boyle stepped up to the table, dressed in the same white shirt and jeans as before, and lugging a brown leather shoulder bag. He sat down two seats over from Tyler, on the other side of Clay.

A different waiter appeared and asked Boyle for his choice of beverage.

"Jack and Coke," he said as he took out his reporter's notebook and smart phone, and placed them on the table in front of him. "And lots of ice."

Clay stood up and extended his hand across the table towards Boyle. "We haven't been formally introduced. I'm Stockton Clay with Automobile Digest. I've been reading your articles for years. I'm a big fan," he said.

Boyle remained in his chair, picking up the smart phone and swiping the screen, ignoring Clay's hand. "That's nice," he replied without looking up.

An awkward silence followed. Clay kept his gaze on Boyle, wondering if the guy was playing some sort of joke— *no one could be this disrespectful, could they?*—but it was evident that he was not, so Clay withdrew his hand, shrugged his shoulders and sat back down in his chair, feeling more puzzled than humiliated.

It occurred to Clay that maybe it was Boyle who left that threatening note in the tablet box, as part of a sick hazing ritual for newcomers. If so, Clay decided that he was not going to give him the pleasure of acknowledging that he ever saw it.

The waiter returned with Clay's orange juice and Boyle's Jack and Coke, carefully placing them next to their side plates when Maki Takano arrived at their table. She was dressed in a black cocktail dress that showed off her shapely figure and exposed her legs from the knees down. She wore her hair loosely, the ends of her strands softly brushing the nape of her long slender neck, but it was the golden tone of her skin that glowed under the lights that mesmerized Clay.

"Good, you're all here," she said. "I think we'll get this party started." She caught Clay staring at her and gave him a friendly wink. With his face red, Clay looked away.

After she had left, Boyle offered his two cents: "She's way out of your league, buddy."

Clay said nothing, partly because he knew it to be true. He watched Maki walk to the middle of the floor and stand next to the object under the blue veil. She spoke into a cordless microphone, which broadcast her voice through six loudspeakers placed around the dining area. "If you can all please be seated, we would like to begin now."

The guests ended whatever conversation they were engaged in and shuffled about the room looking for their designated seats. Within five minutes, all fifty-seven people were in their places, their attention focused on the Japanese woman in the center of the ring. The room's lights dimmed, and a spotlight shined on her.

"Thank you. Kamita Motors appreciates all of you for taking time out of your busy schedules to join us for this special event. We are excited to have representatives from our highest volume dealerships, as well as the top three car magazines from the U.S. here today."

The spotlight shifted to the head table, illuminating the three journalists. A soft round of applause greeted them, initiated by Maki who clapped the best she could with a microphone in her hand. The spotlight then moved back onto Maki.

"As you may know, Kamita Motors is the largest automotive company on the planet with sales surpassing ten and a half million units. Kamita has more than a dozen subsidiary companies all over the world that range from agricultural factories to reusable energy plants to biogenetics labs. But today we are here to talk about cars, and who better to make our big announcement than our president and CEO, Mr. Tetsuro Kanda."

A loud ovation filled the room, with many of the guests standing to show their appreciation for the man who helped them live a life of opulence and luxury—Kamita dealerships were one of the most profitable franchises around. Clay was about to stand up too, but noticed that both Tyler and Boyle kept their bodies firmly planted in their seats. Their expressionless faces reminded Clay that he was supposed to be an unbiased and impartial member of the press, who was there only to report on a story and not to celebrate an individual. Clay leaned back in his chair and took a sip of his orange juice. The spotlight darted to the back of the room where Kanda appeared from an adjoining study, making his way slowly to the center of the ring.

Clay had seen photos of Kanda many times before, but he looked different up close. His weathered face made him look older than his reported age of fifty-eight-years old. He was average height and build, and stood with an athletic posture that complimented his navy Armani suit. His jet-black hair with streaks of silver was slicked back with Pomade, and his large square face was defined by deep creases in the forehead and cheeks. His eyes had a distant, tired look to them, suggesting that he had seen his fair share of hardships in life.

Maki handed Kanda the microphone, bowed, and stepped to the side.

Every guest in the room stopped clapping and sat back

down.

Kanda smiled and nodded his head in several directions. He squinted as the spotlight shone on his face. "Thank you, Takano-san, and thank you all for the warm reception," he said with a commanding voice, tinted by a slight Japanese accent. "Back when my grandfather founded this company, he believed racing was the breeding ground for innovation. And I agree, so I would like to announce that Kamita Motors will return to the highest level of motorsports, Formula One, starting next season with a racecar completely built in-house."

An eerie silence enveloped the dining room, as it took a moment for Kanda's words to sink in. Participating in Formula One racing was a very big deal. Not only was it unbelievably expensive—for a newcomer to be competitive meant committing to a nine-figure annual budget—it also presented a formidable image risk to Kamita Motors. With all the high expectations that would no doubt be placed on them from day one, if Kamita failed to produce results within two or three years, the company would suffer a crushing blow to its corporate image, and subsequently lose whatever sponsors they were able to secure. On the other hand, if Kamita won, its standing as one of the most successful companies of the twenty-first century would be cemented. The dealers clapped louder than ever because success in racing usually translated to more car sales. Clay noticed that even Tyler had joined in, while Boyle scribbled away in his notebook.

Kanda raised his voice over the loud applause. "And to

commemorate the event, we will be introducing a new sports car to the public, a supercar we call the FGT-1."

Again, the audience went silent. The spotlight shifted to the side of the center stage where a couple of leggy models, wearing skin-tight one-piece dresses, walked over to the veiled object. They stopped and stood next to it as Kanda counted to three. On the final count, they yanked on the veil, releasing it from the wires, and pulling away the silk cover to reveal a low-slung sports car, one that had never before been seen by the public.

There were gasps and dozens of open mouths. One man thrust his fists into the air and yelled something that sounded like a Spanish victory cry, prompting another man to scream something in Chinese. Everyone stared at the beautiful piece of metallic art sitting under the warm spotlight. The car, bathed in electric blue paint, featured a slanted nose and wide bulging fenders. A large rear wing made it look as if it were race ready.

Clay marveled at the shape and proportions of the sports car. "I knew it. I knew they were working on a supercar," he said to anyone who was listening.

Chapter 7

A few hundred yards from Le Restaurant Dantès, a lone figure quietly made his way across the courtyard of the Hotel du Var. The sun had long since descended beneath the rolling hills, and a full moon shined overhead. The moonlight cast long shadows of the surrounding trees, and together with a light mist that rolled in off the sea, they gave the hotel grounds a down right spooky feel.

The man wore dark clothes and kept to the shadows, so he was nearly invisible to the naked eye. The red and gray hair that jutted out from under his wool ski mask showed that he was past his prime. He held a small penlight in his gloved hand, pointing its narrow beam of light on the numbers stuck to the guest rooms' doors, until he stopped at the one marked 210, the room assigned to Stockton Clay. He took out a card key and slid it into the slot by the door handle. When the small light flashed green, followed by the snap of an unlocking latch, he pushed the door halfway open and stepped inside.

The room was pitch black, but he elected not to switch on any of the lights for he was not a welcome visitor here. Instead, he depended on his trusty penlight to help him navigate his way into the bedroom, being careful not to step on any loose clothing or disturb the current state of the room in any way. When he reached the bed, the man—who wore thick-rimmed brown spectacles under his mask—took out a magnifying glass and a small plastic container from a belt pack that hung around his waist. Placing the light on the night stand, he used his magnifying glass to examine the pillow carefully.

He quickly found what he was looking for and took out a pair of tweezers from his bag. On the pillow was a strand of hair, which he delicately removed and placed inside the plastic container. He then moved to the bathroom, where he walked up to the shower stall. It was still wet, a sign that it had been used within the last hour. Shining the light into the stall, he removed more strands of hair that had settled on the drain cover.

As he put his equipment away, something in the wastebasket caught his eye. He pointed the penlight into the wooden container next to the toilet and saw a pile of crumpled tissue paper inside with bloodstains on them. He carefully pulled one of the tissues out and placed it in a plastic Ziploc bag, which he stowed into his belt pack with the rest of his belongings.

Satisfied with his gatherings, he tiptoed back to the front entrance and left the room as quietly as he had entered.

* * * *

Kanda held up his hands, quieting the crowd. "I am nearly finished with my speech, so if I can have your attention for another moment."

"You mean there's more?" a guest in the back shouted.

Kanda smiled. "Yes, a bit. There are a couple of people I'd like to introduce. We have just signed them to be the drivers for our Formula One team next year. May I present last year's World Driving Champion, Alfonso Lucci and Ka-mita's own homegrown talent, Marco Senna."

The doors of the FGT-1 supercar swung open and out stepped two men, one in his early thirties and another who barely looked old enough to drive. They were both rugged-ly handsome with dark hair and lean builds. The older man stood about five-feet-nine, slightly taller than the other driv-er. Dressed in matching Kamita T-shirts and blazers, they walked to the front of the car and waved to the crowd. The onlookers greeted them with frenzied applause.

"This is historic," Tyler said.

Clay kept his gaze fixed on the younger-looking of the two drivers. "Mr. Kanda did say Senna, right? I wonder if he's related to Ayrton Senna?"

Tyler squinted and looked carefully at the face of the driver introduced as Marco. "Yeah, now that you mention it, he does look like him."

Marco Senna had curly black hair and a thin beard, but it was the eyes that first caught Clay's attention. He had seen those dark opaque eyes before, in books and old racing foot-age of the glory days of Formula One. They were the same eyes that stared down at him every day from a poster on his apartment wall. They belonged to a competitor dedicated to perfecting his craft no matter the cost; they were the eyes of the late great Formula One champion Ayrton Senna, arguably the greatest race driver who had ever lived, but one whose sheer determination to win alienated many of his colleagues.

Kanda smiled in contentment, as his brief two-minute speech had left the guests buzzing with excitement. "Please enjoy your dinner, and thank you again for coming." He handed the microphone back to Maki and made his way to the head table.

At Kanda's arrival, everyone at the table stood. Clay quickly pulled out a business card from his back pocket and presented it to Kanda Japanese style, with both hands holding the card, arms stretched out in front of him.

"Stockton Clay *desu. Hajime-mashite*," he said with a deep bow.

Kanda took the business card and bowed. "Thank you, Mr. Clay."

Tyler and Boyle also took out their business cards and handed them to Kanda in similar fashion.

"Nice to meet all of you," Kanda said as they all sat down.

Maki took her seat, between Tyler and Boyle.

Kanda reached for his champagne glass, but before he brought the rim to his lips, Tyler raised his own glass. "Mr. Kanda, I'd like to propose a toast. Here's to the most amazing car company in the world. *Kanpai!*" he said.

Kanda smiled, as Boyle rolled his eyes. Everyone at the table swigged their aperitifs in unison. "You're all too kind," Kanda said as he placed his glass back on the table.

Clay felt a knot in his stomach; he wanted to ask Kanda a million questions, but was deathly afraid of possibly making a fool of himself. He decided that he would spend this dinner staying quiet and just observe.

"So tell me, what do you think about our announcement?" Kanda asked his table guests.

Shane Boyle casually leaned back in his chair. "I must hand it to you, Kanda-san, you must have worked overtime to keep all this from leaking out. So when will I be able to drive the new sports car?"

Maki interjected. "We brought three prototypes for each of you to drive tomorrow on the racetrack."

"That's great," Tyler said. "This will be a cover story for us for sure."

Clay sat upright in his chair, his mouth wide open. "We really get to drive it?"

"Yes, but all driving impressions are embargoed for one week. You can publish your stories in print or on the internet after Mr. Kanda officially introduces the car at the Tokyo Motor Show next week," Maki said.

Clay noticed Kanda continually glancing his way, as if he were waiting for him to speak. It made him increasingly uncomfortable.

"And what about you, Mr. Clay, what do you think about our announcement?" Kanda asked.

Clay wiped his wet palms on his napkin. "Um, yes. I think the car is absolutely stunning. It reminds me a bit of the old Italian supercars of the seventies. I've been monitoring the automotive forums every day for the past year, so I kind of suspected you were working on a supercar."

"Yeah right, sure you were," Boyle said.

Clay ignored the remark. "I think it's all incredible, the Formula One announcement, the sports car, everything. The driver Marco, he, um, looks just like Ayrton Senna. Are they related?"

Kanda took a gulp of his champagne and broke out in a wide grin. "I was wondering if anyone would notice. Very impressive, Clay-san. Yes, Marco is Ayrton Senna's son."

The three journalists shot each other quizzical glances. Tyler was the first to speak.

"But Ayrton Senna didn't have any children."

"As a matter of fact, Mark-san, he did. Marco was born a few months after Ayrton passed away."

"Then who was the mother?" Boyle asked.

"A Kamita employee. They met when Ayrton was secretly testing our Le Mans racecar. She had asked us to keep Marco's existence quiet because she knew the media chaos it would cause. She brought Marco to us right before she herself passed away about ten years ago," Kanda explained.

"So where has he been for the past, what is it, twenty-some years?" asked Tyler, ignoring the waiter who had just arrived to take their dinner order.

"Our race manager became his guardian, and he has been racing under a different name in China. We thought that the time was right for Marco to, well, come out of the closet, as you say in English." Kanda chuckled at his own joke.

Any jitters Clay previously felt were wiped away by the earth-stopping revelation. "Oh my God, this is going to rock the world. The greatest racing driver of all time had a secret son."

Boyle picked up his notebook and started to furiously scribble down notes. Maki gently put her hand on his forearm. "This information is embargoed, too," she said.

Drops of bright red blood splattered onto the white tablecloth in front of Clay, and he instinctively took his napkin and held it to his nose. "Oh no, not again," he murmured.

Everyone at the table stopped what they were doing and stared at him.

"Excuse me," Clay said as he stood from his chair.

Maki rose to her feet with a concerned look. "Are you all right?" she asked.

Kanda offered him his napkin. "Please use this."

Clay held up his hand. "I'm okay, it's nothing." He turned around and headed to the restroom, located at the corner of the dining hall, wondering why these episodes always happened at precisely the wrong time.

* * * *

After Clay had left his seat, Kanda raised his right hand and waved it back and forth, calling over a tall Japanese man who stood inconspicuously against the far wall of the restaurant. He was in his early-thirties, with a long face, highlighted by pronounced cheekbones and a pointy chin that sported a cropped goatee. His jet-black hair was slicked back, and his black pinstripe suit hugged his tall and muscular build. Jimmy Bando bent down and put his ear next to his boss' face. Kanda whispered something in Japanese to him as they both watched Clay disappear behind the restroom door.

Chapter 8

Clay awoke before the rising of the sun, his body fully energized with the anticipation of the first ever test drive of a sports car that would surely go down in the annals of history. It was precisely opportunities like this—getting to drive the most exotic cars on the planet before anyone else—that made him want to become an automotive writer. His love affair with cars began when he was eight-years old, the moment he first laid eyes on a Ferrari 458 Italia in a neighborhood church parking lot, which led him to cut back on his video-game playing and hit the books in the hopes of landing a job in the auto industry. His devotion paid off as he was accepted to UCLA's engineering school. Upon graduation, he had high hopes of grabbing a position with a car company, but his better-than-average writing skills landed him an even more desirable job, as a writer for his favorite automobile magazine, Automobile Digest, where he could travel the globe driving the newest cars in the world, and where his articles would be read by hundreds of thousands of people around the country.

According to the itinerary provided by Kamita Motors, he was to be picked up by a hotel staffer at seven o'clock, who would transport him to the racetrack where his test drive would take place. Clay decided to wait outside for his ride and take in the cool fresh Provence air.

Daniel, the same young man who escorted Clay to his room the day before, pulled up in the familiar dark green four-seat golf cart a few minutes ahead of schedule.

"Good morning, *monsieur*. Are you ready to go?" he asked with a smile and a courteous nod.

Clay gave him a thumbs-up sign and slid into the back seat.

The cart ride lasted only a few seconds as Daniel drove around the courtyard to the hotel parking lot, stopping next to a mini shuttle bus. Clay stepped inside the fourteen-passenger bus and noticed he had the vehicle all to himself. *Now that's VIP treatment.* As he took a seat in the front row, Daniel fired up the bus's diesel engine. The racetrack was less than a mile from the hotel, so the trip took all of two minutes. Daniel pulled the bus to a stop when they reached the main pit building at Circuit Paul Ricard.

"Please, this way," Daniel said as he stepped out of the shuttle.

Clay followed him through the front entrance of the main building. The main lobby of the Le Circuit Paul Ricard was nothing like what he expected. While most offices at race facilities looked as if they belonged in a fast-food restaurant, the reception area here was immaculate, resembling something out of a billion-dollar Wall Street firm. A giant counter sat in front of a winding staircase with steps made of polished cut stone. The wood-paneled walls were decorated with framed photographs and posters of racing legends, from Juan Manual Fangio to France's own Alain Prost. On the lobby floor sat a replica of the 1961 Ferrari 156 F1 that took American Phil Hill to the World Driver's Championship. Clay took out his smart phone and snapped a photo of the historic car's long lean body and shark-nose front end.

Daniel led Clay through the lobby and down a short hallway that ended at the rear entrance of the garages. These garages served as a base where engineers and mechanics worked on their cars during testing and racing. The facilities were mostly empty, apart from a couple of formula cars sitting under a thick canvas cover.

"Are those the new Kamita F1 cars?" Clay asked.

"I wouldn't know *monsieur*."

Mark Tyler and Shane Boyle were already gearing up to drive. Mark, wearing jeans and a polo shirt, whistled a Beatles song as he tried on different racing helmets off a large metal rack at the corner of the garage. Boyle, wearing what looked to be the same white shirt and jeans from the previous evening, stood outside talking to a tall Japanese man who had slicked back hair and was dressed in a pinstripe suit.

A middle-aged Caucasian man, wearing a Kamita Racing windbreaker walked up to Clay with a big grin on his face. "Good morning, young lad. You must be Clay. I'm Ian Lackey, the race manager for the Kamita Formula One racing team," he said in a thick Scottish accent.

Clay immediately recognized him. Ian Lackey had been his childhood hero. Lackey was one of the most colorful racecar drivers of the Indy Racing Series, and although he won only one race in his five-year career, his aggressive driving style and frequent use of profanity earned him a bad-boy reputation and a legion of loyal fans; one of them being a shy ten-year-old Stockton Clay. After Lackey hung up his racing gloves, he started his own Indy-car team, which went belly-up after two seasons. A year later, he was hired by Kamita Motors as a special consultant and subsequently vanished from the public stage. Clay, as well as most people in the world, had no idea what had become of him, so he was glad to see that the racing legend was still gainfully employed and, despite being more than fifty years old, looked fit enough to outwrestle a bear. He had the air of a modern-day Richard the Lionheart, his short white hair spiked with styling gel, and his thin white goatee complimenting his designer aviator shades.

"It is a pleasure to meet you, sir. I was a big fan," Clay said shaking Lackey's hand.

"Well lad, go get yourself a helmet, and get into your car. We've been told you are all experienced drivers, so we'll skip the boring safety talk. Just be responsible out there."

Clay nodded and walked over to the helmet rack, realizing that it was probably Lackey who had raised Marco Senna and groomed him into becoming a Formula One race driver. The drama was getting juicier by the minute, and Clay was already crafting the headline for his story. "The secret son of the late Ayrton Senna, trained by Indy-car legend Ian Lackey." The mere sound of it gave him goosebumps.

"Hiya." Tyler greeted Clay with a pat on the shoulder. "You okay? You know, your nose thing last night."

"Yeah, nothing serious. Sorry I caused a scene. It was so embarrassing," Clay said as he grabbed a helmet off the rack.

Lackey, who saw Clay take the helmet, hurried over to him. "You should at least try that on, lad."

Stockton held up the helmet to Lackey. "I have this exact one at home, a medium full-face Arai GT6," he said.

"Ah, my apologies. So, you race back in your home country?"

"Not really. I do a few autocrosses a year. I wish I could race, but it's too expensive."

Lackey laughed and nodded. "Too right. You're better off not racing if you have to pay for it yourself. Now go find your car, and let's get driving." Lackey pointed to a large whiteboard in the corner of the garage, where a message was scribbled with a black marker:

"Welcome to the test drive of the FGT-1. This is not a race, so there is absolutely no overtaking. You have four total laps each. There are photographers positioned at different points of the track, so please watch out for them. The car assignment is as follows: Mark Tyler, silver FGT-1; Stockton Clay, red FGT-1; Shane Boyle, yellow FGT-1."

Stockton walked outside onto pit row and saw three beautiful examples of the supercar introduced the night before. The driver-side doors were opened, inviting the three journalists to step in. He went to his assigned car, the red FGT-1, which sat second on the grid. Before he reached it, Shane Boyle ran over and jumped into its driver's seat.

"Excuse me. The board over there says I'm in this one," Clay said.

"Nope, you're in the yellow one," Boyle answered.

"I don't think I am. It says there, *you're* in the yellow one."

Boyle, ignoring Clay, pulled on his helmet and buckled

the chin strap.

"Come on Shane, my boss wanted the red car for our photos."

"Join the club. We also know red cars on the cover and the homepage get the most traction. And besides, that guy in the suit over there said for me to drive this one. He said it was important that I be in this car."

"What guy in the suit?"

Boyle leaned out of the car and pointed toward the garage, but the only person present was an elderly janitor sweeping the floor. "He was there a minute ago. It was this tall Japanese guy in a black suit. Listen, you're wasting my time, so just go to your own car already."

Boyle reached for the door and started to pull it shut; Clay stopped it halfway.

"You know what? You're a real dick," Clay said and slammed the door shut for him, with extra force thrown in.

Chapter 9

Clay walked over to the yellow FGT-1, which looked stunning under the early morning light. Yellow cars attracted plenty of views too, so he wasn't too bothered by the fact that he was forced to switch. He slipped into the car's tight leather bucket seat, which was equipped with a four-point racing harness. Clay, who had previous experiences with this type of restraint system from his autocross activities, buckled himself in after putting on his helmet. In the meantime, Lackey went to each car to help the other drivers get strapped in. When Lackey reached Clay's car, he grinned when he saw that the belts were already properly latched.

"It's always good to have people who know what they are doing," he said as he gave the shoulder harnesses one final tug, nearly crushing Clay's chest.

"I can barely breathe," he gasped.

Lackey gave him a thumbs-up sign. "You're good to go."

Lackey shut the door to the bright yellow sports car and walked to the pit exit, where cars entered the track. After sitting on a wooden stool next to a light signal with its red light illuminated, he pointed to the first car in line, the silver one with Mark Tyler sitting behind the steering wheel. The light turned green, and Lackey pointed toward the racetrack, sending the car blasting down the front straight. The light quickly turned red as Boyle crept to the start line, awaiting his turn to enter the track.

Roughly thirty seconds later, the signal turned green,

and Lackey motioned Boyle to go. He smoked the rear tires and took off like a cannonball. The light turned red again as Clay drove his yellow car up to the start line.

Clay's eyes were fixed on Lackey as he tightened his grip on the steering wheel. Lackey pointed to the yellow car as the light flashed green, prompting Clay to mash the accelerator pedal. The supercar went hurtling down the front straight, but it made little noise, just a high-pitched whirring sound coming from under its hood.

The FGT-1 was equipped with a fuel cell, meaning that hydrogen was the main fuel that powered its electric motors. This meant that the car emitted no dirty emissions because the exhaust that emanated out of its tailpipe was water vapor; therefore, the FGT-1 wasn't dependent on oil, and it left a very small carbon footprint, if any at all. Still, critics contended that the process of producing hydrogen was just as bad for the environment. But Clay knew that Kamita Motors was working on establishing a clean hydrogen manufacturing system to solve that problem.

Although it was Clay's first time on the Paul Ricard track, he was familiar with all of the corners because he had driven it a number of times on his PlayStation driving simulator at home. He wanted to go fast, but he definitely didn't want to push himself or the car too hard and become known as the first person in the world to wreck an FGT-1. There was no shame in taking the first lap slow, to become more comfortable with the vehicle, before increasing the pace gradually. The supercar was so easy to drive, and unlike many exotics that required a high degree of driving skill, this one seemed to steer itself, so Clay found himself increasing his pace with every passing second.

About halfway through the second lap, Clay saw the red FGT-1, driven by Boyle, a few corners ahead. The red sports car was slightly off the driving line for the faster corners and braked way too early for the tight turns.

"Time to reel you in *sucka*," Clay said under his helmet.

Clay took on a more aggressive driving style, letting the shift indicator go all the way to red before grabbing the next gear. Halfway through the third lap, Boyle's car was only a few hundred feet in front of him. As they approached the penultimate corner of the track, Clay accelerated right up to Boyle's rear bumper, just short of tapping it.

Caught you.

He saw Boyle flip him the bird through the rear window of his car. Feeling like he made his point loud and clear, Clay slowed his car down until he was at least four car lengths behind Boyle's when they went through the final turn.

As soon as Boyle's red FGT-1 exited the corner and drove onto the long front straight, it suddenly accelerated from forty to one hundred and forty miles per hour. When it was halfway down the straight, the right front tire locked up, sending white tire smoke into the air and leaving a long skid mark on the gray asphalt. The car skidded left, but didn't slow down. Then the right rear locked up causing the car to go into a wild fishtail slide, with its rear end swinging violently from side to side, totally out of control. Clay watched in horror as the car skidded one way and then the other before crashing into the only section of concrete wall on the track…at full speed.

The gruesome sound of crunching metal and shattering glass filled the air, as the bright red car bounced off the wall and flipped three times across the width of the track. When it finally came to rest, the red FGT-1 sat upside down, the roof partially caved in, and the entire vehicle engulfed in blue and orange flames, spewing different colored fluids onto the ground.

Clay hit the brakes hard, invoking the ABS system. As soon as he undid his belts, he jumped out of the driver's seat and ran to the passenger side of his car, where he grabbed a small fire extinguisher bolted to the floor. Getting close as he could without getting burned, he ran up to the burning vehicle. The stench of burning chemicals and melting rubber burned his nostrils, causing him to cough violently as he pointed the nozzle at the flames and sprayed. But it was no use, the blaze was too big. As he took a step back fearing the possibility of an explosion, an emergency track vehicle arrived. Two workers jumped out of the truck with much larger fire extinguishers and covered the vehicle with a powdery white substance that snuffed the fire out within a couple of minutes. Clay could see Boyle, nudged in the cockpit upside down, his helmeted head pressed up against the ceiling.

The emergency workers pried the driver's-side door open with a large metallic bar and pulled the unconscious driver out of the car. From the track gates, an ambulance drove up with its sirens blaring and light bar flashing. Both doors swung open and two paramedics rushed out of the vehicle to Boyle's limp body. They kept his helmet on, and with the help of the track workers, lifted him onto a rolling stretcher and then into the back of the ambulance.

Clay offered to help, but the ambulance driver held up his hand. "Thank you, but there is nothing you can do."

As one of the paramedics cut the strap that held the helmet to Boyle's head, another paramedic slammed the rear door shut, shouting "*Allez, allez*." Clay watched solemnly as the vehicle sped out of the main gates on its way to the nearest hospital.

One of the emergency track workers motioned for him to jump into his truck. "Please leave your test car where it is, we will take you back to the pits," he said.

Clay pulled off his helmet and jumped into the bed of the full-size pickup. When the truck pulled up to the main pit building, Lackey was there to greet him, his face set in a tight grimace.

"There is a media center on the second floor. Please wait for further instructions there," he said.

Clay acknowledged him with a nod, then walked to the main building, climbed the stairs, and entered the large room with several rows of tables. Tyler sat in one of the plastic chairs in the front row.

"What happened out there?" he asked. "A track worker stopped me halfway around the track and had me sit in my car for fifteen minutes. They said there was an accident."

Clay nodded. He pulled out a chair next to Tyler and sat down, burying his face in his hands. After a prolonged moment, he said, "Shane's car…it sped up and crashed into the wall. It was bad, man. Really bad."

"Was it through the final corner? That one was tricky."

Clay shook his head. "On the straight, the easiest section of the track. I can't explain it. The car just sped up and went straight into the wall."

"Shane wasn't particularly fast, but he was a competent driver. I wonder what happened?"

Clay squeezed his hands together to keep them from shaking. "I'd rather not talk about it right now."

The next half-hour was spent largely in silence, with Clay staring blankly at the ceiling and Tyler fiddling on his smart phone. The door to the media center opened and Maki Takano stepped in, followed by the tall Japanese man with slicked back black hair and a pinstripe suit. Maki looked pale, but stood tall when she spoke.

"As you can imagine, we are all horrified about what happened," she said. "We've decided to cancel the remainder of the event. You will be taken to the airport in private cars later today. I'm sorry we have to cut your drive short, but I'm sure you understand."

"How is Shane?" Clay asked.

Maki said nothing. She looked at him with serene, melancholy eyes.

"Is he conscious?"

Maki took a deep breath and exhaled slowly. "I'm sorry. He was pronounced dead at the hospital a few minutes ago," she said in almost a whisper.

Tyler leaned back in his chair, his hands grabbing the top of his head. "Holy shit."

Clay's eyes opened wide. "Oh my God…"

Maki stepped to the side. "This is Mr. Jimmy Bando, head of security for Kamita Motors."

Bando stepped forward and spoke in a loud commanding tone, showing no hint of emotion. "Just for the record, we studied the data telemetry aboard the car. It records everything, like a black box on an airplane. It showed that the accident was caused by driver error. Simply put, Mr. Boyle was driving over his head."

"Thank you, Bando-san," Maki said as she turned her attention back to the two journalists. "There's a shuttle outside to take you back to the hotel when you are ready."

The two Kamita employees quietly left the room. After a silent minute had passed, Tyler stood up. "I admit, I didn't much like the guy, but losing one of our own like that…it's hard to take," he said as he moved toward the door.

Clay sprang up and grabbed Tyler's arm. "Mark, I saw the whole thing, and that was not driver error."

Chapter 10

Clay walked along the courtyard pathway that led from his room to the main lobby with his roller suitcase in tow. The late afternoon sun shone overhead, and he stretched his arms in the air, when he noticed a large black Mercedes-Benz S500 sedan pulled to the side of the driveway. A stocky Asian man, with wavy hair, rimless spectacles, and dressed in a dark brown suit, stepped out of the driver's seat and walked over to him.

"Here, let me help you with that," he said in perfect English. "I was hired by Kamita Motors to take you to the airport." He took the handle of Clay's suitcase and rolled it to the back of the sedan, where he opened the trunk and lifted the Samsonite with one hand as if it were filled with feathers. He then placed it carefully into the luggage compartment.

"Thanks, I still need to check out, so I'll be right back," Clay said as he turned toward the lobby entrance.

From around the corner of the building, Maki, dressed in a purple blouse hanging over semi-tight designer jeans, walked up to Clay. "Why didn't you send for the concierge?" she asked. "They would have picked you up and transported you here."

"Please, it's only a few hundred feet. And I don't think I can handle yet another golf-cart ride. If you can excuse me, I'm going to go pay for my incidentals now."

Maki stepped in his way. "Everything has been taken care of. You're all set. Mark Tyler was on an earlier flight, so he left a couple of hours ago. He told me to give you his regards."

"Oh, he did? That was nice of him." Clay felt a bit disappointed he didn't have a chance to say goodbye. He genuinely liked the guy, and it wasn't often that he liked someone he had just met.

"If there is anything you need, don't hesitate to contact me," she said.

Clay nodded. "Oh, and Ms. Takano, our magazine policy forbids us to accept gifts that are too expensive, so I left the tablet in the room."

"You should have kept it, but I appreciate your integrity. We will donate it to a charity in your name then. And please call me Maki," she said with a smile.

"I'm really sorry about the accident."

"Yes, we're all still in shock. Have a safe trip back." She walked him to the open rear door of the sedan. "Will we see you at the Tokyo Motor Show in a few days?"

Clay shook his head. "No, I'm too low on the pecking order for that, although I would love to go someday." He stepped into the rear seat of the car as the Asian driver closed the door for him and made his way to the driver's seat.

Clay looked out the window and waved goodbye to Maki as the car pulled out of the hotel driveway.

She returned his gesture with a deep bow, her shiny black hair brushing the sides of her face.

From the half-open window, the cool mountain breeze hit Clay's face and swirled in the rear cabin of the limousine. The sky had turned into a pinkish blue as the sun slowly descended towards the hills. The road to the airport was extremely narrow, but the driver expertly navigated the over-size sedan through the meandering pathways that wrapped around the rocky cliff edges of the area. They passed a number of roadside cafes where locals gathered around outdoor tables to sip coffee and talk about the latest soccer match. The car came to a stop at a T-junction, and a sign showed an arrow pointing left for the airport. Bracing for the hard left turn, Clay was hurtled the other way when the car steered right.

"Excuse me, sir, but that sign said the airport is the other way," Clay said as he straightened himself in his seat.

The driver didn't answer.

Clay leaned forward. "Excuse me. That sign said the airport is the other way."

"We need to make a quick stop," the driver said without looking back at him. "You'll get to your flight in plenty of time."

"Are we picking up another passenger?"

The driver said nothing and took the next few turns at even a faster clip.

Clay squeezed the overhead grab handle, contemplating issuing a complaint to Kamita officials on his smart phone.

The Mercedes-Benz turned into a tree-lined driveway that led to a quaint single-family residence. The outer walls of the small two-story house were covered in stone façade, making the residential building look like it came straight out of a Louis Malle movie. A small metal bench and large tree decorated the front yard.

The driver pulled the Mercedes to a stop, jumped out,

and opened the rear door of the car. "Someone inside of the house wants to speak with you," he said.

Clay looked up at him. "What are you talking about?"

"Just get your ass out of the car and follow me into the house."

"No, I think I'll just stay right here."

"Not an option. We don't have much time." The driver pulled out a leather cardholder and flashed a CIA badge. The name on the card read Charles Wong.

Clay looked up at Wong's face. "What's all this about?"

"Just follow me," Wong said as he walked up to the front entrance of the house. He gave the wooden door two hard knocks. "It's Charlie, I brought the package," he said.

Wong opened the unlocked door and motioned with his head for his guest to step inside. Clay, wanting to run in the opposite direction, paused, afraid that once he stepped into the house, he may never come back out.

"Hurry up and get in if you don't want to miss your flight," Wong said.

That Wong mentioned there was still time to make his flight provided a small sense of reassurance to Clay that he was ultimately going to the airport, so he cautiously stepped through the open door and found himself in a large living room with no furnishings except a large foldable plastic table—the kind one would take to a picnic—and a few chairs. On the table were a couple of laptop computers, several cell phones, walkie-talkies, and a small black handgun. A Caucasian woman in her mid-thirties sat behind the table. She wore her straight blonde hair pulled back and was dressed in a dark blue blouse and jeans. She had an attractive face, with light makeup that accentuated her naturally high cheekbones. She could have easily been mistaken for a local, if it wasn't for the gun sitting on the table.

"Stockton Clay?" she asked matter-of-factly, putting her cell phone down.

"Yes."

"Sit down," she said.

Clay tentatively sat down in one of the folding chairs. "Can you please tell me what this is all about?"

"I'm Beth Flowers. I'm part of a special task force division of the CIA. The man who drove you here is Agent Charlie Wong. We wanted to talk to you because we have reason to believe that your life is in danger."

Flowers reached into her pocket and flashed her CIA identification card.

"I don't understand," Clay said.

"The car that crashed today, we think it was originally meant for you," she said. "We have reason to believe it was rigged to collide against the wall."

"There must be some kind of mistake. I mean, I've never done anything to have someone want to hurt me."

"Were you or were you not supposed to be in that red car today?"

"Well, yes, but Shane Boyle took it away from me."

"That was his misfortune. And you saw the crash, did you not? Did it look natural to you?"

Clay shifted uneasily in his chair. "Well no, but the Kamita people said it was driver error."

"Look, we've been investigating Tetsuro Kanda for illegal activities that I can't get into right now, and your name kept coming up, so we think you may be in danger."

"I really think there's been some kind of mistake. I'm just a normal kid from California who writes for a car magazine. This is the first time I've ever been to a Kamita event. And I just want to go home."

"Then why did Mr. Kanda specifically invite you to this event? We have it on good authority that he wanted you here to kill you," she said.

"That's insane. I just met the man only yesterday."

"Well, I hope you're right, and we are mistaken. In any case, we're going to do everything we can to protect you, but you must contact us if you find anything out of the ordinary, do you understand?" she said.

"Like, I said…"

Flowers cut him off. "Do. You. Understand?"

Clay shifted his eyes away. "Yes, of course."

"Good. Do not tell anyone about our meeting here because everything related to this investigation is classified. Don't even tell your family. We will be in touch if we find anything more that concerns you. Please call this number if you run into anything suspicious or out of the ordinary." Flowers handed him a business card and turned her attention back to her cell phone.

Wong grabbed Clay's right arm and pulled him up out of his chair. "Okay, let's go. You're done here," he said. He escorted Clay back out to the car, letting him open his own door this time.

"But why would Mr. Kanda want to kill me?" Clay asked.

"We don't know for sure," Wong said after slipping into the driver's seat. He started the engine and quickly drove the car off of the property, back onto the main road, this time diligently following the signs to the airport.

"So what am I supposed to do?" Clay said, relieved to be on his way home.

"Just do things you normally do. If we see any unusual activity, you will hear from me or Agent Whitaker in California." Wong glanced into the rearview mirror at Clay's face. "You probably haven't noticed, but we've been watching over you for the past week. Judging from the track incident today, it seems like maybe our hunch was right and someone is trying to hurt you. Therefore, we thought it prudent to bring you in and inform you of the situation. Although we'll always have someone close by, be cautious and keep our contact information handy."

"I still think there's been some big mistake."

Wong pulled the Mercedes-Benz to a stop in front of the departures terminal at the Cote d'Azur Airport. "OK, we're here," he said, making no move to get out. He reached for a lever to pop the trunk open, prompting Clay to get out and collect his belongings. After Clay grabbed his suitcase, the Mercedes-Benz revved its engine and disappeared into a sea of taxis down the airport road.

* * * *

A small white Renault Clio sat along a curb across from the departures terminal at the Cote d'Azur airport, its engine idling, blending in with the other compact cars parked near-by. In the driver's seat sat Maki Takano, wearing a silk scarf around her neck, her hands on the steering wheel and the window rolled down. From behind her oversize Prada sun-glasses, she watched Clay as he got out of the limousine and entered the terminal building through the sliding glass doors. She stepped out of the car and walked to where she had a better view of the inside of the terminal through its large windows, keeping her gaze fixed on the young journalist. Once Clay disappeared behind the security line, she returned to her car, restarted the engine, and briskly drove away.

Chapter 11

The thought of Shane Boyle's death weighed heavily on Tetsuro Kanda as he shuffled through a stack of papers in his private office at Circuit Paul Ricard. Kanda's office occupied the top floor of the main pit building, overlooking the entire facility with large windows all around, providing a 360-degree view of the racetrack. His furnishings exuded a part-Western, part-Japanese theme, all strategically placed according to his Feng-Shui interior designer. His grand walnut desk sat at the far end of the room, with a large leather sofa and coffee table occupying the middle of the office. An old painting on a large folding screen by famous Japanese artist Kano Eitoku stood near a small self-serve bar, stocked with Kanda's favorite liquor, Yamazaki whiskey. Next to it was a large sliding glass door that led to the balcony. An 80-inch video monitor hung on a side wall. On most days, the blinds to the windows were open, but during those rare instances when Kanda occupied the office, they were kept shut.

Tetsuro Kanda was born to Hiroyuki Kanda, whose father—and Tetsuro's grandfather—was the founder of Kamita Industries, Kojiro Kanda, who began the company as a clock manufacturer in a small town called Hamamatsu, located about a hundred-and-fifty miles south of Tokyo. After World War II, the company switched from making clocks to manufacturing scooters and motorcycles—a very necessary commodity in Japan during the rebuilding era—then segued into producing automobiles in the late fifties. The company nearly went bankrupt in the early eighties when the Japanese economic bubble burst and struggled to stay afloat through the next two decades, but things quickly turned around when Tetsuro took over the reins at the tender age of twenty-five after the untimely death of his father. He renamed the company Kamita Motor Company, relocated its headquarters to Tokyo, and cut unnecessary waste from all its operations, even closing down plants and laying off workers, acts never before seen from a large Japanese company. At first, the media attacked him for being cold, dishonorable, and un-Japanese, but within several years, when Kamita Motors had grown into the largest carmaker in the world, he was heralded by those same critics as a prodigy and national treasure.

Kanda heard a loud knock on the office door. He leaned back in his chair, sipped a glass of whiskey, and pressed a button on his desk that automatically unlocked the door.

"Come in," he said.

Jimmy Bando stepped inside and bowed.

"I'm sorry for disturbing you, Kanda-san, but I felt it necessary to update you personally on the cleanup."

Bando was the only one who could bypass Kanda's secretary for an impromptu meeting. He had twenty-four-hour access to the boss, serving loosely as his main bodyguard and all-round handy man. Bando was born into a yakuza family, destined to follow his father's footsteps into a life of organized crime; however, he was never allowed to fulfill that fate after his father was killed in an altercation with a rival clan member while Jimmy was still in diapers. Kanda took a liking to Jimmy's mother, who worked as a hostess in an upscale Ginza nightclub, and agreed to financially take care of her and Jimmy. For the next twenty years, Bando worked devotedly for Kanda, indebted to the man who rescued him from a lifetime of servitude to the Japanese mob.

"All the investigators have left, sir. Everything is in order," Bando said.

Kanda nodded his head approvingly. "Good. Did you allow them access to everything?"

"Yes. The track investigators, local police, and those from the French government combed over the wreckage. Lackey-san allowed them to review all the information on the data telemetry system."

"And what did they find?" Kanda asked.

"They all came to the same conclusion. Driver error," Bando said with a wry smile. "The local police station even tweeted that it appreciated the cooperation of Kamita Motors."

Kanda knew that the incident would leave a small smear on Kamita Motors' public image, but he was confident that it would pass and people would forget, for it was the only fatal accident at a driving event in the company's long history. Earlier in the day, he instructed Maki Takano to send a letter of condolence to Shane Boyle's family, which he insisted he would sign personally. He asked his chief financial officer to prepare a donation to Boyle's live-in partner, a fellow automotive writer he was planning to marry in the coming weeks. Kanda relaxed his shoulders and leaned back in his chair.

"I'm glad to hear that everything went smoothly."

"*Hai.*" Bando bowed his head.

"That will be all," Kanda said.

Bando bowed again and left the office without uttering another word, shutting the door tight behind him.

Glancing at the wall clock, he shifted uneasily in his chair, as he bit off a piece of his thumbnail and spit it out into a nearby wastebasket. He gazed at his artwork, admiring the details of the brushwork until a ringtone from his laptop computer broke the silence.

Kanda hesitated before clicking the answer button, but after three rings, he picked up. The face of an elderly man with thick-rimmed brown glasses, messy red and gray hair, and a white beard appeared on the monitor.

"Yes, Dr. Kranchek?" Kanda said in English, a bead of sweat trickling down his temple.

Dr. Henrik Kranchek, Kanda's personal physician and former consultant to Pax-Gen, Inc., a biotech subsidiary of Kamita Motors, stared back at him with gray eyes. He looked much like your stereotypical mad German scientist, only he was half German, the other half of his ethnic makeup being Dutch. In a high-pitched voice, his words sounded through the laptop speakers.

"Kanda-san, we were successful in collecting the samples from his room," he said.

"When will you have the results?"

"As soon as I get them back to my lab in Tokyo," Kranchek said.

"Let me know as soon as possible."

Kranchek then tightened his lip and took off his glasses.

"I'm sorry, but I have some very bad news."

Kanda stared intensely at the face on his computer monitor. "What is it, doctor?" he asked in a soft, barely audible, voice.

"We found out why your son Kenji has been prone to mild convulsions recently. He has a rare spinal disorder that can't be cured," Kranchek said.

Kanda pounded his fist pounding on the desk. "No, that can't be. He's only five. There must be a mistake."

"We ran and reran the tests. He will most likely be paralyzed from the neck down in a couple of years, and then he will lose functions of his organs. I'm truly sorry sir, but we are still running tests, and it doesn't look prom..."

"Cure him, doctor."

Kanda clicked the "end call" icon, cutting his physician off. He stood up and grabbed a small figurine of a samurai warrior on his desk and hurled it at the window. It broke in half against the glass before falling to the floor. As he screamed at the top of his lungs, he swiped his arms across his desk, sending paper fluttering through the air and knocking over a Tiffany lamp, causing its colorful glass lampshade to shatter in a hundred pieces. After his private outburst had subsided, he sat back in his chair huffing and puffing, staring blankly at the computer monitor. Tears streamed from his eyes, and he buried his face in his hands, sobbing loudly. With a shaking hand, he took out a cell phone from his breast pocket and punched in Jimmy Bando's number.

Kanda did not wait for a greeting. "We must not let the Russians have their way with the Clay boy."

He ended the call and wiped the tears from his face with a personalized handkerchief that he kept in his breast pocket. After putting the handkerchief away, he got up, straightened his suit, and walked out the door, leaving his office in a state of disarray.

Chapter 12

Despite the cacophony of honking horns and pissed off shuttle drivers shouting obscenities at each other, Clay felt a wave of relief when he stepped out of the Delta Airlines arrival terminal at LAX. The familiar scene of the frenzied swarm of cars, taxis, and shuttle buses vying for position under the colored passenger-pickup signs told him he was home. The Lyft driver he had summoned pulled up in a Toyota Camry and helped Clay load his luggage into the trunk. The driver, a young mulatto-skinned, dark-haired man with a black bushy beard, said something to him in a foreign tongue when Clay sat down on the soft fabric seat.

"What did you just say?" Clay asked, knowing full well he had been misidentified.

"Oh, I'm sorry," the Lyft driver said in an Arabic accent. "I thought you were Egyptian. Are you Asian?"

"Does it matter?"

"You looked Egyptian at first, so I was asking you what town you were from. Sorry if I offended you."

"No, you didn't offend me. I've had a really exhausting trip. Just take me to my destination."

"Sure, boss," the driver said as he pulled away from the curb. He looked at the navigation app on his smart phone mounted to his car's windshield. "Off Ocean Avenue in Torrance, right?" Without waiting for an answer, he guided the Camry onto Century Blvd. and onto the I-405.

Clay wondered why the traffic was so heavy on a Sunday evening. It didn't take long to see the reason for the congestion when the Camry passed a car sitting upside down on the side of the road near the shoulder. There were three patrol cars, a firetruck, and an ambulance blocking two of the right-hand lanes.

"Wow, that thing is totaled. I hope no one was hurt," the Lyft driver said as he drove slowly by the accident, rubbernecking to get a better look.

The sight of the crashed car brought back images of the accident at Paul Ricard, making Clay shake uncontrollably. He envisioned Boyle's limp body being carted to the ambulance, and he could have sworn he smelled the sour odor of burning chemicals and charred rubber.

The Lyft driver glanced into the rearview mirror and saw Clay's ashen face. "Hey, are you all right, boss?"

"Yeah, just get me to my destination," Clay replied with a trembling voice.

The driver kicked the Camry into another gear, while constantly jumping in and out of the car pool lane and threaded through slower cars as if they were stationary cones on an obstacle course. Nothing else was said during the fifteen-minute ride from LAX to Torrance, until the car pulled into a small tree-lined cul-de-sac and stopped beside a wooden two-story house. Clay then collected his things and walked up to the front porch, past his Nismo 370Z parked in the driveway. He gave the front door three hard knocks.

A woman's voice sounded from the other side: "Who is it?"

"It's me, mom," Clay said.

The lock to the door unlatched with a loud click, and a

white middle-aged woman greeted her adopted son with a warm smile. "You said you were coming back Tuesday, it's only Sunday," she said as she opened the door and gave him a big hug.

"Yeah, the trip was cut short."

Clay always wondered how such a small woman could hug so tight. The top of her head only came to his chin, and although JoAnne Clay had gained some weight in the past few years, she was still in great shape for a woman of fifty-five, especially one who didn't exercise regularly. Her warm friendly eyes and constant smile always cheered him up when he was down, but he knew that underneath her skin was one of the toughest persons he had ever known. JoAnne had lost her mom to cancer when she was fourteen, and all but raised her younger brother and sister by herself. She survived ovarian cancer when she was still in her early twenties, but the condition had left her sterile. Despite all the hardships and obstacles, she was still able to realize her dream of being a supportive wife and mother, when she married the love of her life, Howard Clay, and adopted Stockton a few years later.

Stockton walked into the house, which smelled of freshly cooked Bolognaise sauce. His father sat at the dining table fiddling with an iPad. Howard looked up at Stockton, his reading glasses hanging on the edge of his nose. "Hi son, how was your trip?"

An ex-military man, Howard sat straight in his chair, his excellent posture and lean build contradicting his sixty-two years. He spent twenty of them serving as a pilot in the U.S.

Air Force, and most of those were in cargo planes, although he originally wanted to be a fighter pilot—unfortunately for him, his six-foot-three-inch frame kept him from fitting into the cramped cockpit of an F-18. Long since retired, he now spent his days performing chores around the house, running five miles every other day, and playing golf once a week with some of his old military buddies. It was a lifestyle he had come to enjoy.

"The trip was pretty crazy," Stockton said as he took off his light quilted jacket and sat down at the table. "What's for dinner? I'm starving."

"I just made some spaghetti," JoAnne replied as she brought a steaming plate of meat and pasta, and placed it in front of him on the table.

Stockton grabbed a fork and dug in, shoving nearly half the serving into his mouth with the first forkful. His mom's rich tomato sauce was always a bit sour, but that's what he liked about it. And there was plenty of garlic inside, which he also loved.

"So how was your trip?" asked Howard again.

Stockton kept his eyes fixed on his food. "There was an accident, a journalist was killed," he said. He had contemplated not telling them about the incident because he didn't want to worry them, but when he couldn't come up with an alternate story, he decided to just blurt out the truth.

"Oh, my Lord, are you all right?" JoAnne gasped, her hand covering her mouth.

"I'm fine. A car went off the track and the driver was killed. It was an accident."

JoAnne and Howard shot nervous looks at one another as Stockton finished the rest of his spaghetti, washing it all down with a large glass of water. He loosened his leather belt that held up his slim fit Levi jeans and paused before he spoke again.

"Mom, Dad, I know you told me that the identities of my real parents are sealed, but is there anything you know about them that you haven't mentioned to me? You know, if they were possibly involved in bad things, like I don't know, drugs or crime or something?"

"No, of course not. You know that we had you under a closed adoption process," JoAnne said. "We can't find out even if we wanted to. Why are you asking, Stockton? What's wrong?"

"It's nothing. It's just that I had a lot of time to think on the plane, and I realized that it's about time I found out who I really am. Not knowing where I came from or what my lineage is, it's hard to figure out where I belong in this world, really hard…" Stockton sighed deeply. "Forget it, I'm not making any sense."

"Stockton, you belong to us. You're our son," JoAnne said.

Howard crossed his arms. "We've never told you this, but when we took you in, the woman handling the adoption said you came from abroad."

"Howard, none of that matters," JoAnne said.

Stockton's head perked up. "So I wasn't born an American? That's new."

"Yeah, they didn't tell us from where. In fact, they said

they didn't know either, but your mother fell in love with you as soon as she saw you, so it didn't matter to us one bit," Howard said.

"You mean there's no record of my birth?"

Howard shook his head. "Not that we know of."

JoAnne cracked a nervous smile. "I've always imagined that you may have royal blood running in your veins."

"Or criminal blood," Stockton said.

"How can you say such a thing?" JoAnne shouted.

"Pretend I never brought it up." Stockton put down his fork, threw on his jacket and grabbed his suitcase and back-pack. "I need to get back home. Thanks for letting me keep my car here."

Both JoAnne and Howard walked Stockton to his car. They took turns hugging him. "Don't work too hard. Make sure you get your rest," JoAnne said.

Stockton loaded his stuff into the tight luggage compartment of his sports car and climbed into the driver's seat. He started the engine, waved goodbye, and drove off into the evening.

As Clay sped in the fast lane of the I-405 onramp, he contemplated his origins. He had been adopted by Cauca-sian parents soon after his birth, and they raised him with plenty of love and support; however, there were times when he was reminded that he wasn't like everyone else. To this day, he would recall Back-to-School nights in elementary school when his Asian classmates looked at his light-haired, blue-eyed parents with curiosity, while the Caucasian chil-dren from church avoided him altogether because they said he looked like a terrorist. Perhaps this was why he longed for acceptance and a higher meaning in his life. But now, all he really wanted was just to live a halfway normal life without anyone telling him someone wants him dead.

Chapter 13

Clay entered his small second-story studio apartment, located in a quiet, middle-class neighborhood in Glendale, ready to keep the promise he made to the mail boy, Craig Riley, about playing Combat Shooter. And besides, he felt he needed the escape right about now—an intense gaming session would provide a welcome distraction from the events of the past two days. He took a quick shower and plopped his body down into a well-worn single sofa chair that faced a trio of flat-screen televisions. He owned all the latest consoles, from Sony, Microsoft, and Nintendo, bought on long-term credit as his meager automotive journalist's salary couldn't offer him the luxuries of life just yet. The only other items here were an Ikea double bed, tucked in the far corner of the room, and an unframed poster of Ayrton Senna hanging on the wall.

Like many young men of his generation, Clay was a gamer, although he disliked this label because the term had a negative connotation when applied to anyone past puberty. For him, gaming was a serious activity for it gave him the chance to fight life-and-death battles without the risk of actually getting injured…aside from the occasional sprained thumb. He got enough physical activity from judo, which he started as an elective class at UCLA and still practiced twice a week on campus. It was a good way to stay in shape, without going to a gym. His goal was to get a black belt, still at least two years away. As for gaming, he once toyed with the idea of pursuing a career in E Sports, but he quickly realized there were many better and more dedicated gamers out there, and earning a comfortable living playing video games was reserved only for a select few.

He felt a tinge of excitement as he powered up the latest version of the PlayStation gaming console, for he was in the final stages of testing a new video-game controller, shaped like a very real-looking handgun, as part of a study group for a new online shooter game. He and Craig were among a hundred pre-sale beta-testers selected from around the country—a distinction that gave both of them a sense of accomplishment for being recognized as leaders of their often ridiculed field.

The televisions glowed to life as Clay placed the wireless Logitech headset over his head. *All systems check, join the game in progress.* Craig was already in the midst of the action, playing from his own home four blocks away.

"Well, look who finally showed up," Craig greeted him through the game's intercommunication system. "How was your trip?"

"Crazy. I'll tell you all about it someday."

Clay didn't waste any time getting into the action. He pointed the fake gun at the television monitors and took down Nazi bad guys two, sometimes three, at a time. The gun-shaped controller had a special mechanism that enabled it to recoil like a real firearm with every shot. It even had a reload feature when it ran out of ammo. Within a minute of playing, he had already cleared the level, leaving Craig and the other online testers in the dust. Clay's character, a digital rendition of a mercenary soldier, ran, jumped, tucked, and rolled like a real person, as it came upon the Level Three Boss, a giant Demon Hitler with long fangs who shot fire-balls out of its mouth. Clay took him down with five well-aimed shots.

"Whoa, that was awesome. Man, with moves like that, you should've been a Navy Seal or something," Craig said.

"I would have never passed the physical. I'll see you tomorrow at work."

"What, quitting already? Let's get the Level Four Boss," Craig said.

"Tomorrow, man. I need to get some Red Bull and chill." Clay pulled off his head set and switched off the tele-vision and game console. He grabbed his jacket and headed out the door.

He walked two blocks to a Seven-Eleven store, which often served as his primary source for nourishment. When he entered, the lone Hispanic man working the counter gave him a friendly nod. Clay walked down the middle aisle of the empty store and grabbed two cans of Red Bull from the refrigerator on the back wall, when he heard a "thump" and what sounded like a man grunting.

As he turned around, the cashier was not at his post. He then heard a "click," recognizing the sound of a door being locked.

"Hey, I'm still in here," Clay said loudly.

No answer.

Clay took another step towards the counter, where he saw a large man at the far end of the aisle, dressed in a black knee-length coat and a ski mask pulled down over his face.

The man pointed what looked like a gun with a silencer attached to it at Clay.

It's said that when a person sees the wrong side of a gun, it elicits one of two different reactions: either you freeze from sheer terror, also known as "a deer in the headlights affect," which usually results in getting killed, or the body acts to protect itself out of pure instinct. Fortunately for Clay, he was part of the latter group, as he instantly dropped to the floor and barrel rolled to the rear of the aisle, mimicking a move of one of his favorite video-game characters. The man aimed the gun at Clay and squeezed the trigger twice. One of the bullets embedded itself into the floor, the other tore a small hole in Clay's jacket, missing his flesh by a hair's width.

By some miracle, Clay had made it to the back of the aisle and took shelter behind a rack of potato chips. He hoped that the man would clean out the register and just go away, but then he heard the sound of approaching footsteps.

Panic set in, as Clay's hands shook uncontrollably. He took three deep breaths, relaxed his shoulders, and concentrated on coming up with a plan. As far as he could tell, he had two options: one was running for the door and trying to make it out of the building before being shot in the back; the other was to charge the killer and take his gun away. Neither choice had much chance in succeeding, but he decided to go with the first option and, if by some miracle he made it to the door, he hoped there would be enough time to unlock it and escape. Clay crouched into a sprinter's position and readied his body to spring forward, but stopped when he saw something that defied description. Appearing out of nowhere, a matte black Dodge Charger plowed head first into the store, shattering the glass doors into a thousand pieces.

Using his arms to shield his body from the flying debris of glass shards, Slim Jims, and Corn Nuts, Clay leaped to the back of the store. The Charger took out a piece of the front counter before ramming its front end into the man in the black coat. Clay heard the grotesque sound of crushed bones as the armed man screamed under his mask. He took the full brunt of the car's force before disappearing underneath its front bumper. The Charger stopped, and the passenger door of the car swung open. A thirty-something African American man in the driver's seat leaned across the console.

"Russell Whitaker with the CIA. Get your ass in the car now," the man said as he flashed his government ID.

Clay looked at the card, but didn't move.

"Boy, get your ass in the car," Whitaker shouted.

Clay surveyed the scene and slowly walked towards the open door of the Charger. He climbed into the passenger seat and, as he reached out to close the door, he saw the body of the Seven-Eleven worker on the floor near the half-broken front counter. The Hispanic man was on his back, his eyes open, and a large black hole marked his forehead.

Before Clay could buckle his seat belt, Whitaker shifted in reverse and punched the accelerator. The Charger backed out of the store and peeled rubber out of the parking lot onto the main street. In less than five minutes, they were on the I-5 freeway, as Whitaker regularly monitored the rearview mirror to make sure they weren't being followed.

"You just killed a man. What the hell is going on?" Clay shouted with his voice an octave higher in pitch than usual.

"Hang tight, my man. I'm taking you to someone who'll be able to answer a lot of your questions."

Chapter 14

Clay felt his heart racing, and he trembled with the realization that he had actually been shot at for the first time in his life. He studied the man seated next to him, Russell Whitaker, who sat reclined in the driver's seat with both hands on the steering wheel. Whitaker was a big man, looking more like a professional football player than a government agent. In fact, Clay would later discover that Whitaker did play ball, as a second-string defensive end for the USC Trojans back in the day. And although his six-foot, four-inch frame carried a little more heft than when he was in his college days, he looked like he could still mix it up with the best of them on the gridiron.

Whitaker pushed a button on the dashboard and spoke into a small microphone attached to the rearview mirror. "This is Whitaker. Requesting a clean-up crew at a Seven-Eleven on the corner of Olive and Victory. Two dead; one unfriendly."

"Roger that," a female voice said through the speakers. "We have cars on the way."

"Thanks. I left a big mess. Out." Whitaker ended the transmission.

Clay turned towards the husky agent. "You were the one who cut off the Jaguar the other day, aren't you?"

Whitaker nodded. "Yeah, you suddenly pulled off the freeway like a maniac, so it took me a while to catch back up with you. Freaked me out."

"That guy back there? Who was he?"

"We won't have an I.D. on him for at least a few more hours. Do *you* have any idea who he is?"

"Of course not."

"Well, he really seemed to want you dead." Whitaker abruptly changed lanes and slowed the Charger's speed down to about thirty miles per hour. He studied the rearview mirror for any sign of a tail.

Clay slapped the top of the dashboard. "I keep telling you guys, this is one big mistake. I'm just a normal guy who likes cars and video games. There's no reason for anyone to want me dead."

"So how do you explain what happened back there?"

"I can't. Maybe he was robbing the place, and I just happened to be in the wrong place at the wrong time."

"Yeah, you keep telling yourself that. My orders are to make sure you're unharmed. You're officially under my protection now."

Clay rubbed his temples, his head starting to ache as he tried to fit all the unknown pieces together in an impossibly surreal puzzle. "None of this seems right…people trying to kill me for who knows what reason, the CIA…Wait a minute, I get it. This is one of those hidden camera pranks, right?"

Whitaker shot Clay a condescending look. "No more questions." He then pressed his foot down on the accelerator pedal.

Clay leaned back in his seat and remained quiet as Whitaker, his eyes still darting from the road ahead to the rearview mirror, pulled off the freeway and onto a narrow, empty street lined with a couple of hamburger joints and a furniture store with a "Going Out of Business" sign in front. It could have been anywhere, but judging from the direction they had traveled, Clay guessed it was one of the many unincorporated areas of Los Angeles County.

The Dodge Charger pulled up to a windowless one-story office building, with drab brown walls and no door in front. The sign on the wall read Blackbridge Labs.

"Okay, we're here," Whitaker said as he stepped out of the car.

Clay followed the CIA agent to the back of the building where a dim light illuminated a heavily reinforced door with a small number pad near the doorknob. Whitaker punched in a six-digit code, which prompted a small buzzing sound and a loud click. He opened the metal door and stepped inside.

"Come in, and make sure you shut the door behind you," he said.

Clay stepped into the building. The room was well lit with rows of fluorescent lights embedded in the ceiling, revealing what looked like a state-of-the-art science laboratory, complete with strange-looking machines and computers against every wall. An elderly Asian man appeared from the back office, his short black-and-white hair combed to the side, and dark-rimmed spectacles hanging on the bottom of his nose. The white lab coat that draped over his skinny five-foot, six-inch frame seemed like it was at least a size too big, flapping like a cape whenever he moved. His large round head and his long thin neck made him look like a life-size bobblehead doll. He wore a big smile on his face as he greeted his recently arrived guests in the middle of the room.

"Ah, it's you Agent Whitaker. This must be Stockton Clay," he said in perfect English.

"This is Dr. Nakajima. He works with us. He's the one who wanted to see you," Whitaker said.

"Nice to meet you, doctor. Can you tell me why I'm here?" Clay asked.

"Please call me George," Nakajima said as he shook Clay's hand. "I just finished with your DNA tests. Would you mind having a seat?"

Clay found an office chair at the nearest corner of the lab and sat down. George sat in from of him.

"I understand that you were adopted, is that correct?" Nakajima asked, with his face inches away from Clay's.

"Yeah, so?"

"Do you have any recollection of your real parents?"

"No, I was still a baby. Can you get to the point?"

Nakajima nudged his glasses upwards with his index finger. "Well, Mr. Clay, I'll come right out with it. This may come as a big shock to you, but you are the biological son of Tetsuro Kanda, the president of Kamita Motors."

Chapter 15

Clay paused, not sure if he heard the doctor's words correctly. "I beg your pardon?"

Nakajima reached back for a metal clipboard on a nearby counter. "All the tests line up; there's no mistake. I assume you know who Tetsuro Kanda is."

"But that's impossible."

"I'll take that as a 'yes.' Here are the DNA test results. See for yourself. The one on the top is yours, the bottom one is Mr. Kanda's." Nakajima held out the clipboard.

Clay had never seen a DNA test result before, but the two separate graphs on the sheet of paper had what appeared to be identical blotches of ink.

"Where the hell did you guys get my DNA?" he asked.

"We got it from your apartment," Whitaker replied.

"You broke into my apartment? Isn't that illegal?"

Whitaker put up his hands. "Look, I was just following orders. And…I haven't had anything to eat all day, so if you fellas don't mind, I'm going across the street to get some grub. Y'all want anything?"

Nakajima shook his head. Clay kept glaring.

"Okay, I'll be right back. And don't even think about leaving this building." Whitaker clasped his hands and hurriedly walked out of the building, making sure the door clicked shut behind him.

Nakajima placed his hand lightly on Clay's shoulder. "Actually, Stockton, may I call you Stockton?"

Clay nodded as he returned the clipboard to Nakajima.

He then took off his jacket and held it in his lap. He felt something warm run over his lips and noticed drops of blood on his shirt.

"Oh shit, not again," he mumbled as he pinched his nostrils shut.

Nakajima reached into his front pocket and handed him a handkerchief. "Here, use this."

"Thanks," Clay said as he wiped his nose and upper lip before tilting his head back.

"When did the nosebleeds start?" Nakajima asked.

"About a couple of weeks ago."

"This isn't good."

Nakajima stood up from his chair and took out a pair of latex gloves from a nearby drawer. He retrieved his now bloody handkerchief from Clay and carefully placed it on a tray, which he carried to a workstation at the far end of the lab. Clay couldn't exactly tell what the scientist was doing, but he could see the once-friendly face was fixed in intense concentration. The elderly doctor rolled his office chair from one table to another like a bouncing pinball, punching a keyboard here, mixing liquids in a test tube there.

Several minutes later, he returned to where Clay sat, his brow furrowed. "It's what I suspected. This didn't show up on the DNA tests. You have Andor's Disease. It's a very rare disorder that affects your blood cells, most notably around the brain. If you don't get healthy blood cells from a direct relative soon, your life will end."

"What? This is a joke, right?"

"I'm sorry, but it's not."

"First you tell me that Mr. Kanda is my father, and now, you're telling me I have a fatal disease? What the hell?"

Nakajima remained quiet; the melancholy look in his eyes was enough to tell Clay that he was dead serious.

"How long do I have if I don't get those healthy blood cells?"

"It's hard to say. You might have a few weeks; then again, you might only have a few days. The disease is already in the second of three stages," Nakajima said. "You're free to get second or third opinions, but because this disease is so new, it may take them weeks to come back with results, and you don't have weeks."

"What is it? A form of cancer?"

"No, it's caused by a genetic imbalance. Piercing headaches, as well as your bloody noses, are symptoms of Andor's Disease. They're caused by the inflammation of cells in your anterior ethmoid, which makes the muscles and veins in your temples pulsate, gradually at first, then stronger until the blood vessels explode, killing the host."

"That sounds just delightful," Clay said. "Why can't I just get a blood transfusion from like from a blood bank? I hear about those all the time."

"A standard blood transfusion won't work because this disease works at the cellular level. We need to introduce healthy cells into your system that are an exact match with what you currently have, and that requires a direct relative," Nakajima said.

Stockton stared blankly at the ceiling. "But I don't know of any direct relatives."

"You do now."

Clay turned towards Nakajima. "You mean Mr. Kanda? There's got to be some mistake. There is no way Tetsuro Kanda is my father."

Nakajima looked deep into Clay's eyes. "Stockton, there is no mistake. He is your father. And without a transfusion from him, you will die."

"Okay, if what you say is true, then all I need to do is get blood from him, right? And then I'm cured."

"That might not be so easy. Mr. Kanda is being investigated right now by the CIA, and he is one of the most reclusive men in the world, so tracking him down will be difficult. We'll brief Agent Whitaker as soon as he returns."

"I think I remember hearing that Mr. Kanda will be at the Tokyo Motor Show, and if I'm not mistaken, press days start tomorrow."

"That's good to know. Getting you that transfusion should become the CIA's main priority, but knowing them..." Nakajima left the sentence unfinished.

"Does any of this have anything to do with that man who tried to kill me?"

"I'm sorry, but I'm not at liberty to say."

"We're talking about my life here. Whether I live or die. You need to tell me what the hell is going on."

The doctor removed his glasses and wiped a few beads of sweat from his face with a handkerchief. "You must understand that there are things I can't discuss because of national security."

Clay threw his hands up. "National security? What the

hell do I have to do with national security?"

"There are things that are better for you not to know. And, it's my sincere wish that you can return to the life you were living. That's why I'm assisting them on this particular project. And Agent Whitaker was assigned to watch over you around the clock, without disrupting your daily activities."

"Well, my daily activities have been thoroughly disrupted. And why did you run a DNA test on me, anyways?"

"I was asked to verify your identity. A special task division of the CIA has been searching for Mr. Kanda's lost son for the past several months and when they located you, they asked me to compare your DNA with Mr. Kanda's, to make sure you were the one."

"So why was this CIA task force looking for Kanda's son?"

"I'm sorry, that's all I can say right now."

"At least tell me who that guy was trying to kill me?"

"I'm sorry, Stockton. I wish I could, but I can't because I don't know."

"Then who's my biological mother?"

Nakajima took a deep breath, as his eyes focused on a spider crawling on the wall. After he watched it disappear through a thin crack, he turned to Clay. "I don't know Stockton. Mr. Kanda had many lady friends back then."

The door to the office opened and Whitaker stepped in, holding a greasy paper bag full of French fries. "You guys miss me?"

Nakajima stood up and walked over to the bulky government agent. "Agent Whitaker, as you know, we have confirmed that Stockton here is indeed Mr. Kanda's biological son. But more important, I just discovered that he has a serious disease that requires the presence of his father. Time is of the essence. Is there any way you can bring Mr. Kanda here? Stockton has reason to believe that he will be in Tokyo tomorrow."

"What kind of disease?" Whitaker asked, placing the bag of French fries on a nearby table.

"A very fatal one," Nakajima said.

Whitaker grimaced. "Shit. That certainly throws a kink in our plans."

"The first press day of the Tokyo Motor Show is tomorrow, and I know that Mr. Kanda is going to be there," Clay said.

Whitaker put up a hand. "Slow down, buddy. I need to discuss this with the boss. I was ordered only to watch over you." Without waiting for a response, he took out his cell phone, punched in a four-digit number, and walked into Nakajima's office, closing the door behind him.

A moment later, he cracked the door open and stuck his head out. "Hey doc, the boss wants to speak with you."

"Excuse me, Stockton," Nakajima said, passing in front of Clay as he made his way to the office.

Clay could hear the muffled voices of Nakajima and Whitaker through the shut door. He took out his smart phone and, as he searched for flights to Tokyo on his browser, Whitaker and Nakajima emerged from the office.

Whitaker was the first to speak. "I'm sorry, but he said that we can't expose ourselves to Mr. Kanda just yet. But at the first chance, we'll get him to you."

"And when will that be?" Clay asked.

Whitaker took a bite into a couple of French fries. "Can't say, but we'll do our best."

"That doesn't sound so reassuring. I need to discuss this with my parents." Clay took out his smart phone.

Whitaker reached over and grabbed it. "We'd rather you not disclose the information presented here to anyone just yet, especially to your parents. It will seriously compromise their safety. We don't exactly know who or what we're dealing with yet, so the fewer people involved, the better," Whitaker said.

Clay closed his eyes. "Well, I can't just sit here and wait for you guys to bring Mr. Kanda in at your own leisure."

"Stockton's right. We don't have much time," Nakajima added.

Whitaker shrugged his shoulders. "Not my call."

"Then, I'm going to go to Japan and talk to him myself," Clay said.

Whitaker gulped down his fries and shook his head. "That's not a very good idea."

Whitaker's cell phone buzzed. He looked at the caller ID before answering. He then stepped back into the office, but this time he kept the door open, keeping an eye on Clay as he spoke on the phone.

Clay looked solemnly at Nakajima. "What do you think, doctor? Honest answer."

Nakajima rubbed his chin. "As I said before, time is of the essence. I told his boss that they should locate Mr. Kanda and bring him here immediately, but he said that doing so right now would jeopardize their entire investigation."

"Good to know that they care about me so much," Clay said.

"Still, I don't recommend you going out and trying to find him on your own."

"Listen doctor, I just found out who my real father is. Do you know what that means to me? I've been wondering about my real parents all my life. And when I see Mr. Kanda, I want to ask him a million things, like where I was born and why he gave me up. But more importantly, I want to get that transfusion because I sure as hell don't want to die yet."

Whitaker placed his phone in his pocket and returned to the main room. "That was the boss again. Here's the deal: we strongly recommended that you stay here and let us watch over you while the good doctor here monitors your condition. Bringing Kanda to you will be Priority One after we conclude our investigation."

"And if I say screw you?"

"We're not authorized to detain you against your wishes, so I can't force you to stay."

Clay nodded. "Then it's settled. I'm going."

"I was afraid you were going to say that," Whitaker said

Nakajima stepped forward and handed Clay a business card. "Be careful, and call me as soon as you find him. I will be ready to perform the procedure when you do."

"Thank you, doctor."

"Call me George, please. Oh, and let me give you something to stop those bloody noses, at least for now." The doctor walked to the corner table and opened a drawer. He took out a plastic container and filled it with pink-colored capsules, before tossing the bottle to Clay, who caught it with one hand.

Clay eyed the bottle suspiciously.

"Take two of those every time you feel a headache coming on or get a bloody nose. You can trust me, Stockton, I would never betray you."

"Why are you helping so much? You don't even know me."

Nakajima wagged his finger. "You're wrong about that. I know you better than you think."

Clay flashed the doctor a confused look before heading out the door with Whitaker. Something seemed out of whack, giving him the odd feeling that he was being set up, but by whom and for what purpose, he had no clue.

Chapter 16

Clay's third international plane ride in as many days touched down on the runway at Haneda International Airport just as the sun rose over Tokyo's craggy horizon. As he stepped off the plane and strolled through the terminal, he took note of the cleanliness of the airport, and how the workers, dressed in neat matching uniforms, performed their duties like programmed robots—no socializing with one another, their entire concentration focused on the job at hand. The man behind the immigration counter, dressed in a light blue shirt and tie, carefully studied Clay's passport, looking up at his face several times before letting him pass.

Wearing a fresh polo shirt and a pair of faded jeans, Clay emerged from the customs area holding his modest belongings—a North Face jacket and one Oakley backpack that held a change of clothes and toiletries. When he stepped into the arrivals terminal, he noticed that a few faces looked at him with disappointment when they realized he wasn't the one they were waiting for. Then, he let out a big yawn—he was tired for he only managed to sleep for a couple of hours on the twelve-hour plane ride; his mind too occupied with the recent discovery of his real father.

That he was discarded by his real parents didn't come as a surprise, for he suspected that that was the case ever since his foster parents told him he was adopted. It was the identity of his real father that was the real shocker. Clay was fairly sure that Kanda would deny the relationship, most likely because it would probably expose a secret affair. But whether he owned up to it or not, Clay was determined to get the old man back to America for the transfusion.

Clay scanned the arrivals terminal for anyone holding a sign with his name on it, but the only placards he saw had kanji characters written on them. He walked around the terminal, past the stores and restaurants that weren't yet open for business, until he was sure no one was there to greet him. Agent Whitaker did mention that someone here would be keeping an eye on him, but it seemed like the CIA had misled him again. He made his way to the money exchange window and traded his forty dollars for five thousand Japanese yen, wondering how he was going to pay back the credit card company for his one-thousand-dollar plane ticket.

As he approached a large sign across the way with "Information" written on it in English, a young woman with her hair in a tight bun topped with a small yellow hat welcomed him from behind the counter with a bow.

"*Okayku-sama, douka nasare mashita?*" she asked, sitting abnormally straight in her high office chair, with her gloved hands resting on the desk in front of her.

"English please," Clay said.

The woman's expression went from friendly to horrified, as if she had just offended her guest. She bowed deeply. "I am so sorry. May I help you?" she said with a thick Japanese accent.

Clay smiled, amused at the fact that he looked Japanese to her. "Yes, I want to go to the Tokyo Big Sight. You know, where the Tokyo Motor Show takes place."

The woman smiled and held out her white-gloved hand

in the direction of the escalators. "Please take the Keihin Kyuko bus. It takes you straight there in about thirty minutes," she said.

Clay turned and saw a large sign over the downward traveling escalator marked "Airport Bus."

He thanked her and made his way quickly down the escalator to the bus stop.

The bus pulled up to the curb outside the main terminal building on the exact minute it was scheduled to arrive. Clay boarded the fifty-passenger vehicle, which, despite the early morning hour, was packed with people. He had no choice but to stand, holding onto a grab-handle that hung from the vehicle's ceiling. He wasn't complaining though, as he had a clear view out the large front windshield, treating him to a ground-level view of Tokyo. The sun cast bright yellow streaks of light through sparsely clouded skies that illuminated this wondrous place of efficiency and order. Clay had seen many photos of Tokyo before, he even ran through its streets virtually in a video role-playing game called "Grand Theft Auto: Yakuza," but it was different seeing it all in the flesh. The bus turned left, driving onto a high overpass, where he was treated to an elevated view of an endless sea of buildings that seemed to go on forever. There were no visible flat patches of land anywhere; it appeared that every square inch of this wondrous city was covered in concrete and steel. Although the green foliage of nature was peculiarly absent, the city exuded a strange peacefulness, and was it ever clean. There was no trash anywhere nor was there any graffiti to be seen.

The bus driver announced something in Japanese into a microphone that broadcast his voice through several speakers inside the bus. Clay clearly heard the words "Big Sight" mixed within the babble. As the bus came to a stop, he leaned over and asked the driver, "Is this the Tokyo Big Sight?"

The driver nodded.

Clay threw his backpack over his shoulder and stepped off the bus. Large colorful banners that marked the entrance to the Tokyo Big Sight loomed across the street. Located smack in the Koto ward, the Big Sight played host to small- and medium-sized events while the larger conventions took place at Makuhari Messe in the neighboring Chiba prefecture, about an hour outside of the city. The Tokyo Motor Show was once a grand show that required the expansive halls of the Makuhari Messe, but once China became Asia's largest automotive market, its significance declined, playing second fiddle to the Beijing and Shanghai Auto Shows. For the past few decades, it had been relegated to the smaller venue.

An endless number of cars and buses pulled into the convention center's parking lots as Clay made his way to the media registration center. His timing couldn't have been better as he had arrived about fifteen minutes before the doors opened for the first of two media days, where only journalists and invited guests were allowed in, giving them full access to the cars and opportunities to chat with company executives. The show opened to the public three days later.

Clay got in line at the media registration desk, wondering how on earth he was going to sneak his way in because he didn't have any credentials, and he knew that the Tokyo Auto Show didn't allow walk-ups.

Chapter 17

"I'm sorry, but my credentials were lost at the airport," Clay explained to the young man working the media registration stand. The worker wore a red staff uniform and didn't seem to be in a particularly good mood as a long cue had formed in front of his station that wrapped around the far corner of the building. It was going to be a very long day.

"Do you have identification?" the stand worker repeated.

"No, that was also in my luggage with my credentials, and the airlines misplaced everything. As you can see, I only have this backpack," Clay said.

"And your passport?"

"The baggage person who was trying to help me locate my luggage still has it," Clay continued his lie.

"What is your name?" the young man asked with a hard, pronounced glare.

"Peter Lee," Clay answered with a straight face.

The young worker shot him a suspicious look.

"I'm half."

It was a risk using Lee's name, but Clay was fairly sure that his colleague was registered for the show because Jeremy Simmons mentioned a trip to Tokyo with Peter a few days before, and the Tokyo Motor Show was the only event in town. A small part of him hoped that he was wrong because he couldn't help but feel some envy towards Lee if he was indeed asked to cover the motor show over him, a show that he had wanted to visit all his life.

The worker punched Lee's name into the laptop. "Ah yes, here it is. It says here we mailed it out last week, to America."

"Yes, as I said, I had the pass in my luggage, and my luggage was lost."

"I'm sorry, I can't issue you another one without proper identification."

Clay leaned forward, his elbow resting on the countertop. "Listen, I have a very important interview with Mr. Tetsuro Kanda in a few minutes, and if I don't make it on time, I'm going to hold you personally responsible. It's for a big cover story."

The young man stood his ground, not intimidated by Clay's aggressive body language. "Do you have proof of your appointment?"

"No I don't have proof, but if you call Maki Takano, she will verify it right away."

The young worker paused at hearing Maki's name. "You know Ms. Takano?"

"Yes, she is expecting me any second now, and I will not hesitate to mention your name if I miss my meeting," Clay said as he read the name of the man's identification badge out loud. "Mister Ryohei Suzuki."

Suzuki paused. A bead of sweat rolled down his temple, which he wiped away with a handkerchief. "I will speak to the manager, please excuse me."

He disappeared behind a curtain at the back of the stand. This wasn't good, Clay thought, because the longer this process took, the more likely his bluff would be revealed. He considered leaving the media center and come up with another plan altogether, when Suzuki returned, accompanied by an older man dressed in a cheap beige suit.

"Mr. Lee, here is your pass. I'm sorry for the delay," the manager said, presenting a plastic card with Lee's name on it.

"Thank you," Clay said coolly, trying to conceal his disbelief. He took the pass and attached it to a lanyard he took out of a large box on the counter, and then he placed the cloth loop around his neck.

"It is my pleasure. We don't want to be any trouble for Kamita Motors. They are our biggest sponsor," the older man said smiling. "Please enjoy the show, Mr. Lee."

Clay bowed and quickly walked out of the media center, pleasantly shocked that his plan had worked. He joined the flow of people headed to the front entrance. Once there, an attendant made a visual check of his credential and handed him a flyer that showed a timetable of the press conferences taking place during the day. The Kamita Motors press conference was first up, and it started in fifteen minutes in the West Hall. Clay studied the floor plan on the flyer and headed directly for the Kamita Motors booth.

The West Hall featured Japan's "big four" automakers, and their respective booths were extravagant to say the least. Although they were referred to as "booths," in reality, they were more like small pieces of real estate with their own mini-office building, complete with lounges, a kitchen, and meeting rooms. Displayed up front were the wildest vehicles a person could imagine. There were always plenty of head-turning concepts, super sports cars, large vans, and everything else one could envision riding on two, three, and four wheels.

As Clay strolled through the arena, he walked past the Nissan booth that featured a model of a residential neighborhood powered by a car's fuel cell, while the Mazda display across the way showcased its self-driving sports car. Further into the hall, Toyota and Honda had displays that touted their concept hover cars, with the latter demonstrating a walking, talking robot. But one thing each manufacturer had in common was that their respective floor spaces were attended by shapely female models who flashed their tantalizing smiles to all the visitors. Trying to keep his concentration on the task at hand, Clay advanced deeper into the hall, until he spotted a large Kamita Motors sign against the back wall. Although he was still a good fifty yards away, he could tell that a crowd of people were already gathering around the large booth; he quickened his pace to make sure he got a spot up front.

"Stockton? Stockton!"

Clay cringed when he heard the all too familiar voice of Jeremy Simmons calling out to him from behind. He turned slowly around and saw his boss stomping his feet towards him with Peter Lee diligently flanking his rear. Clay flipped his credential over so the side with Lee's name was hidden.

"Oh, hey Jeremy," Clay said with an unnatural wave.

"What the hell are you doing here?" Simmons asked.

"I can explain."

Simmons' face turned red and his nostrils flared. "I

don't believe this. You can't just show up here without my approval. What the hell do you think you're doing?"

Clay held up his hands. "You're absolutely right, but there's a really good reason for this, which I can't get into right now."

"Don't bother. You're fired. As soon you as get back, clean out your office."

"Jeremy, there's a lot more going on here than you realize. Please."

Jeremy turned to Lee. "Peter, I hope you enjoy having your own office because your roommate is history."

A wide grin broke out on Lee's face. "Yeah, I'm excited."

Simmons walked past Clay without saying another word. Lee followed closely behind his boss and flashed a devious smile at Clay as he passed by.

"You little shit," Clay said under his breath. He momentarily considered tackling Lee from behind and pounding his face into a bloody pulp, but instead he settled for flipping him the bird. Sure, it was immature, but it made him feel better, despite the fact that Lee didn't see it. Clay turned around and rushed over to the Kamita Motors booth.

The interaction with Simmons had cost him valuable time. The crowd in front of the Kamita Motors booth was already overflowing with journalists and corporate executives. Every chair in front of the main stage was occupied. At the risk of offending a few dozen VIPs, Clay forced his way towards the front, squeezing through a sea of suits until he was about fifty feet from the stage, but off to one side.

The stage was enormous, consisting of metal and wood, and set quite high, about five feet from the ground. A few technicians darted across the width of the platform holding cords in their hands, making sure everything was plugged in and cleared away. Clay spotted Maki Takano, dressed in a chic dark pink business suit, standing behind a roped off section holding a notebook in her hand and directing people to their places. She had on a wireless earpiece and spoke into a small microphone pinned to her lapel. Clay waved his hands frantically, but she didn't look his way. If anyone could lead him to Kanda, it was Maki, so he decided to make his way to her immediately, even if that meant pushing the Prime Minister of Japan out of the way, which he thought he might have done. He made slow progress through the throng of people, and got to about five rows from the front-left corner of the stage when suddenly, loud dance music blared from a dozen giant speakers around the booth. The show was about to begin, and the people surrounding him bunched tightly together with their attention fixed on the stage. There was no room for him to advance any further; he had no choice but to hold his position and wait.

Chapter 18

Bright lights in a variety of colors flashed throughout the rear section of West Hall, until gradually, they all came together at the middle of the stage, lighting it in a deep golden sparkle. From above, ropes dropped seemingly from midair, as their edges dangled a few feet above the ground. The onlookers gasped as acrobatic circus performers, dressed in matching skin-tight costumes and heavy makeup on their faces, slithered down the lines, some using only their feet and legs. As soon as these performers dropped onto the stage, they stood in a ring formation. From inside their circle, a small stand slowly ascended from beneath the stage floor. Tetsuro Kanda, dressed in a navy Hugo Boss suit, rose above the ground like a sacred deity as he stood proudly on the stand, a smile fixed across on his face. An enthusiastic wave of applause filled the air.

The music slowly faded out, as a single spotlight focused directly onto the president of Kamita Motors. One of the circus performers appeared from the surrounding darkness doing a series of back handsprings. He theatrically handed the company president a microphone before cartwheeling off the stage.

Kanda took a moment to survey the large crowd that had gathered to hear him speak. Every person in the arena was silent; the air was thick with anticipation.

"Thank you for coming," Kanda said as his voice echoed off the walls. "As you know, Kamita Motors has always been dedicated to a certain kind of race, and I'm not referring to those run on racetracks. I'm speaking of the human race. We have and will continue to break new ground in the automotive world, yes, but we are strategically positioned to also help society in a number of different fields. For example, our energy subsidiary, Ki Electric, has broken new ground in the safe use of nuclear technology, and Daiwa Research, another of our companies, continues to develop new drugs to fight diseases like cancer and ALS."

Kanda paused, following the instructions that flashed on the teleprompter. The guests showered him with a warm round of applause. He soaked it all in, and nodded his head several times in appreciation before he continued: "But our specialty has been and will always be making cars. We will be contesting in the Formula One racing series next year with our own chassis and engine. And we will commemorate that occasion with our newest product, the FGT-1 super car."

The crescendo of Kanda's speech was accompanied by a triumphant fanfare that resonated around the hall. Dry-ice smoke emanated from either side of the stage, covering the floor in a thick white mist. Then the entire back wall slowly rose. From the darkness, the electric blue FGT-1 that Kanda had introduced in France days before slowly drove forward as the circus performers returned, performing back handsprings next to the supercar until it came to a stop in the middle of the stage. Confetti rained from the heavens; the multi-colored squares of rice paper sprinkling onto the heads of everyone in attendance. The back wall, now hovering about twenty feet in the air, became a large video screen, which played a clip of the new car in action. Clay was entranced by the elaborate spectacle, watching the entire show in awe. He had never witnessed a car introduction so glamorous and grandiose.

When the short video faded to black and the music died down, the main lights flickered back on, signaling the end of the press conference. As the circus performers retreated to their dressing rooms backstage, Clay cursed to himself loudly. Kanda was nowhere to be seen.

Chapter 19

Tetsuro Kanda made his way through a secret passageway that led under the main stage to a private meeting room located behind the booth, away from public view. A security guard, who manned the entrance to the meeting rooms, immediately recognized Kanda and unhooked the roped barrier, bowing as he passed by.

Kanda opened the nearest door, which had a large paper sign with the kanji characters "立入禁止" stuck onto it. It meant that no one besides authorized personnel was allowed inside. The room was essentially a lounge, complete with a white leather sofa, several chairs, and a long wooden table against a wall that held coffee, sandwiches, and several rows of bottled water. An 8K Ultra HD television monitor that hung from a wall showed a live feed of the Kamita Motors press conference.

Kanda unbuttoned his suit jacket and poured himself a cup of hot coffee. He smiled as he watched the excited journalists gather onto the Kamita stage on the television monitor, as they vied for a spot around the FGT-1 to get a photograph of the car. A few of the company shareholders were there too, being interviewed by reporters in his absence. The enthusiastic response from the media should make them feel easier, he thought, as a few of them had expressed reservations about making the huge investment into Formula One racing.

His coffee break was interrupted by a soft knock at the door.

"Come in," Kanda said in Japanese.

Jimmy Bando, Kanda's personal assistant, entered, dressed in his customary black pinstripe suit and his jet-black hair slicked back.

"Jimmy. I need to go see Dr. Kranchek. Can you take me to his lab first?"

Bando remained standing near the door and bowed. "Yes sir."

Kanda's smart phone buzzed in his pocket. He took it out and looked at the message on the screen: "DNA tests are positive. They match with yours. Kranchek."

Kanda shoved his phone back into his pocket. "Change of plans. We need to find that Clay boy. It's important."

"He must be back in the States by now. Do you want me to fly there and track him down?" Bando asked.

Kanda shook his head. "No, we'll go together. I must meet with him directly."

Bando bowed and opened the door, stepping to the side to let his boss pass first. He followed Kanda out of the room and down the short hallway. From there, Bando quickened his pace and positioned himself in front of his boss. Suddenly, an obese man with a messy beard, dressed in a baggy corduroy sport coat, and holding a recording device in one hand, blocked their way.

"Mr. Kanda, may I ask a few questions regarding the Formula One decision?" he asked.

Bando grabbed the reporter's arm and pushed him to the side. "I don't know where you've been hiding, but Mr. Kanda does not do unscheduled interviews. If you take another step towards him, you will be very sorry," he said through gritted teeth.

The reporter looked back at Bando with a terrified expression. He quickly turned around and scurried away towards the show floor.

"Some of these journalists, they're like hyenas," Kanda said.

Bando bowed. "Or worse."

Bando stepped through the exit door that led to the VIP parking lot and stopped abruptly once he stepped outside. Kanda, who was following close behind, ran into the back of his assistant.

"What are you doing?" Kanda asked.

Bando didn't respond. He stood in place with both arms raised near his head. When Kanda looked up, a Tokarev handgun with a large metal cylinder attached to its muzzle was pointed at Bando's head. A muscular Caucasian man, dressed in a blue suit, whose thick black beard covered his long, chiseled face, stood next to him. Kanda recognized Oleg Ivanov, one of the security guards at Pax-Gen, dressed in a tight-fitting navy suit. He looked a decade older than his actual twenty-three years, partly because of the beard and also because his pale complexion was excessively weathered. Ivanov held the pistol steady in his hand, while another Caucasian man, in his late fifties, with a shiny bald head and sun-tanned face, stood next to him. He also wore a suit, though his was light brown and did not fit his stocky build so well.

"No sudden moves, brother," Ivanov said in a Russian

accent as he reached into Bando's jacket and pulled out a Beretta 3032 Tomcat from a shoulder holster. He shoved the small Italian handgun into his pants pocket and lowered his Tokarev to chest level.

"Ah. Mr. Kanda. It's so good to see you," the bald man said with his arms open. "I knew if we waited here long enough that you would show up."

"Who the hell are you?" Kanda asked.

The bald man bowed. "I am Colonel Viktor Sokov. We've come to take you to Deputy Minister Dmitri Novak."

Kanda's face twisted in anger. "Do you know what you're doing? I will have you sent to the Gulag for this."

Sokov sighed. "Your threats have no effect on me, sir. Now let us go for a quick ride, shall we? My boss is waiting. Come this way."

They walked to a small empty alleyway where a black Audi A6 waited, its engine idling.

Bando slowly lowered his hands.

"Keep your hands where we can see them or my associate will put a bullet into your skull," Sokov said.

Ivanov smiled.

"Don't listen to him Jimmy. That dog wouldn't dare shoot us in a public place like this."

Sokov chuckled. "Mr. Kanda, you really have no idea what sort of people you are dealing with, do you? Now get in the car."

Kanda spit on the ground. "Never."

Ivanov pressed the muzzle of his firearm at Bando's temple. "If you don't do what the Colonel says, I will open a small hole in your assistant's head."

Kanda, sensing that Ivanov meant what he said, held up his hand. "Fine, I will go meet Mister Novak. Now put your gun away."

"If you can step into the back seat, Mr. Kanda, and you too," Sokov said as he opened the rear door of the A6.

Kanda and Bando ducked their heads into the cabin and took their places at the rear of the car. Sokov walked briskly to the other side of the A6 and plopped down in the front passenger seat. He took out his own Tokarev, turned in his seat and pointed the gun in their direction. Ivanov jumped into the driver's seat, placed his pistol between his legs and drove the A6 out of the alleyway toward the exit of the VIP parking lot.

Chapter 20

Stockton Clay emerged through the same door that Kanda and Bando had passed through minutes before, just in time to see them in the rear seat of the Audi leaving the premises. A few minutes earlier, Clay had found his way to the meeting rooms at the back of the Kamita Motors booth and pleaded with the security guard to allow him in, telling him that he had an urgent appointment with Mr. Kanda. The guard, who spoke little English pointed to the rear door. "Kanda-san, outside," he said.

Clay rushed to the exit, hoping to catch Kanda before he left, but he was a minute too late. He scurried after the car on foot, hoping to stop it before it made it out onto the main road. Although he ran after the black German sedan, waving his arms, screaming at the top of his lungs, the A6 kept its course, continuing on its path toward the exit. It turned left and onto the main road.

Clay ran out of the parking lot and saw the Audi stopped at a nearby stop light. He knew he had no chance of reaching the car by foot before the light turned green, so he searched for a taxi. He was in luck as there was a taxi stand fifty yards away with several cabs parked against the curb; they had gathered for the auto show rush, as hundreds of potential customers would come pouring out of the Big Sight headed back to their respective hotels. Clay ran to the first taxi in line and knocked on the driver-side window.

An elderly man with shiny white hair and tinted spectacles sat in a reclined position with his eyes closed in the driver's seat. He sprang to attention when he heard Clay knock. He buttoned the top of his wrinkled shirt, rubbed the sleep from his eyes, and pulled a lever on the dash. The rear door opened automatically. Clay had no time to be impressed with the automatic door, although it was the first time he had ever seen one. He jumped into the taxi and shouted, "Follow that black car."

"*Okyaku-san, eigo wakarimasen yo,*" the driver said.

Clay had no idea what the old Japanese man had just said, but he guessed it was something along the lines of not being able to speak or understand English. He remembered reading on the internet that most of the older Japanese people living in Tokyo didn't speak a lick of English, and this man fit that bill to a tee. Clay considered ditching the cab for another one, but if he were to come across another non-English speaker, Kanda and the A6 would be long gone. He couldn't take the chance, so he pulled out his smart phone and activated the translation app.

"Please follow that black car," he said slowly and deliberately into his phone, carefully pronouncing every syllable. He then held the phone up to the driver.

"*Soko no kuroi kuruma wo otte kudasai,*" a pleasant female voice said in perfect Japanese.

The taxi driver nodded and pushed the engine start button of his car. "*Hai wakarimashita,*" he said as he pulled the cab away from the curb.

It didn't take long for the orange and white Toyota Prius to get right up on the rear bumper of the black A6 as they slowly made their way through Tokyo's notorious traffic.

The Audi then came upon a yellow light in the Shimbashi district, a heavily-congested part of town, when it suddenly sped up to make it across the intersection before the light turned red.

Clay noticed his taxi slow as it approached the same intersection, the traffic light flashing from yellow to red. He pounded the backrest of the front passenger's seat. "Don't stop. Go. Please," he said.

The driver hesitated.

"Tomaru-na. Ikeh. O-negai-shimasu," the female voice said through the smart phone's speakers. Clay realized that he had not switched off the translation app.

The taxi driver grimaced, as he tightened his grip on the steering wheel. Clay had heard about the older generation of Japanese people's insistence to play by the book and never take on a single risk. They were indoctrinated to be invisible, and Clay imagined that this man was like most others of his generation: a former "salary man," who gave his life for the good of the company he worked for, only to be rewarded by total disassociation by his colleagues upon retirement. Those without families lived out their lives in isolation and loneliness; some, whose bank accounts got thin, went back to the countryside. Clay wondered if this man had a family or any friends.

As the taxi came to a stop, Clay dropped his head and cursed under his breath. He contemplated pushing the old man out of the driver's seat and taking the wheel himself, then, with a sudden jolt, he was tossed back into his seat as the Prius took off like a bat out of hell. The small four-cylinder powerplant let out a growl as the driver floored the throttle pedal, eliciting the front wheels to let out a small chirp. The taxi sped across the intersection well after the light had turned red, navigating around three vehicles that had already started crossing, provoking their drivers to lean on their horns.

"Yes," Clay shouted, pumping his fist. "Thank you so much."

The driver responded with a small nod. Clay didn't know what had prompted him to break out of character—perhaps he got caught up in the thrill of secretly tailing a mysterious car—but whatever the reason was, he wasn't about to complain.

The driver continued to follow the Audi until it pulled up to a large Japanese residence, guarded by a high white wall. The ornate metal gates that led into the property slowly spread open, allowing the Audi to drive in. As soon as it passed through, the gates closed, leaving the Prius to come to a slow stop a few hundred feet down the road.

"I will get off here. Thank you," Clay said as he took out his wallet from his back pocket. "How much?"

The driver pushed a button on the fare machine. It spit out a white piece of paper, which he tore off and handed to his passenger. It showed two thousand yen or about twenty dollars. Clay opened his wallet and handed half of his cash to the driver.

"*Domo arigato*," the driver said as he took the fare and pulled the lever on the dash that opened the rear door. As Clay stepped out, the driver said in his best English accent,

"*Goodo luckoo.*"

Clay smiled and gave the driver a friendly wave. The driver closed the rear door and, with a thoroughly contented look on his face, drove off in search of his next fare.

Chapter 21

Tetsuro Kanda glared at Viktor Sokov, who sat with his gun pointed at him from the front passenger seat of the Audi A6. Not a word was uttered inside the car for the duration of the trip from the Tokyo Big Sight to Shibuya ward. It was evident that the Russians had done their footwork because the driver, Oleg Ivanov, knew the quickest way to Kanda's home without having to rely on the navigation system.

"Why are we at Mr. Kanda's house? I thought we were going to Mr. Novak's apartment," Jimmy Bando, who sat next to Kanda, said.

"The minister is here, waiting inside," Sokov replied.

A chill went down Kanda's spine. It was not the answer he had expected or wanted to hear. "He's in my house?"

"*Da*. When he explained to your wife that you and he were old business partners, she asked him in for tea. What a trusting woman your wife is, Mr. Kanda," Sokov said.

Kanda wiped his brow with his handkerchief. "Jimmy, don't do anything that will endanger my family, please," he whispered before stepping out of the car.

Kanda's home was once a Shinto temple that had been converted into a residence in the early nineteen sixties by Kojiro Kanda, his grandfather and founder of Kamita Industries. The front of the house was a blend of eastern and western design elements, with a cobblestone driveway that led to a portico with large wooden double doors. But inside the three-story home, things took on a significantly different flavor, as the interior exuded a distinctly Japanese motif. The floors were completely covered by a special walnut wood flown in from Indonesia, and the eight rooms on the ground floor were separated by sliding shoji doors constructed from bamboo frames with rice paper panels. The outer rooms were bordered by a narrow deck that looked out to a giant backyard complete with a swimming pool, a bonsai garden, and guest house. A small staircase near the main entrance led to the second level where the guest bedrooms were located, and the entire third story was dedicated to the master bedroom. The floor plan of the house mimicked the residences of feudal lords from the samurai era.

Kanda walked down the main hallway, ahead of Bando. Sokov and Ivanov followed close behind with their guns pointed at them under their jackets. Kanda slid open the shoji door to the living room, the largest room on the ground floor located toward the back of the house. Unlike the other rooms in the house, the living room was furnished Western style, with a large Fabio leather sofa that sat atop an exquisite Persian rug. One wall was dominated by a giant flat-screen television, the other by a framed Van Gogh painting. A compact wet bar, stocked with Yamazaki whiskey, occupied the far corner of the room. Above the bar countertop, a security monitor that showed the gated entrance was mounted on the wall.

Kanda's wife, Nena Larsson-Kanda, and their five-year-old son, Kenji, sat on the lush rug playing with Russian nesting dolls. Watching them with a wry grin on his face was Dmitri Novak, sitting with his legs crossed on the sofa, dressed in a dark suit, the top of his light blue dress shirt unbuttoned and a silk Gucci tie draped loosely from his neck. He had gray hair that just brushed his large ears and a long, drawn face with deep-set wrinkles cutting through both his cheeks and forehead. His thick salt-and-pepper eyebrows matched his bushy mustache, and his large bulbous nose held a pair of rimless green-tinted spectacles that partially covered his piercing gray eyes. Even while seated, it was evident that he was tall, and at seventy-years old, fit for his age.

"Ah, Mr. Kanda. It's nice to see you again," Novak said when he saw Kanda enter the room.

"Daddy," Kenji shouted. Wearing a Yomiuri Giants baseball jersey and Gap Kids jeans, he sprang up from the floor and ran to Kanda with his arms open wide.

Kanda squatted and hugged his child tight. "My son. I love you so much," he said with his eyes shut. "Nena, are you all right?"

Nena Larsson-Kanda stood up, her long legs stretching out beneath a knee-cut Prada skirt. She pulled her shoulder-length blonde hair back and clipped it in place with a diamond broach. Kanda first met Nena when she worked as a floor model for a Kamita Motors dealership in Sweden. Despite the thirty-year age gap, Kanda was instantly mesmerized by her appearance and warm personality, and asked her to dinner after their first meeting. Several months later, they were secretly married on a small volcanic island just outside of Tokyo called Miyakejima, nearly twenty years after the death of Kanda's first wife and son. Kanda's close friends were relieved that he had finally put his tragic past behind him. Less than a year into the union, the Kandas welcomed a baby boy, Kenji, into their family. Kanda was delighted that Nena willingly abandoned her modeling career to be a full-time wife and mother.

"Welcome home dear," she said as she greeted Kanda with a kiss on the cheek. "The minister brought Kenji some wonderful Russian toys. He was telling me how you two worked together at Pax-Gen."

"Yes, that was nice of him. Will you and Kenji excuse us dear, I need to talk to our guests," Kanda said.

"Of course. We'll be at the park. Come on Kenji, daddy has to work," she said as she held out her hand to Kenji.

"Daddy, can we play with these dolls when I get back?" Kenji asked.

"Sure we can. Now go with Mommy."

Nena led Kenji out of the room, making sure to close the shoji door on her way out.

As soon as they left, Novak flashed a wide grin, displaying his crooked rows of yellow teeth.

"You have a lovely family," he said.

"What is the meaning of your visit?" Kanda asked.

"Oh, come now, why so serious, Kanda-san? What, has it been five years since we last saw each other?"

"I don't recall."

"Of course you do. It was when you shut down Pax-Gen and essentially fired me without notice."

"What do you want? We agreed never to meet in person again."

"Can't I simply say hi to my old boss?"

Kanda glared at him. "You lied to me. You didn't tell

me the true identity of the Clay boy when you asked me to invite him to our event in France. You nearly made me an accomplice to the murder of my own son."

"There is no proof that he is your son, and he may hold secrets that we do not want revealed yet, so the safest thing to do is to eliminate him."

"I had his DNA tested against mine. He's my son, you lying bastard. I'm going to notify the authorities about your crimes."

"You will do no such thing," Novak said as he pulled a Zastava Tokarev M70A pistol out of his jacket pocket. He pointed the gun at Bando and, without any hesitation or warning, squeezed the trigger. A loud pop filled the room; Bando screamed and dropped to his knees holding the side of his stomach.

A large grin formed on Novak's face, one that revealed the level of pleasure he felt in harming another human being. He then pointed the gun at Kanda.

Chapter 22

Drops of blood fell from Bando's shirt onto the floor. Kanda put his hand to his mouth. "Oh my God. Are you mad?"

"Shut up and listen to me, or you will get one too," Novak said. "And don't worry, this is a small gun, he's not dead, at least not yet."

Kanda rushed to the side of Bando and kneeled down. Bando was still conscious, sitting upright and clutching the side of his torso with both hands, his eyes opened wide in shock.

"Are you all right, Jimmy? I will call the ambulance," Kanda said.

Novak made a subtle gesture with his head to Ivanov, who responded with a curt nod. Ivanov walked over to Kanda and pulled him up by his armpits, forcing him away from his fallen assistant.

"Let go of me, you filthy dog," Kanda said as he tried to break free of the Russian's hold.

Novak walked over to where Bando sat. "Look at you, you poor helpless animal."

Bando's eyes began to gloss over; his breaths came in short, pronounced intervals.

"There have been concerns recently, disturbing reports that the CIA are snooping around your company," Novak said.

"I know of no such thing," Kanda answered.

"Perhaps you don't, but it is very troubling just the

same. Also, Viktor and Oleg tell me that you have not been fully cooperating with us."

"That is a misconception on their part."

Without warning, Novak kicked Bando in the face.

A loud snapping sound indicated that Bando's nose broke on impact, sending blood from his nostrils onto the Persian rug. Bando dropped flat on his side, one hand covering his face, the other still over the bullet wound.

"Stop it, what is it you want?" Kanda asked.

"Don't think me a fool, Kanda-san. We had it all set up for that punk to drive the red car, and this little shit of yours switched him out of it at the last minute. Isn't that right, Jimmy?" He kicked Bando's hand away and put his foot down over the bullet wound. He pressed down and twisted, causing Bando to scream in agony.

Kanda struggled to break free of Ivanov's hold, but to no avail. "Stop, please. It's not his fault."

"Kanda-san, have I not honored my side of the pact?" Novak said lifting his foot off the bleeding wound.

Not waiting for an answer, Novak walked over to the wet bar where he took out a small glass from the cupboard and poured himself a fifth of Yamazaki whiskey. He sniffed the smoky brown liquid and took a sip, letting it sit in his mouth for a moment before slowly letting it slide down his throat. "Not bad," he said raising the glass towards Kanda. "Not as smooth as our vodka, but not bad at all."

"I'm glad you approve," Kanda said, shifting his gaze from Novak to Bando.

Novak took another sip and swirled the whiskey around

in the glass. "At your behest, I worked day and night to de-velop my technology and help make you a historically sig-nificant man: But you are a fool and I will no longer play the part of your pawn. In time, people will marvel at my accomplishments."

"Despite your flawed character, I do agree that what you have done so far is miraculous," Kanda said.

Novak walked toward the large shoji door that led to the backyard and slid it open, the sunlight hitting his face. "It's too late to play nice because I have a new benefactor that doesn't want any evidence of this technology out in the open. They want this exclusively to themselves, and your boy, who should be dead, has the potential to ruin every-thing, not just for me, but for you, too."

"You're doing this for money? When I first met you, you told me you were working on the behalf of humanity."

Novak laughed. "Don't be ridiculous. It was what you wanted to hear, so I said it. What do I care about humanity? Humans are all selfish, rotten forms of life on a crash course to extinction."

"You're mad."

"There's a thin line between genius and madness, Mr. Kanda, and I can't expect you to discern which side of that line I fall. And, I'm afraid I can't expect you to be loyal to my cause, so I must insist that you stay under my jurisdiction for the foreseeable future. I can't have you running around causing problems for me."

Kanda let out a small laugh. "You are kidnapping me? People will know right away that I am missing, and they will send the police after you. Do you not remember who I am?"

"Ha," Novak burst out. "You are nothing. And besides, you're a recluse, a hermit. No one ever knows where you are. Your family doesn't even know where you are half the time. Tell your wife that you're going on an extended business trip."

"I will not listen to you," he said.

Novak smirked as he placed his glass of whiskey on the countertop and walked over to where Bando lay with his eyes closed and taking slow, shallow breaths. "Do you know what it is about inflicting pain that's so intoxicating? I will tell you Kanda-san, because I have studied pain extensively during my time with the KGB. When you have the ability to inflict pain on someone, you have complete power over them. The desire and ability to inflict pain translates to power, straight and simple. It shows lesser beings who is superior; true power has nothing to do with birthright, wealth, or race."

"Leave Jimmy alone," Kanda said.

Novak drove his index finger into the bullet wound, causing Bando to let out another deafening scream. He chuckled loudly. "For example, do you know why raping a woman feels so good? For some, they may do it to relieve sexual tension, but for others, like me, it's seeing the terror in their eyes as you overpower them, and what better way is there to overpower someone sexually, man or woman. When you rape a person, you have complete power over them. And if you happen to get bored with your subjects or when they no longer respond, then simply get rid of them and move on to the next."

"You're insane, you must know that."

Novak stood up and pointed the barrel of his gun at Bando's head. His lips curled into a smile as he looked into Bando's terrified eyes. He pulled the trigger, and another loud pop echoed throughout the house. The bullet entered the side of Bando's forehead, with the force of the blast causing his head to bounce off the floor. The sharp odor of gunpowder filled the air, and Bando lay motionless on the floor.

Kanda's face turned white; he fell backwards staring at his assistant's dead body.

"Time to move onto the next victim. Will it be you Kanda-san?" Novak put his gun back under his jacket and sat on the sofa. "Can't you see the big picture? The existence of that boy can incriminate us both. What we were doing won't be looked upon favorably, and we might be put on trial. It is for the good of both of us that he is eliminated."

"You killed Jimmy," Kanda murmured. "You killed him…"

Novak nodded. "Yes, and I will kill your wife and your boy next if you continue to disrespect me. There is also the small matter of some files Dr. Sato stole from Pax-Gen, files he was asked to destroy. He told us before he died that he hid them inside your business server."

"Yes, they are stored in a private, protected server that can only be accessed from my office computer."

"Then one of my assistants will accompany you to your office after hours. You will give him access to those files so he can wipe them clean. All of my men are very talented hackers, being Russian of course, so it should not take them long. I can't have anyone else having the fruits of my technology," Novak said.

Kanda slowly rose to his feet. He turned away from Bando's corpse and walked slowly towards the wet bar. Once there, he reached for the whiskey bottle with a trembling hand. As he poured himself a glass, about half of the whiskey spilled onto the counter. Then something on the small security video monitor caught his eye; a lone man standing in front of the main gate. As he looked at the image more closely, he gasped when he saw Stockton Clay peering into his estate through the front gate's iron bars. Kanda dropped the whiskey glass, which bounced on the hard wood floor.

"I'm sorry. It slipped from my hand," he said as he switched off the power to the monitor, confident that none of them had noticed. "If you will excuse me for one moment, I need to visit the restroom."

Novak nodded. "It's your house."

Kanda walked out of the living room and closed the door behind him. Sliding his feet as quietly as he could, he moved past the restroom to his study at the end of the narrow hallway. After glancing back to make sure he wasn't being followed, Kanda entered his study and shut the door quietly. Once inside, he threw off his coat, thrust his hands into the inside breast pocket and pulled out a platinum business-card holder, where he removed a small stack of business cards and shuffled through them searching for the one with the Automobile Digest logo. There it was: Stockton Clay, Associate Editor.

Kanda heard the sound of the living room door slide open, followed by the thumping sound of approaching footsteps. One of the men was coming; he needed to act fast, so he took out his smart phone and entered Stockton's cell phone number. Once he finished, he typed a seven-word message and hit "send" just as the door to his study slid open. It was Ivanov, wearing a particularly disgruntled look on his bearded face.

"What are you doing? I thought you needed to go to the bathroom," he said.

"I had to answer an urgent email," Kanda answered, clutching his smart phone in both hands.

Ivanov stepped into the room and pried the phone away. "Give me that."

"What are you doing?"

Ivanov looked at the screen and saw the message that Kanda had just sent. "You betraying dog, I knew we couldn't trust you."

"Give that back to me," Kanda said.

Ivanov answered him with a swift backhand to his right cheek that sent the old man down to one knee. Blood oozed from the side of Kanda's mouth as he looked up at Ivanov's grinning face.

"Come with me," the Russian said as he grabbed Kanda's arm and forcefully yanked him up to his feet. He led him out of the study, the smart phone in one hand and Kanda in the other. He threw him into the living room where Novak, seated on the sofa, and Sokov, who stood next to him, waited.

Ivanov handed the phone to his boss. "Look what I caught this big rat doing," he said.

Novak took the gadget and read the contents on the screen. He shook his head. "Oleg here noticed that you had a visitor right after you left," he said pointing to the monitor on the wall above the wet bar, which was now switched on. It showed Clay still standing in front of the main gate.

Kanda stood motionless, not saying a word.

Novak stood up, straightened his jacket and shoved Kanda's phone into his own pocket. "Well, we should consider us very lucky that the kid came to us. He saved us the trouble of looking for him. Mr. Kanda, you and I shall take a ride to my apartment. Oleg, go and kill the boy now."

"*Da papa*," Oleg said as he left the room.

Chapter 23

Clay walked up to the front entrance of the magnificent Kanda estate and peered into the vast grounds through the bars of the ornate iron front gate. A long driveway led to a building that looked like a Shinto temple. He could tell the property was expensive, but he couldn't even begin to guess what it was worth, knowing that Tokyo always placed among the top three spots of the most expensive cities in the world to live. On the white concrete wall, an intercom hung next to the gate. Under it was a wooden plaque with the kanji characters "神田" written artfully in black ink. A small security camera mounted atop the eight-foot-high wall pointed directly at him, but there was no sign of a security guard or even a watchdog. Japanese executives were pretty lax about their security, he thought. The truth was that Japanese company presidents and CEOs were not the big shots that their American counterparts were: they earned a fraction of American CEOs' salaries and were considered just another part of the company cog; therefore, they rarely required any security because kidnapping a CEO of a Japanese company would hardly demand a big ransom.

Clay stood in front of the gate, contemplating the best way to get inside. He considered scaling the wall and jumping over, but decided against it in case a passerby saw him and called the police. Without coming up with anything better, he decided to just ring the bell, ready to explain to whomever answered through the intercom that he needed to see Mr. Kanda; that it was a life or death situation. If that didn't work, then he would climb the wall.

Clay's index finger was about to press down on the small blue button when his smart phone buzzed. He found it odd that he would be receiving a call for he had blocked everyone on his contact list from getting through to avoid international roaming charges. Out of sheer curiosity, he pulled the phone out from his front pocket. A text message flashed across the screen in capital letters from an unfamiliar number. "YOUR LIFE IS IN DANGER, LEAVE NOW."

At first, he thought it was some kind of strange spam mail, but when he considered all the crazy things that had happened in the past few days, he decided to play it safe. He shoved his smart phone back in his pocket and backed away from the front gates, keeping a watchful eye on his surroundings. He headed across the street to observe Kanda's house from a distance. When he was about halfway across the street, the side gate flung open and a tall Caucasian man, who Clay would later come to know as Oleg Ivanov, stepped out. Their eyes met.

It was clear from the man's scowling face that he didn't come out to invite Clay in for tea and crumpets. Clay then noticed that he held a gun, which prompted him to instinctively get to the ground and do a judo roll in the opposite direction, a move he had used back at the Seven-Eleven near his home. *Aren't guns illegal in Japan?*

The unordinary sight of a grown man doing what looked like somersaults in the middle of the street made Ivanov pause, giving Clay the time needed to take cover behind a parked car. Ivanov pointed his gun in Clay's direction and fired. The bullet took out the car's passenger-side window.

Clay ducked, as his heartbeat raced. He didn't know what to do. He felt a notion to stand up and tell the man there's been a huge misunderstanding. But then again, this guy didn't look like he was interested in chatting. Clay decided to run, now convinced without a doubt that his biological father wanted to murder him. It all made sense now; he now knew the reason why he was the only one at Automobile Digest who received the invitation to the big Kamita Motors event. The CIA agents weren't lying after all. But why on earth did Kanda want him dead? It couldn't be about the money. Did he want to get rid of evidence of a past affair?

Using the car as a shield, Clay headed down an adjacent street, with several small boutique shops and a dozen pedestrians strolling along the sidewalk. There was still some distance between him and the main road where he could lose his attacker in a crowd. Running at nearly a full sprint, Clay looked back and saw Ivanov in pursuit, his right hand tucked under his unbuttoned jacket.

Clay continued along the semi-crowded road weaving his way past a couple of mothers pushing their baby strollers and several middle schoolers dressed in their *gakuseifuku*, school uniforms, on their way home from class. Sticking to the outer edge of the sidewalk to keep his pursuer from having a clear shot at his back, he glanced over his shoulder once again. Ivanov had closed the gap, now about two blocks away, and his hand was still tucked under his coat. Up ahead was an ornate arch, which usually decorated the entrance of a busy shopping street, so Clay headed straight for it, hoping to find a big crowd of window shoppers. When he got there, he realized that he had made a terrible mistake. The arch marked the entrance to a narrow road, lined with small drinking establishments, and being midday, most of them were closed, leaving the entire area all but deserted. Heading deeper down this path would make him an easy target, but he knew he couldn't turn back, so he scanned the area for a place to hide. About a block away was a small bar with its door half open. He quickly ran towards it.

It was a small rectangular two-story building with an unlit neon sign hanging on a wood paneled door with a large window. The sign read "Bambina." Clay pushed the door open and walked into a large, dimly lit room. The air reeked of cigarette smoke, hard liquor, and stinky perfume. It took him a moment for his eyes to adjust, and through the smoky mist, he saw two heavily-tattooed Asian men, dressed in tank tops and wrinkled cargo shorts, sitting at the bar. They were knocking back Tequila shots. Although he had never seen one in real life, Clay was fairly sure he stumbled into a yakuza girlie club, owned and managed by the Japanese mob, where many gang members passed the time waiting for assignments.

As Clay closed the door shut, one of the men at the counter, sporting a large dragon tattoo on his shoulder, looked over at him and shouted in Japanese, "*Kono bakkyaro. Mise wa shimattenda.*" Despite not understanding the words, the message was clear: He was not welcome. Clay wanted nothing more than to turn around and leave the place, but if he did, certain death awaited him because Ivanov was probably right outside the door by now. The odds favored him staying inside the bar, with the yakuza gangsters.

Chapter 24

The two yakuza men glared at Clay, who stood just inside the main entrance.

"I'm sorry, but can I order a beer?" Clay asked.

"*Ah? Gaijin?*" said the man sitting next to Dragon Tattoo, who had a tattoo of a *sakura*, or cherry blossom flower, on his upper back.

Clay squinted through the smoke and noticed several sofas placed in two neat rows in the middle of the room. Each sofa had a small table in front of it with a small bottle of whiskey. On one of the sofas, two young Japanese women sat and giggled: one had blonde hair, obviously dyed, cut short to about the base of her neck, and the other wore her black hair down to her waist. Both looked to be in their late teens or early twenties.

The blonde girl stood up and walked towards Clay, sticking out her large perky breasts under a loose T-shirt. She shouted something to the man at the bar in Japanese and stood right in front of Clay, studying him from head to toe.

"Hey mister," she said in a thick accent. "We like handsome *gaijin* boy. Do you want to play?" She grabbed his shirt by the collar, pulled his face down to hers, and licked his cheek. Clay instinctively pulled away.

When he leaned back, he felt someone standing behind him. He turned around and saw that it was the other girl, the one with the long black hair, who had quietly moved to his rear, as stealthily as a ninja. She wrapped her arms around Clay's waist and hugged him tightly.

"I like white boy too," she said.

"Shit, this is getting too weird. I'm sorry, I think I made a big mistake." Clay pried the black-haired girl's arm loose, stepped around the blonde girl, and headed for the exit.

He stopped in his tracks when he saw Ivanov's head through the window in the front door, walking slowly past the Bambina entrance, looking in every direction for his prey. If he left the building now, he wouldn't last ten seconds, so he turned back around.

"How much for a beer?" he asked the blonde woman.

Dragon Tattoo cursed loudly and put out his cigarette in an ashtray. He stood up and pushed the girls aside. The two young women muttered something in protest, and then returned to their places on the sofas. Clay, whose knees were now shaking, stood his ground.

"One beer, twenty thousand yen," the yakuza man said, flashing a smile that revealed more than a few gold teeth.

After doing a quick calculation in his head, Clay gave the man a quizzical look. "That's two hundred dollars. Is this some kind of joke?"

"No joke. You pay now, beer or no beer," Dragon Tattoo demanded as he pulled a switchblade knife from his back pocket. Clay noticed the man was missing half his left pinky finger, which he knew was a form of punishment that yakuza members inflicted onto themselves to atone for mistakes. These guys were the real deal.

Clay dug into his pants pocket and pulled out his wallet. He took out his last two one-thousand-yen notes, which he held out to the yakuza with both hands. The Japanese man grabbed the money and, after a quick survey of the cash, shook his head.

"Not enough."

"But that's all I have," Clay said as he opened up his wallet and showed the man it was empty. "How about credit card?"

"We don't take credit card, you idiot."

"Then can I wash dishes or something?"

Dragon Tattoo shook his head and called his buddy over from the bar. "No, then you must pay with pain."

The other man, Sakura Tattoo, stood up, knocking over his stool in the process. He was much larger than Dragon Tattoo, with the build of a professional wrestler. He stood at least six-feet-three and looked like he weighed more than two thirty. His tight shirt strained to hold his thick chest and bulging biceps.

Clay wanted no part of Sakura Tattoo, nor did he want to taste the knife that was pointed at him, but he couldn't yet go outside for Ivanov was probably still nearby. Deciding that he would rather fight two men and a knife than one with a gun, he instinctively thrust his right leg forward, catching Dragon Tattoo squarely in the groin with a front kick. The man screamed and dropped the switchblade on the dirty tile floor. Sakura Tattoo, with clenched fists, moved towards Clay with bad intentions written all over his huge square face. He grabbed Clay by the shirt and threw him like a rag doll across the room. Clay flew nearly ten feet, until he crashed into the opposing wall, knocking a cheap Klimt poster from its hook in the process. The impact temporarily stunned him, as he slowly got off the ground. He had never before experienced such raw physical strength.

"I kill you," Sakura Tattoo said, as he moved toward Clay.

This guy wasn't messing around; killing people with his bare hands was probably part of his job description. Clay now had no choice but to get the hell out of there or have his neck broken by Sakura Tattoo. His judo training wasn't going to be of any help on this guy. As soon as the cobwebs cleared in his head, he made a dash for the front door and busted out of the building, hoping that Ivanov had moved on to another street.

The bright rays of the midday sun temporarily blinded Clay as he burst outside. He looked down the street and saw that Ivanov was about halfway down Bar Row, four blocks away. The Russian had his back turned to the Bambina, but the sound of the door slamming open against the wall made him turn around.

Ivanov looked Clay in the eyes.

Clay flashed him the middle finger and turned in the opposite direction, running to where he first entered Bar Row, under the fancy archway. Ivanov pulled out his Tokarev as the two yakuza men came out of the Bambina building.

"That white man over there is my uncle. He has lots of money," Clay shouted to the yakuzas.

Both Dragon Tattoo and Sakura Tattoo stepped in Ivanov's path. Clay hoped they would slow the Russian assassin down enough for him to jump into a taxi and escape, or better yet, beat him to a pulp. Ivanov didn't even blink as he shot Sakura Tattoo in the leg.

Clay barely heard the muffled gunshot, but the scream of Sakura Tattoo echoed off the nearby buildings and rang in his ears. That cry was followed by another scream, this time from Dragon Tattoo. Without looking back, Clay increased his pace and turned into a small alley. He could now see the main road one block away. A sign on the side of a building read Shibuya Train Station, written in English, with an arrow pointing straight ahead.

When he got to the main road, it was everything he had hoped for: the sidewalks were crowded with people and the train station was within sight. Clay looked back and saw Ivanov still coming at him, shoving people out of his way.

Disappearing in a sea of people would be a breeze, but then Clay realized that more than half the people around him were at least two inches shorter than him, leaving the top of his brown head exposed. He bent over slightly at the waist as he ran, knowing that he looked ridiculous trying to run with his back hunched over. A few school girls giggled and took photos of him with their smart phones, but he didn't care. As he squeezed through the crowds of people on Aoyama Pass, he felt the vibration of his smart phone in his pants pocket. Now was not the time, so he ignored it, but it kept ringing… and ringing. All calls from the U.S. were supposed to have been blocked, and even if they weren't, they were to be sent directly to voicemail, but this particular one did not. Perhaps the call was connected to the message he received in front of Kanda's house, and seeing how it had saved his life, Clay took out his phone and answered the call without looking at the caller ID.

"I really can't talk now," he said.

A female voice responded on the other end. "Don't hang up, where are you?"

"Who is this?"

"This is Maki Takano of Kamita Motors. Where are you Stockton?"

He didn't answer.

"You're in danger Stockton. You need to tell me where you are," Maki said.

"What, so you can send another killer after me? I know that your boss wants me dead."

"You must listen to me carefully, Stockton, if you want to live," she said. "It's not Mr. Kanda who's trying to kill you."

"Oh no? Well, his hitman that's chasing me right now thinks otherwise."

"You have to trust me, Stockton. Follow my instructions. I know Tokyo better than you. I'm on your side. Please trust me, or you will die."

Clay thought about hanging up on her, but when he looked back, he could see the killer making his way towards him. The guy seemed to be a human blood hound. At this point, Clay realized that he had very little to lose in hearing her out. "I'm all ears."

"Can you get into a taxi?" she asked.

"No way. If I stop, he'll catch up to me, and he evidently has no problems shooting people in public. There's a big train station up ahead. The sign says Shibuya." Clay looked back as he held the phone to his ear and saw Ivanov forcing his way through the crowd, edging closer.

"Stockton, listen carefully. Shibuya Station is one of the busiest train stations in Tokyo with lots of platforms. Try to lose him in the crowd and jump onto any train. Get off at any exit and grab the first taxi you see. Tell the driver to take you to Mitsuwa Bank Building in Shinagawa, got that?"

"Okay. Mitsuwa Building in Shinagawa. Got it," he said, and shoved the phone back into his pocket, making a beeline for the train station.

Clay reached Shibuya Crossing, known as the busiest intersection in the world, located immediately in front of the train station. Shibuya Crossing featured five crosswalks— four connecting the corners of the intersecting roads, and one that ran diagonally. Clay got lucky as he caught the green light for the diagonal crosswalk, allowing him to go from the far side of the intersection directly to the entrance of the train station. He looked back and saw Ivanov standing more than a block away with his head swiveling, searching for his prey. Blending in with the crowd had worked, at least temporarily.

Once Clay crossed the street, he hurried to the ticket gates that led to the trains and jumped over the middle gate. Inside was a large monitor that displayed the schedule of departing and arriving trains. The departure schedule showed a train leaving Platform Five in four minutes. He looked back. No sign of the killer.

Clay hurried down the escalator, taking two steps at a time, squeezing past a long line of people standing on the left side of the steps heading to Platform Five.

When he got there, the platform was packed with people who stood in neat lines, making it nearly impossible for him to completely disappear among them. *Why do the Japanese have to be so damned organized?* So he jumped into a line at the far edge of the platform.

Ivanov appeared on the escalator, his hands tucked into his jacket, making his way down to the platform.

How the hell did he know I was here? Fortunately, Ivanov hadn't spotted him yet.

Clay ducked down and bear-crawled to the back wall near a bench where he crouched down behind a large trash bin. When he peered out from behind the blue plastic container, he could see Ivanov stepping off the escalator, looking left and right for his mark.

Clay glanced at his watch. It was another minute until the next train arrived, but he still had to figure out how to board it without being seen. Then he remembered reading on the internet that Japanese trains, along with Swiss trains, were the most punctual in the world, leaving and arriving exactly on schedule, usually to the second. A plan quickly formed in his head, but it all depended on if the information on the internet was factual, which wasn't very reassuring.

Ivanov walked up and down each line, carefully checking every commuter's face, while keeping his hand on his gun under his suit jacket.

Clay watched him gradually make his way towards him. If the information on the internet was correct, the next train should arrive before Ivanov could make his way down every line and check every face.

Then it happened again: Drops of liquid oozed down over Clay's lips. The blood splattered on the ground where he crouched, and he felt a headache coming on. Hurriedly reaching into his pocket, he took out his pill container and dry-swallowed two capsules. The nosebleed didn't stop right away, as Clay let the red droplets fall freely from his chin. He checked his watch again. About thirty seconds more. Then the tunnel echoed with the faint sounds of an approaching train. *Well whaddyaknow*, the internet *was* telling the truth, he thought. If he jumped across the tracks in precisely fifteen seconds, he would be on the opposite platform, on the other side of the tracks, and the arriving train would block his pursuer's path. He just hoped that there wasn't another train coming in on the second set of tracks, or he would be rail kill.

A musical jingle sounded through the loudspeakers, followed by a man's voice announcing the approaching train in Japanese, followed by a female voice that said in English: "The train is arriving, please stand behind the yellow line."

Ivanov was about ten feet away now and closing in; Clay kept his entire body tucked into a tight ball, his eyes fixed on his Casio G-Shock. Thirteen, fourteen, fifteen, now. He sprang forward and leapt off the platform onto the live train tracks. His Nike sneakers crunched the black gravel floor as he landed between the two steel railroad bars. An elderly woman standing nearby screamed as the headlight of the oncoming train backlit the presumed suicide jumper. Ivanov pulled out his gun and pointed it in Clay's direction, but it was too late, the fourteen-carriage train had already stopped in front of him, blocking his intended shot before he could pull the trigger.

The elderly woman fainted, as a couple of high school students came to her aid. Clay had jumped onto the opposite platform just in time. He ran up the escalator and looked over at the recently arrived train; Ivanov looked up at him through the window of the carriage. Clay couldn't help but smile, parts of his white teeth glowing through his blood-stained mouth.

Chapter 25

Clay ran up the stairs and back to the central area of the Shibuya Train Station. He didn't waste any time lounging around, taking an escalator down to another platform he chose purely by random. After jumping into the central most carriage of the first train that pulled in, he grabbed a seat until it pulled into Jimbocho Station. It was another purely random decision, but he decided to get off here, and then snuck past the ticket booth by blending in with a crowd of tall young men dressed in matching athletic warm-ups. He hailed the first taxi he saw and instructed the driver to take him to the Mitsuwa Bank Building in Shinagawa.

Clay did his best to clean the dried blood from his face with his shirt sleeves. But before he could wipe it all off, the cab pulled to a stop next to a narrow glass building with three ATM machines on the outer wall. "Mitsuwa Bank," the driver said.

"Can you please wait here?" Clay asked slowly.

"Yes. No problem," the driver answered in English with a thick accent.

Clay stepped out of the car and scanned every direction for a familiar face. There were a number of small office buildings lined up like dominoes on either side of the narrow street, most of them four to six stories high. A few pedestrians walked in the middle of the road, but none of them were Maki.

"Stockton," a voice called out to him from behind.

Clay swung around and saw Maki Takano emerge from

an outdoor stairwell of a plain white eight-story building on the opposite side of the street. She wore a large hat and dark sunglasses that covered most of her face.

"Are you all right?" she asked as she walked up to him.

"Yeah, that was close, but thanks to you, I was able to get away."

"You're not hurt?"

"No. So what do you know about Mr. Kanda wanting to kill me?" Clay asked, keeping himself a good ten feet away from Maki for he didn't entirely trust her, or anyone else for that matter.

"Stockton, don't be afraid of me. I'm here to help you. I don't know who is trying to kill you, but I'm relatively sure it's not Mr. Kanda. But first, we need to get you to a safe place. Come with me. There's no guarantee that your pursuer didn't follow you here."

"I'd like some answers first, please."

"Stockton, we need to hurry. I'm with a special division of the CIA," Maki said as she showed him an identification card with the letters CIA on them in blue.

Clay's body straightened, his face twisted in confusion. "Wait a minute…what?"

"Now follow me."

"Is everybody in the world a frickin' CIA agent? How do I know that I.D.'s not a fake?"

Maki put her card away. "I work with Russell Whitaker, who I presume you met in the States, as well as Dr. George Nakajima," she said.

Clay relaxed his shoulders. "Okay, I believe you. But

can you help me with the cab fare? I'm completely out of cash," he said, pointing to the waiting taxi.

"Yes. Wait right here."

Maki walked to the passenger-side of the waiting taxi and took out five one-thousand yen notes. She passed them to the driver through the open window, who took the money and handed her a receipt.

"You know, the taxi cabs here take credit cards," she said when she returned.

"Yeah, well I think I maxed mine out on the plane ticket here."

"Come with me," she said as she led him behind the bank and into a small residential neighborhood that consisted of plain-looking one- and two-story single family homes with no driveways or garages. The only parking spaces here were located in cramped corner lots with self-serve pay stations.

They walked quickly, sticking to small streets until Maki stopped in front of a drab two-story office building with brown walls and small tinted windows. A white Lexus GS sedan was parked illegally in front. There were no signs in front of the building, but Clay did notice a number of surveillance cameras mounted on the walls.

"This can't be the offices of Kamita Motors, can it?" he asked.

"This is home base for our task force," Maki said as she stepped up to the front door and placed her thumb on a small metal panel mounted to the wall. The lock on the door buzzed followed by a loud click. She pushed the door open and walked in.

"What is this, a safe house?" Clay asked.

"No, it's a satellite office. There wasn't room for us at the embassy, so we set up shop here. We move locations every three months or so. The main CIA Japan branch is somewhere else."

Clay followed Maki through the front door. Once inside, he walked past a reception area and into a large room that resembled a loft, with crisscrossing partitions that divided the floor space into several office cubicles.

She led him down a narrow aisle between the cubicles, then up a winding open staircase before stopping at the only office on the second floor, where she knocked three times on a plain wooden door.

"Come in," said a husky male voice from inside.

Maki opened the door and stepped to the side, allowing Clay to enter first. She then went back downstairs after closing the door behind him.

Dr. George Nakajima was seated in a chair facing a large wooden desk.

"George? What on earth are you doing here?" Clay asked.

The bags under Nakajima eyes showed that he had not slept much recently; his disheveled hair and wrinkled gray sweater hinted that he had probably just stepped off an airplane. "Hi Stockton. I'm glad you're safe," he said.

Standing behind the desk was a large fifty-something man with curly reddish-brown hair, his ear pressed to a cell phone. He was slightly overweight, and wore his dress shirt with the top button undone. His loose-fitting slacks partially camouflaged his beer gut, but his broad shoulders and thick forearms indicated that he spent a fair chunk of his free time lifting weights. His coat and tie hung on his office chair.

"Don't just stand there, come in," he said as he ended his call.

Clay took a few steps into the room. The office was large, even by American standards. In one corner was a United States flag sitting stoically on a stand next to a black leather couch. On the near wall was a giant map of Japan, with several colored pins stuck to it. Several blurry photos of rough-looking men decorated the far wall.

"I'm Andy Roberts," the man behind the desk said as he thrust his right hand out. "We're with the SSD, a new branch of the CIA. We're working independently from the main Japan station, so I hope you forgive our shoddy dwellings."

Clay softly shook Roberts' hand. "SSD? Never heard of it."

"Special Science Division. We specialize in identifying the production and use of chemical weapons, the spread of manmade viruses, and other nasty stuff our enemies have been concocting. There are a lot of very smart bad guys out there with very bad intentions," Roberts said. "It's our job to keep an eye on them."

Clay walked up to the desk. "Sir, I have absolutely no desire to cooperate with you, or anybody else for that matter, until someone tells me what the hell is going on."

Roberts removed his feet from the desk. "Yes, I don't think we can avoid that any longer. By the way, you work for Automobile Digest, right? Man, that must be such a cool job."

"I don't work there anymore."

Roberts picked up a recent issue of Automobile Digest from his desk and pointed to the cover. "Hey, what do you think about this new Corvette? I'm not a big fan of the styling direction, are you?"

Clay shot him a cold stare.

"Right, we can talk about cars later, I suppose. Then let's get right down to it. Have a seat. I insist."

The tone in Roberts' voice suddenly turned authoritative, prompting Clay to do exactly as he was told. This was Roberts' turf, and he made sure his young guest knew that.

"George, want to fill our guest in from the beginning?" Roberts said.

Chapter 26

Aside from the ticking second hand of the wall clock, the room fell silent for a moment. Clay readjusted his seating position in his chair and fixed his gaze on Nakajima, who smiled warmly at Clay and looked into his eyes when he spoke.

"Stockton, about thirty years ago, while I was in my last year at Harvard Medical School, I was recruited by a company called Pax-Gen. I didn't know it then, but the company was funded by Kamita Motors."

Roberts broke in. "It was a very, very secretive company. It was never publicly listed as a subsidiary of Kamita."

The doctor nodded. "That's right. The facility was located in a remote part of Khabarovsk, in eastern Russia."

Nakajima's commentary was interrupted by a soft knock on the door. Maki entered with a can of Red Bull, which she handed to Clay. He hungrily grabbed it with both hands and immediately popped the top. He took a huge swig, nearly finishing the entire can.

"Thanks, Ms. Takano. I needed that."

"My pleasure," she said as she took a seat in the last remaining chair. "And call me Maki."

"Doctor, please continue," Roberts said.

"Where was I? Oh yes, Pax-Gen." Nakajima cleared his throat. "So at the time, Stockton, I was told that this company was created to find cures to diseases like cancer, using new revolutionary genome techniques. This was right up my alley, so as soon as I graduated, I enthusiastically joined this forward-thinking company, which offered a really high starting salary. It didn't take me long to discover later that the real motive behind Pax-Gen was not just advancing gene research, but developing nanotechnology."

"You mean like tiny robots? I read about that somewhere, but I thought it was all science fiction," Clay asked.

"Well, it's a lot more real than you can imagine. Nanotechnology is the manipulation of material things on the molecular or atomic scale. In short, it allows us to control individual atoms and molecules by programming them like computers. So in theory, with nanotechnology, one material can be completely turned into another, such as steel into gold or water into wine, by changing its chemical makeup," Nakajima said.

"That sounds impossible," Clay said.

"Yes, it does, but it's all in the realm of possibility. While it's still in its infancy, nanotechnology is currently being used in fabrics, and it has even been utilized for turning algae into fuel. But what we were working on at Pax-Gen was really revolutionary. We wanted to use this technology to cure diseases, such as cancer, AIDS, and Alzheimer's. Because of the huge funding from Kamita, Pax-Gen succeeded in developing nano-robots to enter the human body and repair mutated DNA on a molecular level."

"I'm not sure I follow," Clay said.

"Stockton, our bodies are defined by our DNA, that much you should know. And this DNA is always being damaged, but it can repair itself by replication, making copies of the damaged parts automatically. But problems occur when the DNA becomes mutated—accidental changes in the DNA code—and that can't be repaired so easily. The mutation of a single gene leads to genetic disorders like cystic fibrosis, sickle cell anemia, and color-blindness. And cancer usually results from a series of these mutations within a single cell."

"So you're saying I have mutated cells? That's why I'm sick?"

"We all have some mutations from birth. They can be inherited from your parents, and they can naturally happen during your lifetime. Some of these mutations occur during cell division, and some are caused when DNA becomes damaged by environmental things, like UV radiation and viruses."

"Get to the point, doc," Roberts said.

Nakajima rubbed his forehead. "Yes, well, we were working on a way to use nanotechnology to fix these mutations in the DNA by having nanobots replace the damaged cells with healthy ones. If successful, it meant that a person would never become sick or contract a deadly disease because nanotechnology could cure anything. Hell, we could theoretically turn a white man into an African American, change a person's natural hair color, and yes, even perhaps stop aging; nanotechnology had the potential to take any DNA cell and replace it with whichever ones we wanted. The possibilities were endless. Our first trials on diseased lab animals worked like a charm."

"You mean these microscopic robots are the key to curing cancer?" Clay asked. "Is that what you're saying?"

"Yes, that's right. It was quite exciting, and we were

ready to take the next step. Perform our experiments on humans," Nakajima said.

Roberts broke in: "Because of ethical implications, and the fact that this technology isn't yet regulated by a governing body, all of what they were doing was essentially illegal. Imagine if these nanobots were programmed to do harm, such as inflicting deadly diseases like AIDS on a large population. A third-world country could become a superpower with this technology in a few short years."

Nakajima nodded. "That's right, but my immediate supervisor at Pax-Gen, a man named Dr. Yukio Sato, insisted that what we were doing was ethical. And the rest of the staff agreed with him. Just imagine, we could be the first ones to find a cure for cancer. Then, Sato informed us that an order had come from up top that it was time to experiment with human subjects. A few months later, we had created nanobots designed for the human body. We're talking about robots one-billionth of a meter in size, invisible to the naked eye. Our first job was to search the area for infants afflicted with fatal diseases to, for the lack of a better term, use them as human guinea pigs."

"That's horrible, but what does all this have to do with me?" Clay asked.

"Patience, dear boy, patience," Roberts said with a wry grin.

Nakajima continued. "Mr. Kanda and his now-deceased first wife had a son, about a year old, who had a fatal form of Sickle-Cell Disease, or SCD. He insisted that we use his child in the hopes that nanotechnology could save him. The little boy didn't have much time left, perhaps only days to live. I warned Kanda-san that the risks were too great because things could still go wrong, but he was adamant. So this boy became our first human trial—the prototype, if you will. We injected the baby with millions of nanobots and waited. Within a day, the technology started to do exactly what it was supposed to, and in a few months, it had completely cured the child from SCD; however, something else happened. The nanobots began altering other cells in his body, the healthy ones. They started messing with his blood cells, and we couldn't find a way to stop this. So in effect, we created a brand new disease that we had never seen before."

"Talk about your nightmare scenarios," Clay said.

"We knew that there were going to be risks, but we never imagined that we would develop a new disease. As I studied this baby boy, I was intent on finding a cure, but Dr. Sato told us that we couldn't risk the boy developing even more new diseases and possibly spreading it outside the lab, so he ordered for us to terminate the child."

Clay shifted uneasily in his chair. "Couldn't you have just taken the nanobots out?"

Nakajima looked down at the floor. "No, once they were in, they stay there forever. You have to remember that there were millions of them in his body. We programmed them to vaporize when the host died so as not to leave any evidence of our work. You must understand, I couldn't bring myself to end the life of another human being. I made a vow to save lives, not end them, so I snuck the baby out and treated him myself in secret, while lying to my superiors that I had disposed of him. It took a few weeks, but I was able to cure him, or at least I thought I did, and I took him straight to the U.S. consulate. I have not returned to Pax-Gen since."

"What did you tell Mr. Kanda?"

"They told him the operation failed, and his son died of SCD. He took the news hard. In fact, it devastated him and his wife. Then about a year later, Mrs. Kanda was tragically killed in a traffic accident."

Clay winced and pressed his hand to his temple. Small lumps pulsated near his ears randomly like a splattering of light rain, accompanied by a slight headache. He shoved his hand into his pocket, pulled out his pill case and shook out two capsules. After popping them into his mouth, he washed them down with Red Bull, as blood trickled down from his nostril.

Nakajima handed him his handkerchief. "Here, use this. And take one more pill, because if you can now feel the headaches, it means that the illness is getting stronger."

After doing as the doctor ordered, Clay wiped away the blood with the handkerchief. The medicine worked like a charm; the pain in his head subsided and his nosebleed stopped within seconds.

"Thanks George."

"You're welcome."

Maki, who was seated on the opposite side of Clay, joined in the conversation. "Stockton, we have reason to believe that Pax-Gen did other illegal and potentially dangerous things in their lab, including producing clones to use them as test subjects. This would eliminate the need to go find sick babies. In fact, we're sure that Marco is a clone of Ayrton Senna."

Clay nearly spit out his Red Bull. "Marco, the race driver Mr. Kanda introduced? You have got to be joking."

"We had discussed at the onset of creating our own human babies for our trials, but I strongly disagreed with my colleagues," Nakajima said. "But it seems like they went ahead and did it anyways."

"And because of the Kamita connection, they happened to have Ayrton Senna's DNA lying around, huh? Pretty convenient." Clay remarked.

"We checked Marco's body, but there was no sign of Pax-Gen's nanotechnology inside, so we're fairly sure that either he was a trial or they made him just for kicks. But I have no idea how many different clones they made," Nakajima said.

Roberts leaned forward: "When George told us what went down at Pax-Gen a few years ago, we decided to take a closer look; but by then, the company had already been shut down, and all evidence of their work had been wiped clean because Kanda knew if Pax-Gen was investigated, he would go to jail."

"But now, there's something even more sinister going on," Maki said. "Everyone involved with Pax-Gen has been getting killed off, one by one. After the unexplained deaths of two low-level staffers, Dr. Sato was killed in his car in Hokkaido last year, shot through the head."

"What? Why?" Clay asked.

Roberts shrugged his shoulders. "At first, the local police thought it was just a carjack gone wrong, but all his computers were missing, and when Dr. Sato's right-hand man at Pax-Gen turned up dead in a similar fashion in Kyushu a week later with his computers gone too, we knew these were not mere coincidences. So we tried to get to Mr. Kanda himself, but the old fart avoided us like the plague. He's a real hard man to track down. And because we had no proof or legal authority to bring him in, we were forced to open a clandestine investigation."

"I'm sure I was next on the list of whoever was doing the killings," George said. "But thankfully, I've been under the protection of Agent Roberts."

Clay turned to Nakajima. "Why did you wait so long to report this? Why didn't you go straight to the authorities after you left the company?"

Nakajima shook his head. "In hindsight, I should have, but I didn't want to get mixed up in any trouble. I was still young, fresh out of medical school. I just wanted to get as far away from Pax-Gen as possible and pretend none of it ever happened. And I was scared…there really was something evil about that place."

"According to the good doctor here, there was a mysterious director at Pax-Gen who never showed himself, rarely visiting the lab, and when he did, he worked exclusively from a separate highly-restricted top-secret facility. We feel that he was the main man behind the nanotechnology," Roberts said.

"I never saw this facility because I worked in the support lab. The foundation for the nanotechnology was developed in a place we called Station One, which was kept secret from us, all except Dr. Sato and his assistant. Most of the first experimental nanobots were produced there, and our job at Station Two was to fine-tune them, conduct experiments and monitor their effectiveness," Nakajima said.

"Again, what's all this have to do with me?" Clay said.

"We're almost there," Roberts said with a wink.

Maki shot Roberts a cold, hard look, before addressing Clay again. "Stockton, if nanotechnology is perfected and ends up in the wrong hands, not only will it have serious ethical implications, it can have dire health and, more important, political consequences."

"Okay, so?"

Maki turned in her chair to face Clay. "Our mission is to find out who's behind this operation and make sure all of the information is contained. After going undercover at Kamita, it became evident to me that Kanda-san was merely the financier and kept his distance from the day-to-day operations of the company, leaving that up to our mystery man. We need to find that person."

"But we now have something that might bring this evil genius out in the open," Roberts said.

Clay perked up. "You're talking about that baby that George snuck out."

Roberts smiled. "Exactly."

"Because he has the proof in his body. Find him, and you can use him to bait the bad guys. Wait, you don't mean…" Clay suddenly froze with his mouth fully open.

"It's about time you pieced it together. You are a bit

slow on the uptake, aren't you, buddy?" Roberts said with a chuckle.

Maki took a deep breath and looked into Clay's eyes. "That's right, Stockton, that baby was you."

Chapter 27

The words hung in the air for what seemed like an eternity. Roberts reached for his wooden cigar box on the far end of his desk, as he watched Clay's face turn pasty white. Maki and Nakajima held their collective breaths, waiting for the impending reaction, hoping that it would be a calm one.

Roberts took out a fat Cuban Cohiba and caressed the cigar in his hand before clipping the end of it with a silver cutter. He pointed to Clay with his cigar. "That's right, buddy. You're the prototype."

"Me?" Clay leaned to one side in his chair. "You mean to tell me that I was a goddam lab experiment?"

Nakajima put his hand softly on Clay's shoulder. "Stockton, I know how you must feel, but…"

Clay swatted Nakajima's hand away. "Hold on. That means all this time, you guys were using me as bait?"

Roberts let out a long wisp of smoke. "We only found out about you a couple of months ago, and we think Mr. Kanda found out shortly after we did. Your safety was always a concern, so we had you watched until we could get confirmation that you were really the one. We also had one of our men tail you from the moment you landed at Haneda. Unfortunately, our guy lost you when you abruptly left the auto show."

Maki shifted her gaze to Nakajima, who removed his glasses and wiped his forehead with his hand.

Clay stood up. "You set me up, didn't you? You wanted me to come to Japan, so I could help you draw out the bad guys."

No one answered.

"Well, I'm not playing your stupid game anymore, so you can all go screw yourselves." Clay turned and yanked the door open, sending it crashing into the inside wall. He grabbed his backpack and walked out.

Maki stood up and moved toward the door.

"Takano, let him go. Don't interfere," Roberts said. "Remember, our primary job is to identify the culprits and stop them. Let him bring them to us. He'll be safe. I've got Agent Chung watching him."

"He needs someone to talk to. I can't treat him like some sort of convenient tool."

"Takano, I said leave him be," Roberts said, this time with more volume, but Maki pretended not to hear and walked out of the office.

Roberts sighed. "Talk about overreacting. Didn't see that coming," he said, relighting his cigar with a silver Zippo lighter. "I thought he'd be happy that we were watching over him. I mean, we did save his life."

"What did you expect? The boy just found out that he was a lab rat, and that he has millions of tiny robots inside his body that are killing him. I just hope he doesn't do anything drastic," Nakajima said.

"It was yours and Takano's idea to tell him everything. I'm still wondering if it was the right choice."

Nakajima frowned. "You saw what could happen if you kept him in the dark. He would just go snooping around on his own and possibly jeopardize your entire operation, not to mention get himself killed prematurely in the process. We really had no choice but to tell him."

"Or detain him against his wishes," Roberts countered.

"Your entire way of thinking is unethical."

Roberts took another drag from his cigar. "Since when did the CIA become ethical? Hey, at least he won't be dying from cancer, that's gotta count for something."

"We haven't confirmed if his body is resistant to cancer yet," Nakajima said.

"Yeah, well it probably won't matter when all is said and done."

* * * *

Clay ran down the stairs taking two steps at a time. He anticipated a number of husky agents lying in wait for him as he reached the ground floor, but not one person appeared.

He made it outside with no resistance whatsoever. Once he reached the sidewalk, he randomly picked a direction and started walking, not caring where he was headed; he just wanted to get as far away from the spooks as possible and make some sense of what he had just discovered. Under his breath, he cursed Roberts, Nakajima, and even God, whose existence he was beginning to question. As he made his way down the narrow road, he heard the distinctive clicking sound of high heels on the pavement coming from behind him. It grew louder with each passing moment.

"Stockton. Wait, please," Maki called out as she ran towards him.

Clay turned around. "I need to be alone, so without sounding too rude, get lost."

"Stockton, there are people trying to kill you. You shouldn't be outside all by yourself."

"Yeah? Unless you're going to go and find Mr. Kanda, so I can have my transfusion, I think I'll take my chances on my own, thank you. But I'll be sure to call you when I find him."

Maki grabbed his forearm. "Stockton, stop. Look at me."

Clay had little choice but to do as she demanded because he couldn't pry his arm out of her vise-like grip. "For God's sake, what?"

"When I first saw you in France, I felt sorry for you, Stockton. I thought, here's just another ordinary guy, nothing special about him at all. And he's probably going to be killed without ever knowing why. But when I heard you had come to Tokyo on your own and tracked Mr. Kanda down, and then followed him all the way to his house, I was like, here's a guy who takes matters into his own hands. Here's a guy with guts."

"If you're trying to cheer me up, don't bother. Unless you want to shoot me or arrest me, let me go." He used both hands to pry free from Maki's grip and started walking in the opposite direction.

"Stockton, please come back," she said, but her plea fell on deaf ears.

Chapter 28

Kanda stood at the edge of his carport and watched Viktor Sokov throw Jimmy Bando's corpse into the trunk of the Kamita Presidente luxury sedan. Novak motioned with his gun for him to get into the rear seat of the car. Once he sat down, Novak slid in next to him, as Sokov jumped into the driver's seat.

"Where are you taking me?" Kanda asked.

Novak slipped his gun back under his jacket. "To my flat in Roppongi. You'll stay there until one of my other assistants escorts you to your office to wipe your drives. You'll have to excuse me this afternoon as I have a speech to deliver at Aoyama University. They seem to be one of the few institutions in the world open to new ideas."

Kanda recalled the first time he attended one of Novak's lectures. The man's ideas about curing diseases and improving life enticed him, so he sought a private meeting with the Russian. There, Novak had promised him that his technology could save his dying son, so Kanda asked him to secretly head his biotech company, Pax-Gen International. How he regretted that decision now, allowing the madman to have free reign to do whatever he pleased. Only five people in the world knew of Novak's involvement with Pax-Gen: Kanda, Novak, Dr. Sato, his assistant Dr. Mori, and Ivanov. The eight lower Pax-Gen staffers were kept in the dark.

The Presidente traveled along the sparsely crowded Chuo Road eastward towards the heart of the city.

"You're not going to get away with this," Kanda said.

"Why so negative, Kanda-san?" Novak asked. "I provided you with arguably the greatest racecar driver in history, and you do have another son."

Kanda clasped his hand together as his eyes swelled with tears. "I received a call from Dr. Kranchek a few days ago. Kenji has a spinal disorder and may not survive."

Novak uncrossed his legs and turned towards Kanda. "You really do have bad luck with children, you know that. Unfortunately, I can't help you."

"You must have some nanobots left, don't you? Can't you treat him?"

"You destroyed most of my samples when you unceremoniously cleaned out my office and closed my lab while I was away. And the few I have left are for a new client."

"Then make some more."

Novak scoffed. "To do what you're asking would take a lot of time and money. And besides, the technology is still yet to be perfected—I have some bugs still to work out—so curing your son would not be possible."

Kanda grabbed Novak's arm. "Then I implore you, don't harm Stockton Clay. He is my own flesh and blood. The fact that he is alive is a miracle in and of itself."

Novak glared at Kanda from the corners of his eyes, yanking his arm away. "Your firstborn died at childbirth. You need to accept that and move on. By the way, how did you discover that he was your long-lost son?"

"I received an anonymous text last week. I didn't believe it at first, but out of curiosity, I wanted to meet him face to face, so I sat with him during dinner. And then, when

I saw the boy up close, I knew right away."

"You were supposed to be helping us eliminate him."

"You never told me he was my lost son," Kanda shouted.

"So it was you who switched him out of the car that exploded, wasn't it?"

Kanda nodded. "Yes, I had Jimmy switch him out."

"Finally, you admit it," Sokov shouted from the driver's seat. "You dirty scum."

Novak rubbed his chin. "I wonder who sent you that text…"

"I will offer you ten million dollars to call off your killer," Kanda said.

Novak laughed out loud. "Kanda-san, do you have any idea what my clients are offering. They have agreed to pay me one hundred million U.S. dollars the minute I deliver them the technology. And they will pay an additional ten million dollars every year so I can continue my work in perfecting it. Can you imagine my technology in the hands of a regime without restrictions? My creations have the potential to overcome nature; I can be more powerful than God himself. So you see, despite your wealth, you don't have nearly enough bargaining chips to compete with my new benefactors."

"Who are these benefactors?"

"You'll see soon enough."

"You're certifiably insane," Kanda said.

"Oh, come on, Kanda-san, don't be so naïve. You're going to love meeting my new friends. They're putting us up in a spacious cabin with a lovely view of the sea and mountains. And you can be back home in a couple of weeks, and no one will be the wiser. By then, our business will be complete, and you'll be free to do whatever you like."

Sokov's cell phone rang, and after brief conversation in Russian, he turned towards his boss. *"On bezhal,"* he said.

Novak's face instantly went from jovial to sinister. "What do you mean he escaped? Tell that idiot he needs to find the boy and kill him now, at all costs. Send in Karpov to assist him," Novak responded in English.

"Understood," Sokov replied.

Kanda watched as Novak shifted anxiously in his seat, his face still set in a twisted frown. After seeing how casually his assistant Bando was gunned down, he was sure that Novak's next bullet had his name on it, but he wasn't going to make it easy for them. He was intent on fighting them until the very end, or at least until he found a way to save his family, including his firstborn he knew so little about.

Chapter 29

Clay didn't know how many hours had passed since he left the CIA building, nor did he care. Keeping his gaze down on the sidewalk, looking up only when crossing the street, he never felt so alone and insignificant in the world. He once believed that he was at the center of the universe; that God considered him more special than any of the others, but with the realization that God had meant for his life to end long ago, the very thought of his existence seemed meaningless.

As he came upon a small bridge that stretched over the Tama River, a narrow waterway that cut through southern Tokyo, Clay stopped at the halfway point of the bridge and leaned over the railing. Fifty feet below him, the water rushed forward angrily, leaving streams of white ripples on the dark blue surface. The notion to jump crossed his mind, but he instead zipped up his jacket and kept walking.

The sun descended over the vast Tokyo horizon, replaced by a full moon that glowed like a pearl in the clear night sky. Clay's feet ached, and his ankles were sore. As he passed by a train station, a sign told him he was in Kawasaki City, which was no longer within the Tokyo boundaries. Just up the road, a small neon sign flashed the words "Yankee Bar," and judging by the exterior appearance of the shabby entryway, it appeared to be a total dive. *Perfect.*

Clay pushed an old wooden door that creaked loudly as it opened. The place was indeed a dive, and a really small one at that, about the size of his studio apartment. A scarred wooden counter with four empty stools occupied most of the space, while a small fabric sofa sat against the far wall next to a large window that looked out to the street. A Caucasian man, dressed in a green U.S. military shirt with the sleeves rolled up, stood behind the counter. His light thinning brown hair hinted at his forty-something age, and his muscular forearms, wide shoulders, and square jaw covered with razor stubble gave him the aura of a real-life G.I. Joe doll, but his warm smile and gentle eyes refuted his husky physique.

"*Irasshai!*" he said, motioning for Stockton, his only patron, to take a seat at the bar.

"A whiskey," Clay ordered. "Neat."

"Hey, you're American. Well I'll be damned," the bartender said in a distinct southern drawl.

"Sorry, but I'm not in the mood to talk, so if you can just let me drink in peace, I'd appreciate it," Clay said.

The bartender gave him a curious look and poured him a glass of Jim Beam whiskey. "Yes sir. You're the customer."

Clay knocked back the glass in one quick motion. The whiskey felt like a hot iron rod being forced down his throat, causing him to double over on his stool and cough violently. Long strings of slobber stretched from his mouth.

"Whoa, slow down there, partner," the bartender said. "I'm here all night."

Clay pulled himself up straight. "Gimme another."

The bartender slowly refilled Clay's glass and also placed a large glass of water in front of him. "That's a chaser. It'll make it go down smoother," he said.

Clay took it slower this time, taking short sips from his glass. He managed to finish the shot without the help of the water, and then ordered another, and then another. As he started on his fifth shot, the effects of the liquor took over his senses.

"You're American right?" Clay slurred, his vision starting to blur. "What in the blazes are you doing here in this shithole?"

The bartender laughed. "So you do want to talk."

"Yes. Yes, I do."

"The name is Matt Crawford. Nice to meet you," the bartender said, as he poured himself a drink and raised his glass. "And this shithole is my home."

Clay clanked his glass against Crawford's. "Cheers, I'm Stockton."

Crawford finished his shot of whiskey in one gulp, as did Clay, whose throat was now completely numb.

Crawford poured himself another drink. "I used to work at the U.S. naval base over in Yokohama. I retired a few years back, and then opened up this small bar with my wife. But enough about me, what brings you this way?"

"Trust me, you don't even want to know," Clay said as he put his head down on the countertop. "You're a good man, Matt…"

Clay closed his eyes and fell into a deep slumber; his body seated on the stool and his head resting on its side atop the bar counter.

"That could've been the shortest conversation I've ever had," Crawford said to himself with a chuckle, pouring himself another drink.

Chapter 30

Maki Takano had no idea where Kanda was. She was asked to provide an update on the whereabouts of the president of Kamita Motors, but he seemed to have dropped off the edge of the earth after the Tokyo Motor Show press conference. She checked every bar, teahouse, hostess club, and hotel that he was known to frequent, but her search came up with a big fat zero. She paused for a few seconds before opening the door to Roberts' office, contemplating what she was going to report to him.

Maki took a deep breath, knocked once, and walked into the office.

Roberts, who sat at his desk, looked up at her. "Find anything?" he asked.

She shook her head and sat down in one of the chairs. "I recommend contacting the Tokyo Station to assist us in finding him," she said. "He's most likely still in the country because we don't have any record of his private planes leaving."

Roberts shook his head. "The station chief is already peeved that we're working independently in his backyard, and they're too busy with some Chinese drug gang in the Tohoku region, so they won't help us. What about tracking his phone?"

"His cell phone is still turned off," Maki said.

"Figures. Flowers went to Kanda's house, and his wife confirmed that he was indeed there earlier, but that he left for a prolonged business trip."

"Yes, I spoke with Mrs. Kanda this afternoon. She told me that too. She said Mr. Kanda had a meeting with an old colleague earlier in the day. She couldn't remember his name, but she said he was Russian. And apparently, he had a couple of scary looking associates with him."

Roberts rubbed his forehead. "You think this Russian guy is connected to Pax-Gen?"

"It's possible though I've never known Kanda to associate himself with Russian businessmen before. She gave me a simple description of the men, but they didn't match any known former Pax-Gen staffers."

"Well, keep digging. Thank you, Takano," Roberts said.

Maki remained seated.

"Is there something else?" he asked.

Maki leaned forward. "Boss, I suggest we bring Stockton in and keep him hidden until we find Mr. Kanda."

"No way. We're getting so close to exposing the culprits. We're staying status quo. Our boy is finally starting to draw the bad guys out, just like we planned."

"Yes, but he's suffering from an illness that we didn't know he had, and we also didn't know that the people after him were such highly trained professionals."

"You don't know that for sure, Takano."

"Come on, boss. The way they rigged that sports car in France, and the way they shot those yakuzas without blinking an eye, what else can they be? He's a sitting duck out there."

Roberts crossed his arms. "I understand your concerns. Tell you what, I'll double the people watching over him. Will that make you feel better? And as soon as we find Kanda, we'll bring him in right away so that Stockton can be treated. I promise. So let's just wait and see how it plays out, okay?"

Maki shot her boss a hard look. "I think using him like this is wrong. We should take advantage of the fact that George was able to find a possible cure. What you're doing is inhuman and totally insensitive." She stood up and walked out of the office without waiting for a reply.

It was the first time Maki had expressed anger at Roberts. She always considered him fair and even-keeled—although he was often clueless about social tact and etiquette—so her sudden outburst was completely out of character. Stockton didn't mean anything personally to her, but the more she pondered his situation and his past, the more she understood why she felt an affinity for him. She saw a little bit of herself in him.

Being born to a Korean father and a Japanese mother in Osaka, Japan, Maki Takano was considered a *zainichi*, a Korean transplant who had Japanese citizenship and even a Japanese surname. But she was still constantly teased by her schoolmates for being Korean, although she had no direct ties with the country whatsoever. Also, because her father was denied citizenship by the Japanese government—like nearly all first- or second-generation immigrants—he was required to go through customs separately from his wife and daughter, something that had a profound effect on her. She gradually developed a strong distaste for the Japanese tradition of discouraging outsiders from blending in, and instead became infatuated with America. She enjoyed American music and movies like many of her school friends, but she was particularly drawn to the country's openness towards outsiders, where every resident and citizen were not only allowed, but encouraged, to call themselves Americans. So she enrolled in a student-exchange program that assigned her to a high school in Seattle, where she dedicated herself to studying and learning about American culture. Her excellent grades resulted in a scholarship to Princeton University, where she majored in public relations. In her senior year, she became romantically involved with her political science professor, who also happened to be a special consultant for the CIA. He pulled some strings to get her a post at Langley upon graduation. Her first and only boss, Andrew Roberts, was so impressed with her intellect, linguistic skills, and a natural-born talent as a sharpshooter that he arranged for her U.S. citizenship and offered her a position as an analyst with the Company. Two years later, she was assigned to the Special Science Division to go undercover at Kamita Motors to investigate Tetsuro Kanda and Pax-Gen International. In her half year at Kamita, she uncovered a number of important clues that led to the discovery of the lost prototype, Stockton Clay. Because she was ordered to anonymously leak Clay's existence to Kanda, she couldn't help but feel a little responsible for putting him in his current situation. She didn't want his blood on her hands.

It was already dark in Tokyo, as Takano drove her Kamita company car, a 660cc mini sports vehicle called the Maestro, towards her flat in the Meguro ward. She reminded herself that she joined the CIA to promote and enforce justice, and she had made up her mind that that was exactly what she was going to do.

Chapter 31

Clay slowly opened his eyes as the round face of a teen-age girl came slowly into focus. She was a *hapa haole*, just like him—half Asian and half Caucasian—with her auburn hair fixed in a ponytail. She wore what looked to be a private boarding school uniform: a navy V-neck sweater, a blue striped tie, and red knee-length checkered skirt.

"Hello, mister. It's morning," she said.

"Who are you? Where am I?" Clay asked. He looked around and found that he was still in the bar from the night before, lying on the small sofa against the back wall. A thick blanket covered his body. The morning sunlight shot through the large windows, making him cover his eyes and wince.

"Dad, he's awake," the young girl said.

Matt Crawford stood behind the bar, washing whiskey glasses. "Rebecca, you better get back to school. Lunchtime is almost over, you'll be late."

The young girl ran upstairs.

Clay sat up and noticed that Crawford walked behind the bar with a pronounced limp. When he came closer, he noticed why: one of his legs was prosthetic.

"Good morning, Stockton, or should I say good afternoon. Here's a little pick-me-up," Crawford said, handing him a cup of hot coffee.

Clay glanced at his Casio watch, and it showed one o'clock p.m. He took the cup with both hands and brought it to his lips. The coffee didn't taste good at first, but it did manage to clear his head. "Thank you…Matt, right?"

"I'm impressed you remember. After your fifth drink, you passed out right at the bar."

"I'm sorry. I didn't mean to trouble you. I hope you take a credit card because I don't have any cash on me." *Evidently, nanobots didn't cure hangovers.*

The bartender waved off the suggestion. "It was a weeknight, and I hardly get any customers here at all, and besides, it was nice to talk to a fellow American. Come on up to the bar," he said as he returned to his place behind the counter.

Clay got to his feet slowly and sat down on one of the stools. "I hope you don't mind me asking, but your leg…"

Crawford smiled as he poured himself a cup of coffee. "Got blown off in Afghanistan. Don't know if you remember that."

"I was still little, but I do," Clay nodded. "I'm sorry."

"Don't be. It seems like you're kinda down in the dumps yourself. You know, when I start feeling sorry for myself, I remember the places where I was deployed to, like Iraq, and Africa. I tell ya, that's where I saw what real hardship was. People, even kids, killed and maimed every day without reason. It's just tragic knowing that these folks were born into that life of suffering with no hope of escape—it wasn't their choice, you know, to be born there. That's when I remind myself how lucky I am, leg or no leg, that I still have my freedom, and a daughter who cares about me, not to mention a small monthly compensation check from Uncle Sam that keeps us fed and this roof over our heads."

Clay heard the sound of footsteps coming down the stairs.

"Dad, I'm going now." Rebecca burst out the front door.

"She's adorable," Clay said.

"Yeah, she reminds me a lot of her mother."

"By the way, where is her mother? I'd like to apologize to her too for troubling you all."

"My wife died of cancer about five years ago. We bought this place together, so I keep it going just for her. She always wanted to run an American-style bar. Now it's just me and Rebecca, who takes care of our living quarters upstairs, while I take care of the bar downstairs."

Clay looked down at his coffee mug. "I'm so sorry, I..."

"Like I said before, don't be. Life is a gift. It should be treasured, not wasted. I feel sorry for those who don't understand what a special thing it is to be alive."

"How about for someone who's not supposed to be alive?" asked Clay.

Crawford shot him a confused look. "What do you mean?"

"Should someone who's not supposed to be alive share the same sentiment?"

"I don't exactly know what you're saying, but yeah, I would say especially someone who's not supposed to be alive. Hell, I don't know if I'm supposed to be alive after that bomb blast that took my leg. If you've already bucked the odds, life should be that much more precious. Don't you think?"

"You're not angry about what happened to your leg? To your wife?"

"Sure, I've been dealt some shitty cards in my life, but

when I think of all those others who have it worse off than me, all in all, I feel like I'm still sittin' on a pretty good hand."

Clay watched the coffee steam rise into the air. He suddenly felt infinitely small and selfish, ashamed for constantly feeling discontented with his life, always envious of others who had more than him. Never once did he consider the less fortunate, the very people Crawford had just mentioned, and even Crawford himself, who he now felt was the most graceful and tolerant human being that he had ever met. Clay had lived a content life up to this point. Most people in the world would sacrifice everything to be able to have what he had.

Okay, so if I'm not supposed to be alive, then I have absolutely nothing to lose. I could risk everything now and still be ahead. Hell, life could actually be fun if I had the luxury of playing with house money.

"Hey, you listening?" Crawford asked.

"Yeah, I'm listening. I've just realized that I've been an absolute fool."

The front door of the bar creaked opened. Clay did a double-take when he saw Maki Takano standing in the doorway.

"Maki? What on earth?"

Maki, dressed in jeans, black leather boots, and a suede jacket, took a seat next to Clay. "Hello, Stockton. Can I have a coffee please," she asked the bartender.

"Coming right up," Crawford said and placed a small white mug in front of her and filled it up with steaming java.

Maki took a sip and nodded in approval. "That hits the

spot. Thank you."

"How did you know I was here?" Clay asked.

"Check your jacket pocket," she said.

Clay did so and pulled out a small plastic button, about the size of a postage stamp. "What the hell is this? A tracking device?"

"We had to make sure you were safe, but I did want to give you time to sort things out on your own. How are you doing?"

"I'm fine…but you know, this borders on stalking, which seems to be happening to me a lot these days."

Maki flashed a subtle smile. "Stockton, I'm not going to bullshit you. As you said, the CIA has been using you as bait for the past few weeks. They knew that if they stayed close to you, whoever was involved with Pax-Gen would come after you, saving us the time and effort of locating them on our own. You're the only evidence of their wrongdoing and their nanotechnology."

Clay shrugged his shoulders. "Can't say I'm surprised. I knew none of you had my best interests in mind."

"Although we were also protecting you, Stockton, I don't care for what they're doing, so I want to help you. Can you give me your cell phone?" she asked.

Clay looked at her quizzically, then pulled his phone out of his pocket and handed it to her. "Can I have that back as soon as you're done. I need to call my parents."

She shook her head. "I'm sorry, but we disabled your phone from making outside calls since last night. The information we disclosed to you is highly classified, so I'm going to have to trust you to not tell anyone about this yet."

Clay frowned as he didn't like the fact that they secretly hacked his phone, nor did he care for being told he couldn't talk to his parents.

Maki turned his phone on, punched in his secret four-digit code, and downloaded an app that Clay had never before seen.

"What are you doing? And how the hell did you know my passcode?"

"Whoever is trying to kill you knows you're in Japan, so they'll probably look for you by tracking your cell phone," she said. "So I'm downloading a special app that prevents your device from being tracked." She didn't answer his second question.

Clay reached for his phone and grabbed it from her hands. "You know what, don't do that. I want them to find me. Mr. Kanda is with them, and if I don't get to him soon, I'm a goner, so let's let them find me, and maybe they'll lead me to him. I know it's risky, but what do I have to lose?"

"Are you sure?"

"Yeah, I'm sick of running around scared. And my first priority is to find Mr. Kanda."

Maki nodded in approval. "You do have guts. Okay, I'm fairly sure they don't know we're involved yet, so we'll try to draw them out in a crowded area. I have just the place in mind." Maki got up and placed a thousand-yen note on the counter. "The coffee was wonderful," she said to Crawford and stepped out of the bar.

Clay stood up, leaned over the counter and offered his

hand to the bartender. "Thank you, for everything. I'll never forget you."

"The pleasure was mine," he said shaking Clay's hand vigorously. "By the way, your friend left way too much money. The coffee is free."

"I think she's paying for the drinks I had last night. Oh, and for my lodging," Clay said with a smile.

"Well, if that's the case, she didn't leave enough."

"I'll pay you back, I promise."

"I'm just shittin' you. Come on back when you're in town again, all right?"

Clay nodded and stepped outside. He walked up next to Maki who waited for him just outside the door.

Maki looked over at a blue Nissan Tida parked across the street and signaled to the young Asian man in the driver's seat, who pulled the car away from the curb and disappeared down the road.

"Who was that?" Clay asked.

"He's one of us. He followed you from the moment you stepped out of our office. Poor guy spent the night in the car. I'm relieving him now."

Clay laughed and shook his head. "You guys...I'm speechless."

"Are you ready for your special guided tour of Tokyo?" Maki asked.

"Yeah. Let's do this."

Chapter 32

Clay's jaw dropped when Maki walked up to a small low-slung sports car parked on the side of the street in front of the Yankee Bar. He recognized the Kamita Maestro right away, the company's best-selling *kei*-car or minicar.

Kei-jidosha, which translated to "light cars" in Japanese, were marketed only in Japan, designed to provide affordable transportation while easing the country's burden on traffic congestion and parking spaces. The exterior dimensions and engine size were restricted by the government, so the Japanese car companies that produced *kei*-cars resorted to a variety of creative styling themes and new technologies to differentiate their machines from their competitors'. The Maestro was the sportiest version of the genre, with a swooping roofline and rear-wheel-drive, following in the footsteps of the Honda Beat and Suzuki Cappuccino.

"The Kamita Maestro minicar. I've always wanted to drive this," Clay said, carefully examining the bright red car from bumper to bumper.

"Here you go," Maki said as she tossed him the key fob.

Clay caught it in mid-flight, beaming from ear to ear. "Are you serious?"

"Yes," she said as she climbed into the passenger seat. "This is a special vehicle the engineering department customized for me. It has a supercharger built into the engine, giving it way more power than the stock model. So be careful, it can bite you."

Clay jumped into the driver's seat and fired up the

three-cylinder engine, which came to life with a sewing-machine rattle. He slid the manual shifter into first gear and pulled the car away from the curb.

Maki inputted an address into the navigation system. The small monitor on the center dash displayed a three-dimensional layout of the surroundings and a bright orange arrow showing the way.

"Just follow the directions," Maki said.

"Yes ma'am," Clay answered as he reveled in the exhilarating power delivery of the small powerplant, waiting until redline before each upshift. Maki constantly checked the rearview mirror and furiously tapped away on her cell phone, sending what seemed to Clay like a dozen texts every minute.

An hour later, the Maestro came upon the base of the Tokyo Skytree, an architectural marvel built in 2012 that extended more than two-thousand feet into the heavens, making it the tallest structure in Japan. It stood taller than the Eiffel Tower and Tokyo Tower combined. Being extraordinarily tall wasn't the only noteworthy thing about the Skytree. The 450-floor tower also possessed state-of-the-art earthquake-resistant technology that came in the form of "shock absorbers" that soaked up fifty percent of the energy from a tremor, the first time such technology had been used for a building so big.

Maki guided Clay to the VIP lot, where they parked the car and headed to the entrance of the Tokyo landmark.

"I've seen photos of this thing, but they don't do it justice," Clay said.

"It's always crowded here, so it'll be difficult for anyone trying to get to you to do anything reckless. I've arranged for a couple of agents to watch the front of the building. They should be here within a half hour."

Clay and Maki walked inside and took the outdoor escalators to the fourth floor, where the official entrance to the Skytree was located. There, a few hundred people waited in line under the afternoon sun in front of the ticket booth, making Clay wonder if he was going to be here all day. But Maki walked up to the security guard who manned the staff entrance and flashed her Kamita Motors ID card. He gave her a curt bow and allowed her to pass.

"Stockton, this way. Come on," she said.

He hurried after her. "Wow, VIP treatment."

"Kamita Motors is a major sponsor," she said.

She led him to one of four elevators where they joined a few dozen other visitors going to the first observatory deck. The carriage hummed as it shot up three hundred and fifty floors to its destination, the Tembo Deck, the main observation floor where glass walls offered a three-hundred-and-sixty-degree view of the city, and on a clear day like this one, allowed visitors to see up to 50 miles away.

"Excuse me Stockton, but I need to make a quick phone call," Maki said as they stepped out of the elevator.

"Sure, take your time. I'll just look around some."

"Stay close, and if you see anything suspicious, come back here immediately. Do you understand?"

Clay nodded. He joined a crowd of visitors making their way around the walkway. At about the halfway point, he stopped to admire a magnificent bird's-eye view of the west side of Tokyo and the neighboring Kanagawa Prefecture. Mt. Fuji exposed its unmistakable peak in the far distance. It took twenty minutes for him to complete a lap around the deck, back to where Maki waited for him by the main elevator.

"Well?" she asked.

"This is absolutely incredible. I could see Mt. Fuji on one side and as far as Narita airport on the other."

"No, I mean did you see anything out of the ordinary?"

"Oh that. No," he said.

"Good. Since we're here, I might as well take you all the way up to the Tembo Gallery. It's as high as you can go."

"Cool," Clay said flashing a thumbs-up sign.

Maki led Clay to another set of elevators, bypassing the paying tourists who were required to fork over another few thousand yen to enter. The smaller elevator climbed another hundred floors up the side of the monument, letting them off on the 445th floor.

There were less tourists here than the lower floors, making it easy for Clay to get right up against the windows and look straight down onto the skyscrapers below. He snapped away several photos with his smart phone as he followed Maki up the spiral ramp to the 450th floor.

Maki stopped when she got to the end of the ramp and turned around. "Stockton, we'll hang out here until…"

Clay suddenly noticed Maki's face tighten. Something had caught her attention over his shoulder. Before he could turn to see what it was, she leaned her head towards his and spoke in a hushed voice.

"Don't turn around. There's a man in a leather jacket behind you. A white guy, with a buzz cut, wire-frame glasses, short and stocky. He's holding a rolled-up newspaper in his hand. We're going to go back down to the main deck and hide near the gift shop. If he follows us down there, take a look at him and let me know if you've ever seen him before."

Clay's mouth went dry. He nodded.

They took the small elevator back down to the Tembo Deck, where they immediately walked into the gift shop on the 345th floor and took up their position behind a colorful banner, pretending to look at the items on sale. Five minutes later, the man in the leather jacket walked past the shop, still holding the rolled-up newspaper.

Clay got a good look at his face, but he didn't recognize it. "I've never seen that person before in my life," he said.

"They might have multiple people after you in Japan, which complicates things." Maki took out her cell phone from her orange Hermes Kelly handbag and made a call.

Clay kept watching the heavy-set man in the leather jacket, but to him, he looked like a typical European tourist.

"We're coming down in ten minutes, are you in position?" she said into the phone. "The mark is Caucasian, five-foot-six, buzz haircut, brown leather jacket, markings on the back of his hand." She put her phone back into her bag and grabbed Clay's arm. "Let's go. We're going to go to the main elevator."

Clay nodded as he followed right behind Maki, who walked past the man in the leather jacket. "And Mr. Clay, this is as high as we can get," she said loudly in a performance that would get her nominated for an Oscar. "We're standing nearly fifteen hundred feet above the ground. Isn't that something?"

"Yeah, cool," Clay answered.

Clay eyed the man, who started taking photos of the view with his cell phone like many of the other tourists there, paying absolutely no attention to him. He wondered if Maki was being a bit paranoid.

When they reached the VIP elevator, the staffer manning the station informed Maki that it was being serviced and would not return for another twenty minutes. So she led Clay to the main lifts where a long cue had formed with at least two dozen people crowding in front of the middle door.

Maki pulled on Clay's sleeve. "Okay, force your way to the front when the doors open."

When the light above the elevator door illuminated, Maki pushed Clay to the front of the line, driving a wedge into the crowd. While getting nasty stares from the other tourists, they were among the first to step into carriage. As Maki had predicted, the elevator filled up before everyone could get in. The man in the leather jacket quickly made his way towards them.

"Maki, that guy's trying to get in here," Clay said as the doors slammed shut and the elevator descended.

She said nothing, as the two were pressed into the far wall of the carriage by the crowd of people squeezed together like canned sardines. Her body was pinned up against his, and Clay could smell the sweet fragrance of her perfume. As his body warmed with excitement, he brought his arms up to her shoulders and looked down at her. Her eyes were pointed downward, so she didn't notice his stare. With soothing music humming from the speakers, he studied her small perfectly-shaped face, her smooth, clean skin, and full red lips. He wanted to touch her arms and hold her steady, but he resisted the temptation. Maki was the one woman in the world who he didn't want to be rejected by; she had shown him patience and warmth in his darkest hour.

He dropped his arms back down to his side and settled for a deep whiff of her perfume as the carriage came to a stop. Maki quickly walked to the exit, pulling Clay by the hand.

"Listen, there's a high probability the man has a partner. If you see anyone familiar or suspicious, point him out," she said to Clay without looking back at him.

"Yes ma'am."

"We'll go straight to the car. We have agents positioned in front of the main entrance to tail our friend when he comes out. And the chief has okayed for me to take you to our safe house. You'll stay there until we can find out the identity of the guy back there, and if he has any friends. Got it?"

Clay nodded.

Once outside, Maki nodded in the direction of two Asian men in sunglasses and casual clothing, sitting on a nearby bench reading a newspaper. She then led Clay to the Kamita Maestro in the VIP parking lot.

"Maki, can I drive again?" Clay asked.

"Sure," she said. "Boys will be boys."

With a wide grin, Clay jumped into the driver's seat

and fired up the car's engine, as Maki took her place in the passenger seat and promptly punched in an address into the navigation system.

"Okay, just follow the instructions like you did last time."

"Roger that," Clay said.

The navigation system directed him to turn onto the onramp of the Chuo Expressway, which he did. After passing through the ETC toll gate, they immediately came upon heavy traffic that forced them to slow to a crawl. Both lanes of the narrow thoroughfare were clogged, resembling a parking lot, with vehicles lined up for miles.

"Welcome to Tokyo," Maki said.

"And I thought the traffic in Los Angeles was bad. By the way, what made you think that guy back there was a bad guy?"

"Well, for one, it was pretty stuffy in there, so the fact that he kept his leather jacket on may have meant he was hiding a weapon underneath. And the newspaper he was holding was a Japanese language newspaper, which unlike American newspapers, requires at least a high-school-level proficiency in kanji to be able to read. And he didn't seem like the scholarly type to me. I assumed he picked it up to use as a prop. And then there was the tattoo on the back of his hand. A lot of Russian mobsters and criminals mark themselves with tattoos all over their bodies, including their hands and fingers, and it seemed unlikely that a Russian mobster would casually spend the day visiting the Skytree on his own, don't you think?"

Clay nodded. "You're like a modern-day Sherlock Holmes."

The evening rush hour was still an hour away, so the roads became less congested the further they got away from the city center. The lane in front of them began to clear up, prompting Clay to press the accelerator pedal, tapping into the supercharged engine of the sporty *kei*-car.

Maki's cell phone rang. She pulled it out of her bag and answered. "This is Takano…What do you mean he never came out?...Okay, roger that."

Maki cursed under her breath.

"Trouble?" Clay asked.

"Maybe. Our mark never came out. So one of our agents went inside to look for him, but there was no sign of him. He probably went out a window or a side exit. Damn, I underestimated him. Now he's on the loose, and we're exposed without backup."

Up ahead was a road construction sign where a worker in a blue uniform and orange flag diverted all vehicles to the right most lane, forcing Clay to slow the Maestro down. He once again found himself stopped behind a long line of stationary vehicles. A cacophony of car horns blared from behind, which prompted him to look into his rearview mirror. In the reflection was a large black car, an Audi A6, slaloming through the evenly spaced traffic, coming up fast on his tail. He'd seen that car before; it was the same one that he tailed from the Tokyo Big Sight to Kanda's home.

"Maki, I think we just found our friend again, or should I say, he's found us," Clay said.

Chapter 33

Maki turned around and saw the black Audi hurtling towards them, now a hundred feet away, charging hard with reckless abandon.

"He's going to hit us," she said.

Clay threw the gear shifter into first and simultaneously yanked on the steering wheel. "Hang on," he said as he maneuvered the vehicle onto the shoulder; the Maestro's rear tires kicking up loose gravel.

But his actions came a split-second too late as the front end of the A6 smashed into the corner of the Maestro's rear bumper, tearing away a small chunk of fiberglass. Clay gripped the steering wheel hard, and Maki clutched the overhead grab handle, as the jolt tossed them in their seats like ragdolls. The tensioners squeezed the seatbelts tight across their bodies, the pressure of the belts knocking the air out of their lungs. The bumper did its job of deflecting most of the energy of the impact away from the cabin, but not enough to keep the *kei*-car car from skidding sideways. It came to a stop just shy of the guardrail.

Clay saw the all-too familiar face of Oleg Ivanov scowling at him through the Audi's front windshield. Sitting next to him was the man in the leather jacket from the Skytree, pointing a gun in his direction.

"Oh shit. It's that bearded guy again," Clay said.

Maki reached into her handbag and pulled out a black SIG Sauer P226. "We need to get the hell out of here now."

The sight of the firearm made Clay pause, but he floored

the accelerator pedal, sending the red sports car speeding down the shoulder of the expressway.

The Audi pulled onto the shoulder, nudging a compact sedan out of the way, and followed the Maestro. The two cars sped down the expressway, bumper to bumper, passing hundreds of vehicles sitting motionless in the conventional lanes. When Clay glanced into his rearview mirror, he saw the A6 glued to his broken rear bumper. The man in the leather jacket leaned out of the passenger-side window and fired off three evenly spaced shots.

One bullet found its mark, hitting the Maestro's passenger-side mirror, shattering it into a hundred pieces.

"Does he have no regard for innocent bystanders?" Clay asked.

Maki lowered her window, leaned out of the car facing rearward, and fired off four quick shots, three hit nothing but air; one grazed the Audi's A-pillar. "You concentrate on driving," she said. "Try to stay ahead of these guys until our backup can catch up to us."

Clay knew that the little Kamita had no chance of outrunning the A6 in a drag race. The speedometer showed a hundred and sixty kilometers, about one hundred miles per hour, and the thing was maxed out. The German sedan possessed twice the horsepower of the Maestro, if not more, so it was only a matter of time before the Audi caught them and forced them off the road. The only chance they had of outrunning the A6 was on a twisty road, where Clay could use the Maestro's better handling ability and compact size to his advantage.

"We may have a chance on a twisty road. I can't imagine there's one nearby, is there?" he asked.

"Let me see," Maki said as she tapped the touch-screen monitor on the center dash until a map of the entire region came up. She studied the image, shifting the map position by sliding her index finger on the screen.

The shoulder was coming to an end up ahead, forcing Clay to take the next exit.

"I've got to get off here. Do you know where this road leads?" he asked as he swerved the car onto the off ramp.

"These roads all head into a mountainous area," Maki answered. "Head for the signs that read Mt. Asahi or Odarumi Pass."

"Got it."

Clay had heard of Odarumi Pass before. A few of his Japanese drifting friends mentioned that they had honed their driving techniques on this notorious mountain road outside of Tokyo, which was still a popular spot for illegal street racing. Maki leaned out the window and fired off four more shots; one bullet took out the A6's headlight.

After leaving the expressway, they came upon a toll gate where a tired-looking Japanese man wearing a surgical mask, as many Japanese people did during the cold and flu season, stood inside a small booth. The old man waved at the Maestro to slow down, but Clay paid him no heed, blowing right past the shack without paying or stopping. The Audi followed suit.

Clay kept the A6 at bay by using other vehicles on the road as obstacles, often splitting lanes, which caused his fellow motorists to lean on their horns. But the maneuver helped to provide a healthy cushion between the Maestro and the Audi, which, because of its size, couldn't squeeze between the cars.

Finally, he reached the base of Odarumi Pass. The entrance to the twisty mountain road was unofficially marked by a large parking lot where a half dozen souped-up cars, among them a lowered Mitsubishi Lancer Evolution and Mazda RX-7, were lined up in neat rows, some of them with their hoods lifted open, showing off their shiny modified engines. Several young men and women, dressed in T-shirts and faded blue jeans lounged about, smoking cigarettes and swigging energy drinks. Called "*hashiriya,*" they were amateur street racers, notorious for their underground speed contests and blatant disregard for traffic laws. They ruled here; even the police showed them a certain level of respect on "their" mountain.

The Maestro sped by the parking lot followed closely by the A6 as the sound of their engines echoed off the surrounding hillsides. When Clay looked into his rearview mirror, he saw that the Audi was gaining; he also noticed back in the distance, a modified Nissan Silvia and a lightning blue Subaru BRZ peeling out of the parking lot, joining the chase.

Clay kept his right foot planted to the floor, trying to squeeze every ounce of power the Maestro could generate, but he couldn't pull away from the Audi. Although he created distance between the two cars through corners because of the Maestro's superior cornering abilities, the German sedan kept closing the gap on the straights of the narrow two-lane road.

"There's too much of a power gap between us. I can't shake him going uphill," he said. "Do you know if this road ever descends?"

Maki worked the navigation system. "Yes, this road goes down the other side of the mountain and ends up near a main highway. We have a few more kilometers to go."

Shifting his view constantly from the rearview mirror to the road ahead, Clay could see the man in the leather jacket leaning out of the passenger-side window firing off random shots. Maki answered with her SIG, but it did little in convincing them to slow down. Clay kept his concentration on staying ahead of the A6, hoping that he would reach the downhill section of the mountain soon, for he knew that driving fast downhill took infinitely more skill than going uphill, and he felt confident that he could shake the bigger, more powerful car. When he came out of a corner and saw that the road ahead turned into a long uphill straight, he let out a loud *"oh shit"* because he could see that the next turn was about a mile away. Immediately, the speed of the Maestro decreased as gravity and the weight of two adult passengers strained the *kei*-car's 660cc engine.

The Audi came right up on the rear bumper of the Maestro and swerved into the oncoming lane, positioning itself immediately next to the small red sports car. Clay looked over at the Audi, whose steering wheel was on the left side of the car, unlike the Maestro's, and saw Ivanov smile through his scruffy brown beard—their faces were only a few feet apart, separated by two windows and a few feet of rushing air.

It was obvious what was coming next, so Clay braced for the impact. "Maki, hang on," he said.

Ivanov leaned on the steering wheel, sending the left front fender of the A6 crashing into the side of the Maestro, which gave a little ground and remained steady. Ivanov repeated the maneuver, this time with more force. The German sedan lifted the Maestro's front tires off the pavement, sending it toward the guardrail in a long, steady skid.

As Clay lifted his foot off the accelerator pedal, he furiously worked the steering wheel. The Maestro corrected itself, and Clay got back on the throttle.

"If he does that again, we're going over the edge of the cliff. His car outweighs ours by at least a ton."

"Roll down your window," Maki said as she pointed her gun out the window on his side.

Clay did so and Maki unleashed two shots; the loud pops caused Clay to wince as the gunshots exploded right in front of his face. Both bullets broke the driver-side window of the A6. Ivanov ducked in time, but his passenger wasn't so lucky. The man in the leather jacket caught a slug in his right temple, knocking his head sideways. The slide of Maki's gun snapped in the open position.

"I'm out of ammo," she said.

As he sat lower in his seat in case Maki fired off another shot, Ivanov positioned the Audi for a final go. But before the Russian could act, a minivan appeared in his lane, speeding at him from the opposite direction, its horn honking wildly. The A6 kept its line until the last possible moment, until it finally slowed down and swerved into the proper lane, ducking behind the Maestro, letting the minivan pass. As soon as the opposite lane was clear again, the Audi immediately took up its position next to the Maestro.

"Stockton, this is the highest point of the road. It goes downhill from here," Maki said with her finger pointed to a small sign posted to a metal pole.

"It's about frickin' time," he said as he repositioned his hands on the steering wheel; sweat trickling down the side of his face and a smile forming on his lips. Finally, Clay could turn the odds in his favor and use his adept skills in car control to his advantage.

Chapter 34

As the Maestro ran over the summit of the hill, it went slightly airborne. Immediately, the corners became tighter and the road narrower. A rock wall bordered one side of the pass and a steep drop-off, filled with tall trees, on the other. And because this side of the mountain faced away from the sun, a thin sheet of moisture had accumulated on the tarmac in some spots, making the driving surface unpredictably slippery. Clay couldn't have asked for a better situation. With his face locked in concentration, he positioned his hands to work the steering wheel, the paddle shifters, and the emergency brake handle all at once. His feet moved and pressed the foot pedals like those of a seasoned tap dancer.

Through the first corner, the rear end of the Maestro swung out, and although the car seemed as if it was going to spin, it glided through the turn with the grace of a ballerina, drifting in an elegant arc. As the car slid sideways with the rear tires totally lacking traction, the front tires were pointed in the opposite direction of the turn—known as countersteer or opposite lock—guiding the nose of the car through the corner. The free-spinning rear tires spewed white smoke and howled their disapproval, but because Clay kept the engine revs up the entire time, the Maestro exited the corner nearly as fast as it entered it.

"Where did you learn how to drive like this?" Maki asked, holding the grab handle tightly.

"PlayStation."

Maki made a sour face that implied she didn't believe

him, but in truth Clay did learn a lot about car control from spending hundreds of hours playing driving games, long before he received his driver's license. In fact, Clay once applied for the GT Academy, a national tournament sponsored by Nissan and the Gran Turismo driving game where the best gamers in the country competed for a chance to become real-life race drivers—like an American Idol, but for drivers. The winners were awarded a one-year contract with Nissan's factory race team, and many past graduates became famous racers, competing in the most glamorous motorsports events in the world including the 24 Hour of Le Mans. Unfortunately for Clay, he was disqualified because his position at the magazine made his participation a conflict of interest.

The Audi gradually dropped back, as it struggled to keep steady on the narrow road, scraping the guardrail on a couple of occasions, when it went too wide through the corners. Coming up fast behind it were the Nissan Silvia and Subaru BRZ, which flashed their high beams and honked their horns in a gesture for the driver to pull over, but the Audi didn't stop.

"The guy is persistent," Clay said.

"I've got an idea," Maki said as she flipped down the lid to a storage compartment behind her seat and reached inside. She pulled out a quart of motor oil.

Clay shook his head. "That's not going to work. It's not nearly enough to spin him out. And besides, that trick only works in the movies. It doesn't even work in video games."

"Oh ye of little faith," she said as she took out a pen knife and sliced open two large slits on the face of the container. She then twisted the top off. "Let him catch up and let me know when you come up on a tight left-hander."

"You sure about this?"

She nodded and rolled down her window, the cool oncoming air whipping her long black hair.

"Tight left-hander coming up," Clay said.

"Get the car as sideways as possible, now."

Clay yanked the steering wheel left and pulled on the emergency brake handle. The rear tires instantly lost their grip, rotating the car's rear end; however, as it reached just shy of 180 degrees, he cranked the steering wheel in the opposite direction, downshifted, and got back on the throttle. The car slid sideways through the corner in a wide arc, completely crossed up.

The Maestro exposed its entire passenger side to the oncoming Audi. Ivanov applied more engine power, intent on T-boning the minicar in mid-drift. But before Ivanov could hit the Maestro, Maki hurled the oil container out the window, which hit the Audi's windshield with a *thunk,* splattering thick brown oil all over the glass.

Ivanov activated the wipers, but that only made things worse as the oil smeared on the glass, completely blocking his forward vision. He slammed the brakes, and all four tires of the Audi locked up, the anti-locking system having little effect on a patch of black ice. The big German sedan crashed into the guardrail head first, compressing the entire front end like an accordion. Its momentum carried it over the barrier and down the steep cliff.

Clay thought he heard a scream.

The A6 bounced off a couple of boulders on the cliff face before crashing down on its roof on a small embankment at least a hundred feet below. The cabin was completely caved in, but there was no explosion, no fire.

Clay hit the brakes and stopped the Maestro in the middle of the road, where he jumped out of the car and sprinted to the edge of the cliff to see what had become of the Audi. The A6 had landed belly up, with liquid spreading out underneath, making Clay wonder if any of it was blood. Maki rushed over and stood next to him and put a hand on his shoulder.

"It was either him or us. Great driving."

As soon as the Nissan Silvia and Subaru BRX screeched to a stop behind them, the drivers jumped out of their cars and looked down onto the wrecked car. One of them, with dyed orange hair spiked with hard gel and wearing an AC/DC T-shirt, flicked his cigarette to the ground. "*Arewa tasukaranai na*," he said.

Clay leaned towards Maki. "What did he say?"

"That they're goners," she said.

"Oh, you American?" the man asked. "It is bad accident."

His partner, a bald man, with an earring and wearing a bright yellow sweat suit, said, "I will call 1-1-0," but before dialing, he turned to Maki and Clay. "Were they with you?"

Maki shook her head. "Stockton, we need to get out of here."

Clay walked silently back to the Maestro and dropped into the driver's seat. It was the second time in as many weeks that he had witnessed death up close, but this time, he didn't feel the same shock as before. Once Maki belted herself in, he popped the Maestro's gearbox into first and slowly made his way down the mountain road, wondering if he would ever be able to get off this nightmarish roller coaster.

Chapter 35

As the sun descended below the vast Tokyo horizon, Clay guided the Kamita Maestro through Kabukicho in the Shinjuku ward, known for its extravagant nightlife. Bars, pachinko parlors, and hostess clubs, as well as other more risqué dens of inequity, were opening up for business and Clay couldn't keep from rubbernecking at the colorfully lit signs and sales girls dressed in bikinis on a chilly night. He nearly ran over a young man dressed in a neat suit dashing across the street to lure middle-aged businessmen into his drinking establishment. The narrow streets were filled with taxis and more than a few Ferraris and McLarens, and the area was so well illuminated by the bright lights on the buildings that Clay could have easily drove around with his headlights turned off.

"Thanks for bringing us back the long way. The nightlife here puts Los Angeles to shame," he said as he made a left turn around Shinjuku Station, known as the busiest rail station in the world.

Maki glanced into the rearview mirror, as she had done regularly for the entire hour commute from the mountain road. "It wasn't for your sight-seeing pleasure. I don't think we're being followed anymore."

"It sure is tempting to park and look around here a little," Clay said as he admired the pretty girls dressed as college students, race queens, and even nurses, handing out flyers to potential male customers.

"Not a chance. I think it's okay now to go straight to the

safe house," Maki said.

The twenty-five-mile drive from Shinjuku Station to the safe house took about an hour and a half. They drove into Chiba prefecture, onto a small unmarked street that was barely lit, lined with several automotive repair shops on either side of the road, all of them closed for the night. At the far end of the street were several cheap-looking hotels that rented rooms by the hour. Maki pointed to the hotel at the very end, the one that had a small gated driveway. When Clay drove up to it, the steel gate opened automatically.

"Is this it?" Clay asked as he slowly drove the car in.

"Yes. We call it the Nanka Hotel, although it's not really a hotel. It's the property of the United States government and mainly used to accommodate special guests who don't want people to know that they were in the country," Maki said.

The short driveway ended at a shabby three-story rectangular structure with fifteen windows arranged in rows of three. The brown muck on the exterior stucco walls of the hotel seemed like the building had not been cleaned in months. Clay, however, did notice several shiny new cameras mounted on its walls pointing in nearly every direction of the property. As soon as he pulled to a stop at the front entrance, marked by a tinted set of sliding glass doors, George Nakajima came out.

"You guys took long enough," he said as Maki and Clay stepped out of the car.

"Hi George. We had an interesting afternoon," Clay said.

Maki walked around the Maestro, whose engine was

still running, to the driver's side. "Please get a good night's sleep, and I will see both of you tomorrow morning. We'll need to track down Mr. Kanda first thing."

"But I should be looking for him now," Clay said.

"No Stockton, you need to get some rest. You must remember that you are gravely ill," Maki said.

Nakajima put his hand on Clay's shoulder. "She's right, Stockton. You might accelerate the effects of the disease without proper rest."

"This Andor's Disease, you said it's related to the nanotechnology, right?"

"Yes," Nakajima answered.

"So why do I need a blood transfusion from Mr. Kanda?"

"The nanobots are altering not only your sick cells, but your healthy blood cells too. And you need a fresh supply of the exact type of blood to normalize your system. Once that's done, the nanobots should recognize that your healthy blood cells do not need treatment, thus stopping your illness."

"It's crazy to imagine that I have thousands of small robots inside my body."

"They're not exactly robots, Stockton. They're more like programmed molecules."

"Whatever. And who the hell is Andor?" Clay asked.

Nakajima wore a troubled expression. He covered his mouth with his left hand and muttered his response. "It was the name of Dr. Sato's dog."

"You named my disease after a dog?"

"I'm sorry, it was the first thing we could think of, and

none of us were allowed to use our own names."

Clay shrugged his shoulders. "Well, I guess it doesn't really matter. I'll do as you say and shut it down tonight, but I'm going after Mr. Kanda, by myself if I have to, first thing tomorrow morning."

Maki wrapped her arms around Clay and gave him a light hug. "Good night, Stockton."

Clay held his breath as he felt her warm cheek against his. "Good…good night, Maki," he muttered.

She then stepped into the Maestro and drove off without saying another word, as Clay and Nakajima quietly watched the little sports car's taillights disappear down the driveway.

"She's a very pretty lady. You two make a nice couple," Nakajima said.

Clay laughed. "I have no chance in hell."

"Didn't seem like it to me."

"Trust me. She's way out of my league."

"Listen son, I know women. I used to be quite the play-boy in my day," Nakajima said with a wink.

"You?"

The doctor responded with a scowl, which made Clay burst out in laughter. It was the first good laugh that he had had in a long time, and it felt good.

After he wiped the tears from his eyes, Clay turned to Nakajima with a serious face. "I haven't had a chance to say this yet, but thanks for saving my life, you know, when I was a baby."

"You're very welcome, Stockton." Nakajima said, patting him on the back.

Chapter 36

Maki Takano was no stranger to death. Whether it was in the field investigating an assassination or examining a corpse in some county's morgue, she had seen death up close plenty of times; however, this day marked the first time she actually killed a person; in fact, two people. Although she had tried to convince herself that it came with the job, her arms wouldn't stop shaking as she drove away from the safe house onto Keio Road.

Her mind replayed the scene of the bullet blasting a hole in the temple of the man in the leather jacket, and she could still hear the distinctive *crunch* of bending metal as the Audi smashed to the ground. Then her thoughts turned to Clay. She was thoroughly impressed by the way he controlled the car on the winding road, guiding it as if it were an extension of his body. What's more, he stayed cool the entire time. One thing for sure was that he wasn't your everyday nerdy video gamer. There was something special about him.

She deliberately drove past the street that led to her apartment in Meguro, instead following the signs for the Ginza ward. It was still too early for her to call it a night.

The administration building of Kamita Motors Corporation stood on the corner of Chuo Dori and Harumi Dori, in the fourth district of the Ginza ward, the most expensive neighborhood in Tokyo. The area was home to a number of high-end department stores as well as the best restaurants and hotels in the country. Compared to the skyscrapers all around it, the Kamita Motors building wasn't exceptionally large—it only stood twenty stories high—but it was large enough to accommodate its four hundred or so local employees. Locals called the building "The Cylinder," because of its oval shape and metallic facade that made it instantly stand out. A sign at the entrance read "Kamita Gallery," and the entire ground floor of the building was dedicated to a giant showroom where the company's newest vehicles were displayed. Visitors were encouraged to enter and browse, as the floor was staffed by attractive models called the "Kamita Kandies" dressed in pink and white matching office dresses. The gallery also came with a small Starbucks Coffee shop and gift store. The business offices and meeting rooms were located from the second story up.

Maki lowered her car window and flashed her Kamita identification badge to the security guard at the entrance of the employee parking garage, who opened the gate, allowing her access to her reserved spot three levels down. Once she parked the car, she took an elevator up to the ground floor where she walked through a security gate next to the reception counter. A uniformed guard, sitting at his station on the other side of the gates, gave her a friendly nod.

The public relations department was on the tenth floor, but she instead pushed the elevator button for the top floor where the president's office was located. At this late hour, no one would be around, allowing her plenty of time to search Kanda's office for a clue to his whereabouts—perhaps he had left behind a crinkled piece of notepaper on his desk or an undeleted email on his computer—she had to explore all possibilities.

When the elevator door opened, she stepped onto the twentieth floor and strolled to the main reception area. Access to this area required a special badge to enter after hours, and while Maki was not officially permitted to possess one, she was able to secure one, along with the key-code to Kanda's office. Flirting with the head of security paid plenty of dividends—it was amazing what a friendly hand on a thigh and subtle display of cleavage could get a girl.

The reception area was larger than most people's apartments. The secretary's desk was situated to the side of the room, with two large leather sofas against a side wall next to a large window. The walls were lined with walnut wood and adorned with framed portraits of the founder of Kamita Motors and his son, as well as an oil painting of the company's first automobile. As Maki neared the double wooden doors of the president's office, she noticed that it was cracked open; a sliver of light cutting through the dark reception area. Mr. Kanda always kept his doors locked while he was away, so she assumed it was the cleaning woman. Still, Maki didn't want to take a chance on being seen, so she walked on the balls of her feet, her Christian Louboutin boots hardly making a sound on the dark wood floor. She put her back to the wall outside Kanda's office and slowly peeked inside. There, behind the desk was Mr. Kanda, his face fixed in concentration, lit up by the glow of his computer monitor.

As she softly pushed the door open, Kanda's gaze was still fixed on the computer screen as he pounded away on the keyboard, so she then stepped into the doorway.

"Kanda-san?" she said softly.

Kanda gasped, and his body shot straight up, nearly knocking the reading glasses off his nose.

"Ms. Takano, what the hell are you doing here at this hour?" he said, trying to catch his breath.

"I've been looking all over for you, Kanda-san. I need you to come with me right…" Maki noticed Kanda's eyes darting to something behind her. When she turned around, she saw Oleg Ivanov standing five feet away, pointing a Tokarev pistol at her head. Although she only caught a brief glimpse of the man driving the Audi that went crashing into the ravine, she was almost positive that it was he who now stood in front of her. *But how could that be?*

"Who are you? What is the meaning of this?" Maki asked, glancing over at Kanda, who stared back at her with the eyes of a helpless pup.

"Why are you here?" Kanda asked.

The man with the gun took a step forward. "Who is this person?" he asked in a Russian accent to Kanda while keeping his eyes fixed on Maki.

"She is my public relations manager. Please, she has nothing to do with any of this."

"Well she does now."

Upon looking closer at the man's face, Maki realized that although he did look a lot like the Audi driver, there were some minor differences. First, this man had much shorter hair, and his beard was trimmed a bit tighter. He also had a large pink blotch over his right eye that looked like a giant birthmark. Whether that was causing his eye to nervously twitch every two seconds, she wasn't sure.

"What, what do you want with me?" Maki asked, her hands raised in the air.

"Go over to the couch and sit down," he said.

Maki slowly turned around and took a step towards the sofa at the side of the room, visually measuring the distance between her and the man with the gun. If she swung her bag from where she stood, the length of her arm and the strap on her handbag would be enough for the base of the bag to reach his face. The heft of her SIG Sauer P226 handgun in the bag would act like a stone in a sling that should send the man down, or at least stun him long enough for her to launch a follow-up attack. As she let the strap of her bag fall loosely off her shoulder and into her open hand, she took another slow step. On the next step, she brought her foot down hard onto the floor and pivoted, turning her body around one-hundred-and-eighty degrees. Her right hand followed, as the handbag cut through the air and crashed into the side of the man's face. The blow snapped his head sideways, but it didn't knock him down, prompting Maki to follow up with a reverse kick into his torso, and then a jumping kick to his jaw.

The combination would have been enough to bring a sumo wrestler down, but the Russian stood straight up with a smile, blood from a gash in his mouth coloring his teeth red. He struck Maki's ear with a swift backhand that sent her body airborne and onto the couch.

"You're a feisty one," he said as he pointed the gun at her. "I should shoot you right here and now."

Maki couldn't move. She had been struck a number of

times before by larger men, but never had she experienced this much force from an open-hand strike.

"You animal. Leave her alone," Kanda shouted.

"You shut up. Did you access the server?"

Kanda nodded. "Yes."

The man walked over to the desk and pushed Kanda aside. After he confirmed that the files were the ones he was looking for, he wiped the server clean with several swift keystrokes. He then picked up the desktop computer, and yanked the cables and power cord out of the back panel.

"What are you doing?" Kanda asked.

"What does it look like? I'm taking your computer," the Russian answered. He then took out his cell phone and punched in a three-digit number and spoke in Russian.

Thanks to her aptitude in languages, Maki got about half of what he said. She learned that his name was Boris, and he had just called "papa" to ask him what he should do next.

After putting his cell phone back into his pocket, Boris picked up the desktop computer and held it in one arm. He turned his attention to Maki. "You come with us, and if you do any funny stuff, I kill you on the spot," he said.

"Where are you taking me?" she asked as she sat up on the couch, the cobwebs in her head starting to clear.

"None of your business. Just walk and we go in Kanda's car." He motioned Maki to stand up and go out through the doorway.

Maki complied, leaving her bag on the floor in the corner of the room. When they reached the ground floor, she thought about alerting the security guard as they passed his station at the main entrance, but decided against it—an altercation would put the security guard's life in danger, and more important, if Mr. Kanda were killed, Stockton Clay's death would be as good as guaranteed. So she decided to keep playing the role of the helpless public relations manager. Once in the parking garage, she was instructed to sit in the passenger seat as Kanda took the wheel. The Russian sat in the back seat with his gun out. As they drove out of the garage she wondered where and how this was all going to go down.

Chapter 37

Dmitri Novak took out a surgeon's scalpel from a small cloth case on his lap and held it up to the light. It was his favorite tool of torture, and it gave him a warm feeling every time he had a chance to use it. After putting it back into the case, he sat back on his leather sofa in the living room. Sokov lounged across from him, with a Japanese girlie magazine open on his lap, periodically dozing off with his head hanging over the sofa's backrest. The apartment was located a few blocks away from the foreigner-friendly neighborhood of Roppongi, so the complex was usually full of non-Asian tenants, allowing Novak and his men to come and go freely without attracting any unwanted attention.

The front door burst open, and Kanda walked through first, followed by Maki, and then Boris, who held a gun in his jacket pocket.

"Did you bring his computer?" Novak asked.

Boris placed the desktop on the floor.

"You have what you want, and I will do anything you say. So please let Ms. Takano go. She is just a normal employee," Kanda said.

Novak stood up and walked up to Maki. He studied her face, grabbing her jaw and violently twisting her head left and right. "She is quite the creature. Very lovely."

Maki said nothing; she glared into Novak's gray eyes.

"She came into Kanda's office unannounced," Boris explained. "She is the PR manager."

Novak smiled and cupped her breasts and squeezed

tight. "She would make a nice gift to our clients. They have a fondness for Japanese girls, I hear."

"Don't touch me," Maki said as she slapped Novak's arm away.

"She has quite the resolve. We will need to soften her up a little before we can present her," Novak said as he made a tight fist and unloaded a heavy punch into Maki's mid-section, causing her to fall to her knees and gasp for air.

Kanda clasped his hands together. "Please, she has nothing to do with any of this. I beg you, let her go."

Novak pulled Maki up by her hair; her face was twisted in pain. "I'm afraid that that's impossible, Mr. Kanda. She has seen our faces already. But don't worry, her life will be safe. After my main client is finished with her, she will join the rest of his former whores on the black market, sold to the highest bidder and never to be heard from again."

Tears of anger streamed down Maki's face. She scowled at Novak as she closed her right hand in a tight fist, as if she was ready to unleash a punch.

It was immediately evident to Novak that she was one of those rare people who was unafraid of dying. He had seen that look before during his time in the KGB; he knew exactly how far these types of people could be pushed, and at what exact point they would break. The tough, resistant ones with great willpower amused him because breaking them felt so much more rewarding. A smile formed on his lips, as he smashed his fist into her stomach again, causing Maki to drop back to her knees with her mouth wide open. She coughed violently.

Kanda looked down and closed his eyes. "Please stop," he said.

Sokov grinned. "Hey boss, can I get a piece of that action, too?"

Maki yelped in protest as Novak dragged her by the hair like an animal across the apartment floor. "Normally, I would allow that Viktor, but since we're presenting her as a gift, I want to keep her unmarked. Don't worry though, our benefactor will provide us with many women far more attractive and domesticated than this bitch."

Novak threw Maki on a chair in the dining room. He grabbed her chin and spit in her face, which was already smeared with her tears and mascara. "But if you don't do as we say, I will personally break all of your fingers and cut off your ears, do you understand?"

Maki had no will or energy to resist or respond; her head slumped.

Boris walked up beside Novak. His face was pale, and his body drenched in sweat.

"Minister, I'm having another attack," he said in Russian.

"These are becoming far too regular. Keep an eye on her," Novak said to Sokov as he walked over to a small medicine bag that was on the floor next to the couch. He took out a syringe and stuck its needle into a small glass bottle. After giving the syringe two flicks, squeezing the unwanted air out of it, he plunged the needle into Boris' neck. Boris winced, but his body stopped shaking and the color in his face gradually returned to normal.

"Thank you, papa," he said.

Novak took out another syringe from his bag and walked over to Maki, where he stabbed the open needle into her shoulder. "This will keep her quiet until we leave. You two take turns watching our two guests. I'm going to get some rest. Tomorrow will be a truly historic day for all of us, and I don't want anything to spoil it." He stretched his arms over his head, yawned, and headed towards his bedroom.

Chapter 38

Clay tossed and turned in his bed, trying to make sense of the events of the past few days and hoping that sleep would gradually take over his senses, but no luck. He switched on the light in his room at the safe house, which was basically a two-star hotel suite, furnished with a bed, nightstand, a small desk, and a chair. A flat-screen television hung on the wall, and the faint glow of the LCD clock on the night table showed four in the morning. He made his way into the bathroom, where he splashed his face with cold water, and then looked at himself in the mirror under a dim vanity light.

As he studied every curve, every detail of his face, he noticed blood trickling out of his nostrils. Another headache was coming on, and he could tell that it was going to be much more intense than the last one. Visible on the side of his temples were black veins that looked like squiggly lines on a road atlas, and the skin around the area pulsated with M&M-sized lumps.

After stumbling back to the bedroom, he grabbed his blue jeans that hung on a wooden chair and searched frantically through its pockets until he found his pill bottle. He shook out three capsules and popped them into his mouth, washing them down with a bottle of water on the nightstand. The medicine's effect kicked in gradually, as the small lumps disappeared and the black lines faded away. A minute later, the nosebleed stopped.

Clay sat still on his bed until his breathing and heartbeat returned to normal. It was evident that the headaches were getting more intense, which he assumed meant that the disease was getting stronger.

Giving up on sleep, he took out his laptop from his Oakley backpack and connected it to the internet via the Wi-Fi connection. Every page he visited was surely being monitored, but he didn't care; he wanted to know more about Kanda's first wife, his mother. After trying a number of search sites, he found several entries, including one in Wikipedia that outlined her life in an effectively concise manner.

Victoria Brooks-Kanda was an aspiring actress born in Glasgow, Scotland, who moved to New York on her twentieth birthday in search of fame and fortune on Broadway. But her big break actually came from the other side of the world, when she auditioned for a Kamita Motors television spot in Tokyo. Kanda had hired an American firm to provide him with a Caucasian woman that would appeal to the Japanese public. At the time, the Japanese had a fondness for white women with large blue eyes, sandy blonde hair, and an hourglass figure. From a hundred or so candidates, Kanda personally chose Victoria to be his star. The television commercials, which only aired in Japan, were an instant hit, and she became an overnight sensation, with the media referring to her as "Ms. Kamita Motors." This popularity prompted Kanda to hire her as a full-time spokeswoman for the brand. A few months after they first met on the set of the television commercial, she and Kanda started a secret romance, and they were married two years later.

Clay examined every photograph he could find of Victoria, but most of them were taken during her days as Ms. Kamita Motors; Victoria retired from show business after their son Isao was born a year after their marriage. *My real name was Isao Kanda?* The sites reported that two years later Isao died of illness, and Victoria was killed in a traffic accident soon after.

An overwhelming wave of sadness came over him; an empty feeling deep down in his chest, knowing that he would never be able to meet his mother. She was beautiful, Clay thought, as he scrolled through image after image of her. He also searched for photos of Isao, himself, but could find only blurry black-and-white images of him as a baby.

After an hour of web surfing, he turned off his computer. His thoughts quickly returned to his own situation; he needed to find Kanda soon and have the cell transfusion performed. There were many questions to ask him, like why he had been discarded like a piece of garbage. Kanda's actions were unforgiveable, and Clay wanted to confront him about it face to face, and he wanted to do that on his own terms.

The call to action sounded in his heart, and he threw on a fresh polo shirt. As he quietly opened the front door of his room, he popped his head into the hallway. "You aren't a detainee here, so you're free to go wherever you want inside the building," George had told him earlier. The thought was reassuring, but it still made him feel like a prisoner. The hallway seemed clear, so he softly stepped out of his room and closed the door behind him. A sign on the far wall marked the direction of the stairwell.

Deciding against using the elevator because it would make too much noise when it arrived on to the ground floor,

Clay opted for the stairs. He quickly descended the steps to the ground level where he opened the door and peered into the reception area, which was fashioned after a motel lobby: a small lounging area by the front door with a television, a sofa, and a check-in counter. The entire floor seemed empty, so he headed for the sliding glass doors, making sure his Nikes made no noise on the wooden floor.

"May I help you, Mr. Clay?" a female voice sounded from behind.

Clay jumped and gasped. Beth Flowers, the agent who grilled him in France, dressed in what looked to be the same dark blue blouse and faded jeans as before, stood behind the counter with her hands on her hips.

"Holy crap, you scared the living crap out of me," Clay said, clutching his chest with one hand. "I remember you. Agent Flowers, right?"

Her partner, Charlie Wong, stepped to the counter from behind her. "Good morning," he said. "Good to see you again."

"How did you know I was downstairs? Do you guys have my room bugged?" Clay asked.

"Every square inch of this facility is monitored twenty-four-seven," Wong said.

"What can we do for you, Mr. Clay?" Flowers asked.

"I got kind of hungry, so I thought I would get a bite to eat."

"In that case, Charlie can pick up something for you. Yoshinoya is down the street, and they're the only ones open at this hour."

"Don't bother. I'll get it myself," Clay said as he walked up to the sliding glass doors. He stood there waiting for them to open, but they didn't.

Something must be wrong with the sensor, he thought, so he took a few steps back and walked up to the doors a second time. Nothing.

"I'm sorry, but we have strict orders not to let you leave the building," Flowers said.

Clay turned around and threw up his arms. "You can't hold me captive like some kind of hostage. There are laws against that, aren't there?"

"Chief Roberts' orders I'm afraid. I'm sorry for the inconvenience," she said.

"You know, I'm getting pretty tired of being treated like a criminal. It wouldn't hurt for you to show me a little respect."

Flowers sat down in a chair behind the counter and rested her hands on the countertop. "We're just following orders, Mr. Clay. Nothing personal."

Clay walked over to the sofa in front of the television and sat down. "A beef bowl will be great," he said.

"Do you want a large or medium?" Wong asked, stepping out from behind the counter.

"A large, and a Red Bull, too, and make it quick."

Wong shot him a hard look, but said nothing. He quietly walked out through the front doors, which Clay noticed slid open for him.

"I wouldn't provoke Charlie if I were you. Not only is he brilliant—a graduate of Yale Law and speaker of six languages fluently—he's one of the best field agents we have." Flowers said.

Clay shifted his attention to the television, which played a Japanese news program. He was about to ask for the remote when something on the monitor caught his eye. It wasn't the attractive female announcer reporting on location, but the face of a man in the background. He saw the unmistakable features of Oleg Ivanov, his beard a bit trimmed, escorting a distinguished-looking older gentleman through a crowd of reporters.

"Can you understand what they're saying?" Clay asked without taking his eyes off the TV.

"Why, what's wrong?" Flowers asked.

"Please, there's no time. What are they saying?"

Flowers stepped out from behind the counter and pointed a remote at the television. The volume bar on the screen filled to the halfway mark, and the news announcer's voice boomed from the speakers. Clay leaned forward and watched the TV monitor as a tall gray-haired man with sharp piercing eyes smiled at the camera, as his two assistants pulled him to a waiting limousine. Ivanov opened the rear door for his boss, who, with a final wave to the gathered media, ducked into the car's rear cabin, followed immediately by a heavyset bald man. The video faded to black, and the announcer transitioned to another story.

Flowers lowered the volume nearly all the way to zero. "The controversial former Soviet Deputy Minister of Health made some kind of speech at Aoyama University today about improving the human species. That's all I got," she said.

"Today? Are you sure it was today?"

"Yes, the report said it was late this afternoon."

"But that's impossible. He should be dead."

"Who should be dead?" Flowers asked.

Clay pointed to the television. "That bearded guy who was with the old man, he's one of the guys that chased us down the mountain. He's the same guy who tried to kill me in front of Mr. Kanda's house. There's no way that video feed could be from today."

"Are you sure it's the same person?" Flowers asked, eyeing Clay suspiciously.

He nodded. "Oh yeah, I'm sure. I'll never forget that face for as long as I live."

Flowers froze, her mouth opened wide. "Maybe he had a twin, or he could be a…" She ran over to the counter and picked up her phone.

"What is it?" Clay asked.

As Flowers waited for someone to pick up, she turned to Clay. "We might need to make your beef bowl to go because I have a strong feeling that the chief is going to want to speak with you."

Chapter 39

Stockton Clay sat at the end of the rectangular conference table shifting his gaze between George Nakajima, who sat next to him, and Beth Flowers, who was preoccupied with connecting her laptop to a projector. Two hours had passed since Flowers and Clay arrived at the CIA's Special Science Division's temporary offices in Shinagawa after Andrew Roberts called for an emergency meeting.

The door to the conference room opened, and Roberts walked in first, with his hair slightly disheveled, dressed in a light blue dress shirt—the top button undone—and crumpled black slacks. He sat at the front of the table, while Wong, who followed him in, walked over to Clay and took out a large-sized beef bowl from a white plastic bag and placed it on the table in front of him, along with a can of Red Bull.

"Thank you, sir," Clay said.

Wong took his seat next to Roberts.

"Where the hell is Takano?" Roberts asked.

"I left a text with her, but I haven't heard back yet," Flowers said.

"She did have quite the day yesterday," Wong said.

Roberts nodded. "Yeah, well let's get started."

As Clay snapped his wooden chopsticks apart and dug into the beef bowl, Flowers turned on a projector that showed four faces on a white screen at the front of the room. Clay immediately recognized two of them: Ivanov and the man in the leather jacket. Flowers stepped to the screen with a retractable pointer in her hand, placing the tip of the long stick to the photo on the far left, to an image of an older man with gray hair.

"This is Dmitri Novak, the former Deputy Minister of Health for the Soviet Union and former high-ranking member of the KGB. Our intelligence on him is a bit outdated because it primarily consists of his time within the ministry during the Cold War. He's a brilliant scientist with a genius-level IQ, devout Marxist, and a member of an underground pro-communist resistance group. He was unceremoniously kicked out of Russia after the fall of the USSR, and then took up residence in Lausanne, Switzerland, where he still lives today. We're sure now Novak is the mastermind of the Pax-Gen program because of his expertise on human genetics. Also, with his background with the KGB, he has plenty of contacts in the Russian underworld to do his dirty work."

"So do we know what this guy was up to during his time in the Soviet ministry?" asked Roberts.

"Our reports indicate that he headed a secret program to create super soldiers using genetic engineering during the Cold War."

"You mean he was trying to make a bunch of Captain Americas? Or, I guess in this case, Captain Russias." Roberts laughed at his own joke, but stopped when he realized no one had joined in.

"Engineering a super soldier is not a new concept," Wong said. "The Nazis tried it during World War II using drugs, and many experts believe that under the Stalin regime, efforts were made to create enhanced human beings by crossbreeding men with apes."

Flowers continued. "Supposedly, he produced human clones as early as the 1980s, and he was one of the earliest pioneers in nanotechnology research, but in 1992, the Russians kicked him out because of the controversial nature of his experiments. To the public, it was announced that he simply retired, but in reality, they wanted nothing to do with him because he insisted on using live subjects for his experiments. He continued his research and work privately, with funding from a few small universities in China. He also made money making speeches for various genetic conventions around the world and conducting small clinics. That's where we think he was approached by Kanda, or vice versa. Each one had what the other wanted: Kanda had money and a place for Novak to continue his work; Novak had the potential cure to save Kanda's ill child."

"A match made in hell," Roberts quipped. "And what about those other two goons?"

"The one on the left is Oleg Ivanov. According to Mr. Clay and Maki, he was killed in a car accident yesterday on Odarumi Pass. Also killed in that crash was this man, Sergei Karpov, a known member of the Russian mafia. Ivanov is a bit of a mystery. He doesn't appear in any of our files, but he has been spotted at underground military training camps in Iran and Chechnya."

Clay forced a mouthful of beef and rice down his throat and raised his hand. "That's also the guy who chased me from Mr. Kanda's house, and the one I saw on television this morning."

"We'll get to that," Flowers said. She placed her pointer on the image of the bald man. "He's Viktor Sokov, a former Major with the Russian Air Force, and a distinguished military pilot who was dishonorably discharged after killing a fellow officer in a barroom brawl. He now works as a special ops consultant offering his services to the highest bidder. We've tied him to a few minor terrorist groups in Syria recently."

"A face only a mother can love," Roberts said.

"Oh, and Agent Whitaker has identified the man who tried to kill Stockton in Los Angeles," Flowers added.

"You mean the one Whitaker took out in at that Seven-Eleven? Let me guess, Russian?" Roberts asked.

Flowers nodded. "Yuri Astafyeva, from the Miyakova Gang out of West Hollywood."

Roberts smiled. "The dots are starting to connect."

"Ivanov and Karpov's bodies were recovered by local police yesterday, yet Mr. Clay maintains he saw Ivanov on television after his death." Flowers leaned forward and tapped a key on her laptop computer. The image on the screen changed to a frozen shot of the video feed from the newscast, with a grainy superimposed photo of Ivanov's face, which had a large pink blotch over his right eye.

"Are you sure the video was taken after the car accident?" Roberts asked.

Flowers nodded. "Yes, we just confirmed it with the news station and the university."

"Trust me, it's him," Clay said. "But I don't remember that big birthmark on his face."

"Agent Wong and I think that he may be a clone," Flowers said.

"In fact, we're pretty sure about that, sir," Wong broke in. "And the one who died in the car yesterday was probably another copy of the same person. It would make sense that Novak would have made a few clones for himself while at Pax-Gen and used them as test subjects. Judging by their faces, they seem to be about Stockton's age, so they most likely were manufactured before the nanotechnology had been perfected, meaning they have defects like Stockton."

Clay shot Wong a hurt look.

Wong tilted his head. "Sorry. No offense."

Roberts broke in. "None of that matters to me. What I want to know is what's this Novak guy's end game?"

"Our guess is that he's selling the technology to the highest bidder," Flowers said.

"Who would buy this technology from him?" Nakajima interrupted. "I can't imagine a western country in their right mind would touch him with a ten-foot pole. And, human cloning, and probably nanotechnology too, is forbidden in Islam so that leaves out the Muslim countries. Who would want to risk alienating the entire world by dealing with him?"

Wong cleared his throat. "You're right, no country could risk being associated with this man, except one. The North Koreans would be more than happy to offer whatever price he asks, and there are no religious or ideological obstacles to get in their way. They could overthrow other countries with this."

"Yeah, the thought is horrifying," Roberts said.

"Well, now that we finally know who the players are," Roberts said, "let's get busy."

Flowers turned off the projector. "May I remind you sir that orders from Langley are to proceed with extreme caution. Novak still has friends in high places, as well as a network of mobsters and ex-KGB agents all over Asia. And, we don't have solid proof that he's the culprit yet."

Roberts repositioned himself in his chair. "Yeah, yeah, I know. I just spoke with the director, and he told me he only wants us to keep them from leaving the country without causing a stir. At least until we can get some hard proof. Why don't we just walk on water while we're at it."

"We found out that Novak is currently staying in a luxury apartment complex in Roppongi. Should I stake it out, boss?" Wong asked.

"Affirmative, and don't take any chances. They probably don't know that we're onto them yet. The director pulled a few strings with the Japanese police chief to keep the deaths of the two Russians quiet for now, so hopefully, Novak thinks that his two goons are still alive and looking for Stockton."

As Wong hurried out of the room, Clay put aside his breakfast, leaving half of it untouched. "Why not report this Novak guy to the Japanese authorities and have him arrested. Aren't they on our side? I've seen one of their men shoot a man in the street, for God's sake."

"Trust me. We don't want the Japanese government or Japanese police involved in any of this. They would make this into a giant media circus. It's bad enough they've got Ivanov's and Karpov's bodies. Any luck on Kanda's whereabouts?" Roberts asked.

"Maki told me last night that she left a message with his wife, and that she also tried to get a hold of Jimmy Bando, his personal assistant. No luck on either," Flowers said. "Chances are, Mr. Kanda's with the Russians, probably tying up loose ends before the big sale. Maybe he's getting a cut."

Flowers' cell phone vibrated on the table. She picked it up and looked at the caller ID. "Well speak of the devil. Excuse me," she said as she got up and stepped out of the room.

Flowers' voice was audible from the hallway. "Hi Nena. I'm sorry, Maki's unavailable now, can I help you with something?…When did he tell you that?…Do you know for how long?...I see. Thank you, I'll be sure to relay the message to Maki."

She returned to the conference room. "That was Mr. Kanda's wife. She said that Mr. Kanda called her to say he'll be out of the country for a good while."

"Okay, so now we know that Kanda is probably with Novak," Roberts said. "Whether it's voluntary or not remains to be determined."

Clay stood up. "Awesome, let's go and get him."

"Right. Wong will report in if he's indeed at his apartment, and if he is, we'll move in, but if he and Kanda were to leave the country, which airport or harbor would they use?"

Flowers pulled out a copy of a receipt from a folder on the table. "Novak came in on a chartered flight from Switzerland two days ago, but when we checked with the jet company, he didn't make any arrangements for a return trip."

"I can't imagine they would fly commercial," Roberts said.

"Mr. Kanda keeps a plane at Tachikawa Airfield. It's about an hour away," Flowers said. "And Mrs. Kanda said he left his passport at home, so if he does plan to leave the country, he won't be doing it legally, unless he goes back home to get it before he leaves, which I highly doubt."

Roberts rubbed his chin. "Yeah, he probably won't be needing travel documents for where he's going, if it is in fact North Korea. Beth, take Stockton back to the safe house."

"If it's all right with you, I'd like to stay here," Clay said. "There's no chance in hell I'll be able to rest now, and I want to be close by if anything happens."

Roberts let out a slight moan. "Okay, but stay out of the way because it might get really serious really fast. And will someone wake Takano up? I need her here, and I need her here now."

Chapter 40

Agent Charlie Wong, dressed in a white-kimono style jacket and wearing a blue bandana around his head, carefully studied the luxury five-story apartment complex across the street. It was one of three matching structures, a beige rectangular building donned with private balconies with black metal railings. He nodded to his fellow SSD agent to set down their *yatai*, a portable restaurant stall on wheels, directly across from the complex. *Yatais* were Japan's version of a food truck, but much smaller in scale, and were scattered all over Tokyo. The mobile food carts, which were pulled from location to location by the owner, had been around for more than three hundred years, providing travelers and late-night wanderers with hot meals that ranged from yakitori to oden to ramen.

Agent David Chung, a Korean-American ten years younger than Wong, dressed in the same ramen-chef uniform, carefully lowered the wheelbarrow handles of the moveable kitchen until the front stands touched the ground.

"Oh yeah, I like this spot better, too," he said as he proceeded to hook up a can of compressed gas to the stove. "But I do hate having to dress in this getup."

"There's no parking on this street, and this is the only place to survey that building, so stop complaining and get the noodles ready," Wong said as the early morning sunlight shined over the Tokyo Tower.

The sidewalks of nearby Roppongi were dotted with businessmen stumbling out of all-night drinking establishments, most of them in wrinkled suits, with their ties undone and stinking of body odor, cigarette smoke and alcohol. Drinking until the wee hours of the morning was a long-standing ritual for many Japanese "salary men" who found refuge in whiskey bottles and the company of attractive hostesses that temporarily liberated them from the pressures of seventy-hour work weeks. Without this release, they would probably go insane or become gravely ill from stress. In fact, Japanese is the only language in the world to have a term for death from overworking: *karoshi.*

Two thirty-something men, with the fronts of their suit jackets undone and the ends of their neckties sticking out of their trouser pockets, walked towards Wong and Chung.

"We have customers, David," Wong said softly.

Chung nodded and wiped down the counter with a wet towel.

Wong could hear the conversation of the businessmen as they came closer, walking in a crooked line along Gaien Higashi Dori.

"Man, Sari-chan sure was cute. I'm going to ask her out," the taller man slurred.

His *senpai*, or senior workmate, laughed. "All she'll do is make you buy her expensive gifts. You won't even get to first base."

They ducked under the stall's red banner, called a *noren*, and sat down on crude steel stools along the empty wooden counter.

"*Irasshai*," Wong said. "What will you have?" he asked in perfect Japanese. With one hand, he placed a strainer filled with dry noodles into boiling water, while stirring a pot of steaming pork-bone broth with the other.

"I'll have a miso ramen," the senpai said.

"Make mine salt," the tall man said, "with extra *chashu*."

"*Hai, okyakusama.*" Wong scooped up the noodles and placed them in separate bowls of broth, then handed them to Chung, who placed the hot servings of ramen in front of the customers. They snapped apart their wooden chopsticks in unison and attacked the food like hungry bears.

As they slurped their noodles, Wong spied three men emerging from the apartment across the street. He stepped to the rear of the food stall and pulled out a pair of mini Nikon binoculars. The men fit the description of Novak, Kanda, and Sokov, who carried a pair of duffle bags over each shoulder. Behind them was Maki Takano, escorted by a bearded man matching the description of Boris Ivanov, who pushed her into the rear seat of the Kamita Presidente sedan.

"Shit," Wong muttered under his breath. He pulled Chung by the collar to the back of the yatai. "They have Agent Takano with them. Continue to keep watch here, and report any activity."

Chung nodded. Wong pulled off his bandana and sprinted two blocks in the opposite direction to a small self-pay parking lot, where he took out his phone as he stepped into his Lexus GS sedan.

Andrew Roberts picked up after the first ring. "That was quick. What have you got?" he asked.

"They're on the move, and Agent Takano's with them. She seemed okay, but she's definitely being held against her will. They're heading east on Gaien Higashi Dori. I'm currently in pursuit. I don't know if I can catch them; they've got a big head start."

"Takano's with them? Well, the fact that she's alive probably means that either she's managed to break into their group or they're planning to use her as a hostage. If you don't catch up to them, head directly to Tachikawa Airfield. Kanda has his private jet there, and we're pretty sure that's where they're headed. We're leaving now."

"Roger that." Wong threw the phone on the passenger seat and floored the throttle pedal, steering his car in the direction of the Chuo Expressway.

Chapter 41

Clay had lightly dozed off on a sofa in the reception lobby of the SSD office when a booming voice woke him up. It was Roberts.

"Kanda and company are on the move. Takano's with them. We'll take your car, Flowers," he said as he descended the stairs.

Flowers' head popped up from a cubicle partition, and she quickly strapped on her shoulder holster.

Rubbing the sleep from his eyes, Clay walked briskly to the bottom of the stairs, blocking Roberts' path a few steps from the ground floor, causing him to stop and look quizzically at Clay.

"What're you doing? Get out of my way," Roberts said.

Clay held his ground. "I need to go too."

"Um, that's a negative."

"Then you'll have to arrest me because there's no other way you're keeping me from going."

Roberts stabbed his finger into Clay's chest. "Listen kid. First of all, we're not the police here; we don't arrest people. We either watch them, kill them, or capture them. And second, you're just a nobody with no training or a single clue as to what we do, so stand down."

Clay looked him hard in the eyes. "It's my life we're talking about here."

"Chief, we need to get going," Flowers said as she walked up behind Clay.

Roberts tried to step around, but Clay blocked his path.

"I can be of help. They want me, right? Maybe Mr. Kanda will think twice about leaving the country if he sees his lost son face to face. Maybe that Novak guy will too. I just can't sit here and do nothing as the fate of my life is being decided."

Roberts glared at Clay through the corners of his eyes; then he relaxed his shoulders and smiled. "Come to think of it, you might prove useful. If they do start shooting, we could use you to draw their fire. That might give us the time we need to take them down. We can also use you to swap for Takano, if it came down to that. I appreciate your willingness to sacrifice yourself for us." He patted Clay on the shoulder, stepped around the young man who stood frozen in thought and headed out the front door.

For a split-second, Clay reconsidered his request, but he knew that he was running out of time, so he chased after Roberts and Flowers out of the building.

Flowers took the driver's seat of a dark blue sixth-generation Toyota Crown Majesta sedan, with Roberts sliding in next to her. Clay jumped into the rear.

"So what's the plan, chief?" Flowers asked as she pulled the car away from the curb.

"The fact that they have Takano makes the situation unpredictable. I've been trying to figure out why they have her in the first place. Has she infiltrated their group?" Roberts said.

"You know her penchant for doing things her own way," Flowers said.

Roberts rubbed the back of his neck. "Yeah, but never

to this extreme. No, I think we should assume that she was abducted. But what would they want with a lowly public relations woman?"

"Maybe her cover's been blown?" Flowers said.

Roberts tightened his lips. "I thought about that possibility. But if that was the case, she wouldn't be alive now."

Flowers guided the Crown through the empty streets of early morning Tokyo. "Maybe they want to use her as a hostage in case things went bad? That would make sense."

Clay leaned forward, putting his head between the two front seats. "Maki told me last night before leaving the safe house that she was going to check on something that might help us find Mr. Kanda."

"Did she say where she was going?" Flowers asked.

Clay shook his head. "No."

"Either way, we'll greet them peacefully and see how they react. I'm sure they know that we don't have the jurisdiction to detain them, so I can't see them reacting violently unless we provoke them. We'll rendezvous with Wong at the front entrance of the airfield and go in together. And Clay, you stay in the car and keep your ass down," Roberts said.

The trip from the branch office to the airfield took about thirty minutes. As they drove through the unmanned security gates of Tachikawa Airfield, a private one-runway facility owned by Kamita Motors, Kanda's Presidente sedan was just pulling up to the front of a small hangar on the far side of the airfield. A KamitaJet sat on the tarmac with its engines humming, door open, and airstair lowered on the other side of a hangar.

The nine-passenger jet represented Kamita's latest business venture, into the private aviation industry. As with all Kamita products, the jet was state-of-the-art, featuring a carbon-fiber composite fuselage, aluminum wings, and engine pylons that were mounted over the wings. Because it was extremely lightweight, the jet consumed only a fraction of the fuel used by comparably sized aircrafts. It accommodated a crew of three, a pilot, a co-pilot, and a flight attendant, although Kanda never found a need to have a server on his flights because he always commuted with his personal assistant.

Clay knew all about the jet because he had written a feature on it a month earlier. He also flew this model on his flight sim back home.

In the distance, four men stepped out of the Presidente. Sokov went straight up the airstair carrying duffle bags and ducked into the plane first, while Novak stepped out of the front passenger seat and pulled Kanda out of the rear cabin of the car. Boris stepped out from the other side.

Novak and Boris stopped in their tracks when they noticed the Toyota Crown and Lexus GS heading their way down the side road.

The two CIA cars pulled up about a hundred feet from the Presidente, maintaining a cautious buffer between them and the Russians. They formed a V position, blocking access to the side road, the only way out of the facility unless you cut through a dirt field next to the runway. Roberts and Flowers stepped out of the Toyota, staying behind the front doors of their blue sedan, while Wong remained seated alone in the

Lexus with the engine running, ready to chase the Presidente down in case it made for a hasty escape. Crouched low in the rear seat of the Crown was Clay, who took in the action from the space between the front seats, hidden from the Russians' view.

"Good morning. I was wondering if we can ask you a few questions. You are former Deputy Minister Novak, are you not?" Roberts asked.

Novak, dressed in a pressed gray suit and white dress shirt, glared at his uninvited guests through his wire-framed glasses. He had a firm hold of Kanda's arm. "What is this? Who are you?"

"I'm Andy Roberts, and this is Special Agent Flowers. We're with the United States government."

Kanda's eyes lit up when he heard Roberts' words. "Please help me. These men are trying to…"

He was interrupted mid-sentence by Boris' Tokarev, whose loud pop caused the nearby birds to scatter and sent the CIA agents ducking for cover behind their doors. Roberts and Flowers pulled out their pistols, but before they could return fire, Boris let loose two more shots. The first bullet found the Toyota sedan's headlight; the second grazed Flowers' shoulder, causing her to yelp and fall to the ground.

"What were you saying about them not acting violently, boss?" Flowers said.

Roberts ignored her.

Boris shouted something in Russian to Novak as he ran to the front of the Presidente and crouched near its front fender for cover.

Meanwhile, Novak pulled Kanda towards the plane, screaming what sounded like Russian profanities at him. Kanda resisted by pulling back and dropping to his knees, but Novak was too strong, and in a matter of seconds, he had forced Kanda up the airstair, nearly carrying him the entire way. After throwing Kanda into the plane through the open doorway, Novak followed him in. Boris covered their escape with randomly timed shots at Roberts.

Roberts fired a couple rounds from his Beretta 92 at the front fender of the Presidente as Wong jumped out of the Lexus, still wearing his ramen-man disguise, and sprinted to where Flowers was.

"I'm fine, it just grazed me," she said, as she sat up against the Crown's rear fender.

Wong aimed and took a few shots at Boris, but the bullets found only the front fender.

Clay dropped into the footwell of the rear cabin of the Toyota, his heart thumping like a jackhammer. When he raised his head to sneak a peek at the action, he spotted Maki quietly opening the rear door of the Presidente.

Roberts saw her too. "There's Takano. Stop shooting."

Maki took a step out of the car, but Boris sent a bullet flying near her head, causing her to retreat into the cabin.

Without a moment's hesitation, Clay jumped out of the Toyota and into the driver's seat of the Lexus GS. The engine was already running. He had tested the Lexus GS back in the States, so he was familiar with most of its controls and features. After switching off the car's traction control, he threw the shifter into the D position and floored the pedal.

If he was going to die, Clay thought, what better way to do it than trying to save a damsel in distress.

Chapter 42

The GS spun its tires freely, spewing white smoke and loose dust on the asphalt into the air, as it made straight for the Presidente. Boris unloaded three shots at the oncoming vehicle, causing Clay to duck as the bullets hit the top portion of the Lexus' windshield, penetrating the glass and leaving behind a trio of spider-web shaped cracks.

The GS covered the hundred-foot distance in a matter of seconds; its rear end fishtailing and staining the air with dirt, dust, and tire smoke. The rear wheels locked up as the car executed a one-eighty turn a few feet from the rear corner of the Kamita sedan. The thick brown and white cloud temporarily cloaked the white GS as Clay reached over to the passenger-side door and flung it open. "Maki, get in now."

Seeing everything that had transpired from the rear window of the Presidente, Maki jumped out of the car and climbed into the Lexus' passenger seat. Before her entire body was inside, Clay grabbed hold of Maki's arm and floored the throttle, kicking up even more dust. The car sped away as Boris fired shots into a big brown dust cloud. None of the bullets found their mark.

Maki kept her eyes forward. "I didn't expect to see you. Thanks."

Clay pulled the car to a stop at its original position, facing in the opposite direction. "Don't mention it," he said.

"Nice move, Stockton, but if you ever do something like that again, I'm going to shoot you myself," Roberts said after Clay had lowered his window. "What's your condition,

Takano?"

Maki flashed Clay a quick smile. "I'm fine, sir. A little bruised, but good to go."

To Clay, Maki didn't look fine. Her mascara was smudged, her eyes swollen and he noticed a red mark on the side of her face, just above the jaw. Her clothes were the same ones he last saw her wearing the night before, but they were more wrinkled, with half her blouse pulled out over her jeans.

"Good, here's Beth's firearm and her spare magazine. Let's bring these guys in," Roberts said as he handed her Flowers' Glock G43 handgun.

Maki yanked the slide of the small handgun back. "Mr. Kanda is being held against his will. They might use him as a hostage."

"Yeah, I figured that out when he started screaming for help," Roberts said.

Boris fired off another shot at the Crown. The bullet stuck into the door guarding Roberts. Hidden partially by the dust that had yet to completely settle, Boris jumped out from the hangar and sprinted towards the jet, firing shots at Roberts and Wong as he ran. He failed to notice Maki taking aim through the open window of the GS though.

It was surreal how much distance the Russian covered in such a short time. Clay had seen Olympic sprinters training before, but Boris looked to him like he was as fast, if not faster, than any of them. He had already reached the base of the airstair when Maki unleashed three successive shots. Two bullets hit nothing but air, but the third one struck Boris' neck, blasting open his jugular and creating a starburst of blood. He fell to the ground dead.

"Nice shot, Takano," Roberts said.

A prolonged silence followed the kill. Even the birds stopped chirping. As Maki slowly stepped out of the GS, she kept her gun pointed at the plane and took up a position next to the Toyota.

"Cover me, Takano," Roberts said before dashing to the hangar and taking cover around the corner of the building.

Clay got out of the driver's seat of the GS and crouched next to Wong, who was positioned behind the passenger door of the Toyota.

"I'm sending you a bill for the damages to my car," Wong said with a smile.

"I'm flat broke. You'll have to call my parents," Clay said, not getting the joke.

"I'm just kidding. You did good. Now stay back. These guys in the jet might come out firing."

Noticing Wong's clothes, Clay joked, "Can I have a miso ramen with the works when this is over?"

Wong smiled. "You got it."

"Charlie, park your car in front of the plane. Let's block that son of bitch from taking off," Roberts called out from the hangar.

Wong crouched as he duck-walked over to the GS. He stepped into the driver's seat and slowly drove forward, per-forming a wide U-turn, before heading towards the front of the plane. Then a figure emerged in the doorway of the jet, prompting him to slam on the brakes. A slender Japanese man, wearing a pilot's uniform, fell forward and tumbled down the airstair onto the hard tarmac. He was followed by another man, dressed in a similar uniform, who also landed on the ground with a thud. The captain and co-pilot staggered to their feet and limped to the hangar, the expression on their faces contorted in fear and confusion.

"What the hell?" Roberts said lowering his gun.

Maki kept her aim at the jet door. "Sokov was a former Russian military pilot. They don't need anyone to fly the plane."

Sokov stuck his head out from the doorway and saw the Lexus parked nearby. Before Maki could get a shot off, he leaned out of the doorway and fired off several rounds into the grille of the GS. The bullets ripped through the car's radiator and into the engine, causing it to seize immediately. Smoke and steam rose from cracks in the hood.

Roberts held his gun steady and squeezed the trigger. It was pure luck that a bullet from his Beretta found the back of Sokov's hand, who screamed and dropped his pistol, sending it clanking on the tarmac below. Maki followed with three more rounds, but they hit the plane's fuselage, just above the door. With a grimace on his face, Sokov hit a button on the inside of the plane, causing the airstair, which doubled as the lower half of the door, to rise automatically. The top half of the door came down simultaneously, sealing the two panels shut.

The jet inched forward on the runway; the whir of the jet engines growing louder. If the plane took off, Kanda would be gone and all hope for his survival would be lost. Clay had to stop it from leaving.

Maki jumped into the driver's seat of the Toyota Crown and slammed the door. Clay had already taken a seat beside her.

"Let's go," he said.

Maki unleashed the three hundred and forty horsepower of the Crown's hybrid powerplant, sending all four tires spinning wildly on the dusty pavement.

"Give me your gun," Clay said, as Maki guided the Crown directly behind the moving jet.

Maki shot him a brief, non-approving glance. "I can't do that."

"My life is on the line here. Please give me your gun. Both my hands are free; I can take a better shot."

She cursed in Japanese under her breath. "I know I owe you one, so don't make me regret doing this," she said as she placed the Glock on Clay's lap. "I assume you do know how to use it."

Clay lowered his window. "Yeah, I think so. It looks and feels just like the Realware 25G."

"The what?"

"Um, it's a new video game controller I've been testing," Clay said in a low voice. "But it's quite realistic."

Maki shot him a condescending look. "You gotta be kidding. Have you ever shot a real gun?"

Clay chose not to answer, as the Crown flanked the right side of the KamitaJet. But the plane's speed increased with each passing second, and while Maki kept her foot flat to the floor, the jet started to slowly pull away, traveling close to one hundred miles per hour. Clay leaned out the window and pointed the gun at the fuselage. He fired off six rapid shots, emptying the magazine, but the plane didn't slow down.

"Do you have a spare clip?" he asked.

Maki reached into her pocket and handed him a fully-loaded magazine. "Aim for the landing gear."

He grabbed the magazine and reloaded the gun like an experienced marksman.

"Wow. Remind me to play more video games," Maki said.

With his concentration fixed on the plane's landing gear, Clay fired off four quick shots, hoping that one of the bullets would puncture a tire. The first few slugs caromed off the metal struts of the heavy-duty metal braces, producing sparks, while the others missed the aircraft entirely. Clay knew he had only a few seconds remaining until the plane went airborne, so he released the two remaining bullets, sending one ricocheting off the struts and the wheel housing, and the final one finding its way into the rear tire.

Clay flashed a smile, but it quickly disappeared. While the jet should have slowed down or spun off the runway, it increased its pace, continuing its takeoff in a straight line. Then Clay recalled that the KamitaJet's tires had a self-sealing feature that automatically fixed punctures.

Oh no.

The KamitaJet lifted its nose skyward and went airborne.

Clay pounded his fist into the dashboard. He then noticed the end of the runway fast approaching.

"Maki, brakes," he shouted.

Maki, who was also staring skyward at the plane, hit the brake pedal and spun the Crown ninety-degrees, screeching it to a stop a few feet shy of the end of the runway.

Clay jumped out of the car and watched the departing plane, now a small speck against the clear azure sky. He stood there on the open runway, motionless. *It's over. I'm as good as dead.*

Blood seeped down Clay's nose, and his skull suddenly felt like it was being run over by a tractor trailer, causing him to grab his head and drop to his knees. After pulling out his pill container from his jeans pocket, he fumbled it in his hands as he twisted the cap off. He then swallowed five capsules at once, but the pain didn't subside. In fact, it intensified.

Maki jumped out of the car. "Are you all right?"

Clay popped two more capsules into his mouth and swallowed. A few seconds later, he felt the tension easing. Pinching his nostrils shut, he tilted his head back, and then wiped the blood off the bottom half of his face with his free hand.

"That was the most intense one yet. I think the end is getting near," he said.

Maki kneeled beside him and softly rubbed his back. "Oh, Stockton..."

A commercial Nissan van with the Tachikawa Airfield signage pasted across its sides pulled up next to them. Wong was at the wheel; Roberts sat next to him. He rolled down the passenger-side window.

"You still alive?" he asked.

"Barely," Clay replied.

"Good. Get in the back."

Clay struggled to his feet, refusing Maki's attempt to help him, slid the rear door open, and dropped into the back-seat of the van. "Where are we going? Not that it matters anymore."

Roberts turned around in his seat. "We're taking you to George. We can't have you keeling over just yet."

Chapter 43

Not knowing exactly when the end was going to come was the most troubling aspect of being diagnosed with a terminal disease, or so Clay thought. Now that he knew he would soon no longer be of this world, Stockton felt at peace with himself. He had expected to react differently, perhaps cry or throw tantrums, but he knew none of that would change anything. As he watched the scenery blur by through the van's window, he felt he had little choice but to confront his fate with dignity.

A portable magnetic siren on the roof of the Nissan NV500 flashed red and white revolving lights, flanked by the wounded Toyota Crown Majesta, with Maki Takano behind the wheel and Beth Flowers, her shoulder bandaged, in the passenger seat. The two vehicles sped past the Tokyo Metropolitan Art Museum in Ueno ward and pulled into a small medical complex with the sign "Yamamoto Private Clinic" in front.

They drove up a long driveway that led to a two-story white rectangular building with round stone columns that resembled a scaled-down version of a 1940s hospital, tucked away at the rear of the property. The van pulled up to the emergency entrance, as Maki parked the Crown in a nearby space in front of the building.

Clay followed Roberts into a large examination room, complete with a family practice table, a small sink in one corner, and a large medicine cabinet in the other. Posters showing cutaways of various parts of the human body decorated the walls. As Roberts opened the door to leave, Naka-jima walked in, accompanied by a gentleman about the same age as him.

"He's all yours, doc," Roberts said, shutting the door behind him.

Nakajima and his companion both wore white lab coats, but the similarities ended there. The other man was tall and skinny, with a balding head and yellow teeth stained from years of heavy smoking. He had bushy gray eyebrows, a rectangular face, and drawn cheeks, making him look a bit like a Japanese version of the Frankenstein monster, but without the scars.

"Hi Stockton. It's nice to see you again," the tall man said in a slight Japanese accent.

"Again? Have we met?" Clay asked.

Nakajima stepped forward. "This is Dr. Yasushi Yama-moto. We were classmates at Harvard, and he helped me hide you when I escaped from Pax-Gen way back when. He's the owner of this facility. I've asked him to help us, and he has graciously agreed."

"It's nice to see you again," Clay said. "And thanks for taking me in, now and before."

Nakajima took out a penlight and examined Clay's pu-pils, and then measured his pulse rate before taking his head in his hands and looking at his temples through his thick spectacles.

"How much longer do you think?" Clay asked.

Nakajima rubbed his jaw. "Still hard to say, maybe a couple of days, maybe a week."

"When it comes, how painful will it be?" Clay asked.

"You'll feel the headache again, and then you'll black out," Nakajima replied.

"I don't want to die yet, George," Clay said calmly.

Nakajima looked at Clay with a warm expression. "I'm going to do my best to keep you alive as long as possible, Stockton. Don't ever lose hope."

Clay nodded.

Nakajima took a seat on a nearby stool. "Stockton, I've asked Chief Roberts to bring you here because we just performed an examination on Kenji Kanda, Mr. Kanda's second son, who's your younger half-brother. We found that he suffers from a very rare spinal disorder, which there is no known cure for."

"You mean he's going to die too?"

"There may be a way to save him. The process is Yamamoto's specialty, and he has an interesting theory. Yasushi, can you explain?"

Yamamoto leaned against the sink. "There is no cure for Kenji's disease, but there is one way he might be saved. And that is to introduce some of the nanobots inside your body into his. We're hoping that they will repair the mutated cells and cure him of this disease."

"But wouldn't he develop Andor's Disease like me?"

Yamamoto nodded. "Yes, but we will introduce his mother's blood to normalize his system, and the nanobots will hopefully stop altering his healthy blood cells."

"That's great. He's lucky he has a direct relative so close by."

Nakajima grabbed Clay's hands and held them tight. "Stockton, this means that you were not a failure. Do you understand? You're going to be able to save someone's life."

"You have the potential to save a few more sick people, if we can extract enough of those nanobots from inside you," Yamamoto said.

Clay smiled. "Yeah, sure, do whatever you need to do. And what is it that you're doing exactly? You're not going to cut me open, are you?"

"No. And this procedure won't affect you in the slightest. We just need to extract some blood from you, but we're going to be taking it out of your chest, where most of the nanobots are usually residing," Nakajima said.

Clay winced. "That doesn't sound pleasant."

"We'll be putting you under an anesthetic. You'll be out for an hour or so," Yamamoto said.

"What about my life? Is there a chance I can be cured? I don't know if you've heard, but Mr. Kanda is long gone," Clay said.

Nakajima pushed his glasses up the bridge of his nose. "I'll be honest with you Stockton, without Mr. Kanda, it's going to be very difficult."

"Yeah, I know."

"Please lie down on the table," Yamamoto said.

Clay hesitated for a brief moment, but followed Yamamoto's instructions, albeit slowly. Yamamoto walked to a phone on the wall and spoke quickly in Japanese. A moment later, a nurse, dressed in a white uniform, walked in with an I.V. stand, and rolled it next to the practice table.

"Stockton, please believe me when I say that we're doing our best to save both you and Kenji, and I won't quit on you, ever," Nakajima said.

Yamamoto grabbed Clay's wrist and pricked his forearm with a small needle, inserting the I.V.

"Now please count backwards from one hundred," he said.

Clay watched the doctor's narrow face as he started counting. At ninety-eight, his vision went blurry. At ninety-five, he was overcome by a satisfyingly comfortable feeling. At ninety-three, his body relaxed. At ninety-two, everything went black.

Chapter 44

Clay opened his eyes and winced at the light that shot through the small window. It was still light outside, and a digital clock on the wall showed that an hour had passed since he was put under. The same nurse that came in with the I.V. stand sat with her legs crossed on a stool across from him, continually swiping her cell phone screen with her index finger. She wore a pink nurse's cap that topped her short black hair. Her white uniform hung loose from her narrow shoulders. She looked up when she heard Clay shift his body on the table.

"Oh, hello. How do you feel?" she asked in good English.

Clay remained lying on the table. "A little groggy, but not bad."

"Yes, I will let the doctor know," she said. She slipped her phone into a small pocket on her uniform and walked out of the room.

Hardly a minute passed when the door slowly opened and Maki stuck her head through the crack in the doorway.

"May I come in?" she asked.

Clay nodded enthusiastically. When she stepped into the room, he noticed that she had changed into fresh clothes and although she wore no makeup, looked as vibrant as the first day he laid eyes on her. Barely visible was a light bruise below her left ear, which she kept partially concealed with her hair.

"How are you feeling?" she asked as Clay sat up on the

table.

"My chest hurts like crazy."

"You should lie back down."

"No, I'm good. How about you? Should you even be up?" asked Clay.

"I'm fine, just a little sore. I'd be worse off if it weren't for you. That was an awfully brave thing you did back there. I really appreciate it."

Clay's face flushed pink for a brief moment. "Has there been any news on Mr. Kanda's plane?"

"We're doing everything we can to get him back."

It sounded like a rehearsed answer, but he knew that she was telling the truth. He still held on to the hope that some sort of miracle could happen, and he would survive this ordeal, but deep down it was painfully obvious that the situation was hopeless, and he only had a few more hours left in the world. He pondered about how he should spend the short time he had left. Although he desperately wanted to go home and be with his parents, he knew he wouldn't last the twelve-hour plane ride back to the States. And if he was going to stay in Japan, what should he do? He didn't have any friends or family here, at least not that he knew of.

"If you're up to it, there's someone I'd like for you to meet," Maki said. Without waiting for a response, she stood up and opened the door, and showed in Nena Larsson-Kanda and Kenji into the room. Nena wore a red silk blouse with a Hermes scarf wrapped loosely around her neck and a knee-length checkered skirt. Her blonde hair shone under the fluorescent lights. Kenji had on a plain green T-shirt under a pair of brown OshKosh overalls.

Clay's gaze went directly to the face of the young boy.

"Is that who I think it is?" he asked.

"Allow me to introduce you to each other. Mrs. Kanda and Kenji, this is Mr. Clay," Maki said, as she moved next to Clay and put her mouth next to his ear. She covered the side of her mouth and whispered, "She doesn't know about her husband's involvement or abduction yet."

"Why not?" Clay whispered back.

"It's all still very confidential. As far as she knows, you're a distant relative of Mr. Kanda's, and she doesn't know about the nanobots, so don't mention that either."

Kenji stood cowering behind his mother. Clay could see the resemblance to his younger sibling, but the kid wore his hair much shorter than he did at that age, and he seemed a bit chubbier than he remembered himself being.

Nena walked across the room to Clay and grabbed both of his hands, squeezing his fingers tight. "I can't begin to thank you for what you're doing for Kenji," she said, her eyes nearly tearing. "The doctor said your cells are the key to curing my son."

Clay tried to pull his hands back. "No, it's nothing. Really, don't worry about it."

Nena looked down at her son and placed her hand softly on the top of Kenji's head. "Don't be afraid, Kenji. He's your relative. Go say hi," she said in English.

Clay smiled and held out his hand. "Hi, buddy. You must be Mr. Kanda's son. Nice to meet you. I'm Stockton."

Kenji remained half hidden behind his mother, clinging

to the end of her blouse.

Man, this kid is shy. A case of mother complex?

"Yeah, you and me, even though we've never met before, we're like brothers, or half-brothers," Clay said.

Nena took Kenji's hand and guided him towards Clay. "Go ahead, Kenji. Don't be afraid."

Kenji lightly shook Clay's hand. "Hi," he said.

"Kenji, tell Stockton how old you are," Nena said.

Kenji put up five fingers. "I'm five."

Clay rubbed the top of Kenji's head. "Hey, you speak English. Well, I'm twenty-five, so I've got a big head start on you."

Maki interrupted them. "Nena, we should let Stockton rest now."

"Of course. Come on Kenji." Nena took the boy's hand and headed for the door. When she got there, she looked back at Clay. "Thank you again for what you're doing. My husband would be here, too, to thank you, but he's currently on a business trip. I'm sure he will show his appreciation to you when he returns."

"That would be nice," Clay said.

Nena turned to Maki as she walked through the doorway, "As soon as I hear from my husband, I will let you know."

Kenji kept his eyes fixed on Clay until he exited the room.

When the door clicked shut, Maki put her hand on Clay's forearm. "I hope you haven't given up because I haven't," she said.

Clay closed his eyes and rested his head against the wall. He cursed himself for wasting the best part of his life feeling sorry for himself and taking refuge in video games; those days should have been spent discovering more of what life had to offer, such as traveling to new places and meeting new people. If only he could have a second chance. He couldn't remember the last time he cried, but he felt like breaking down right then and there.

"Can I call my mom and dad now? I need to talk to them before, you know," he asked.

"Yes, the chief said he will allow you to get in touch with them, and he's even offering to have them flown in. But we can't mention a word about your condition to them, so he's brainstorming with Agent Wong to come up with something feasible to tell them."

"Thanks. That'll be great," Clay said.

He looked up at the ceiling. He wondered what he would tell them. For all they knew, he was on a job interview for Kamita Motors. When he told them that he was going to LAX because the world's largest car company was flying him to Japan to interview him, they sounded so proud. He felt a pang of guilt for not telling them the truth, but Agent Whitaker had warned him that revealing anything about the discovery of his real father could potentially put them in danger. Knowing his foster parents, Clay could imagine them making a mess of things to protect their son, especially his mom.

Clay turned and looked at Maki. "Although we've known each other for only a few days, you've been amazing to me. Without you, I would have never made it this far. If only I could have another ten years, or even five, I would have lived them differently than before. There are so many people I haven't yet met and so many places I haven't gone."

"Where would be the first place you would go?" she asked.

"I've never been to Hawaii," Clay answered. "Yeah, Hawaii sounds pretty good right about now."

"It's a wonderful place. I'll have to show you around sometime."

Clay wasn't sure if Maki meant what she said, or if it was just casually thrown out there to temporarily comfort a dying man, but the prospect of spending a day with her on a resort island sounded inviting to say the least. "Is that where you usually go with your boyfriend?" he asked.

"No. I'm not dating anyone right now," she said.

Clay's eyes lit up. "How can someone as attractive as you not have a boyfriend?"

Maki smiled, showing her perfect teeth. "Are you trying to hit on me, Stockton?"

Clay quickly looked away, his face turning wine red. "No, no of course not. Why, do you say that?"

Maki put her index finger to her chin. "To be honest, I've had two relationships in the past four years, but neither of the men could handle that my job always came first."

"I'm sorry to hear that," Clay said, still avoiding eye contact. "But I'd like for you to be nearby, you know, when the time comes."

She walked over to him and gave him a peck on the

cheek. "That's very sweet of you, but you're gonna make it." She went over to the chair and picked up her jacket and purse. "I'll let you know as soon as we hear something. Try to get some rest, Stockton."

"Sure," Clay said, knowing full well he wasn't going to be able to. His mind was focused on how he could sneak out of the hospital and track Kanda down. If he perished on the way, so be it, but he had long ago decided that he wasn't going to die in a cold hospital room.

Chapter 45

Andrew Roberts took off his jacket and threw it onto his office chair, thankful that the only casualty he came away with from the gunfight at the airfield was a small hole in his slacks. The sleeves of his blue dress shirt were dirty and rolled up, and his red curly hair was a disheveled mess. He dropped down into his chair and reached for his wooden cigar box on the edge of his desk. He opened the lid and pulled out a Cuban-blend Monte Cristo, purchased at a tobacco shop across the street. "What a frickin' morning," he said to himself as he kicked his feet up and lit the cigar with his Zippo lighter.

Agent Charlie Wong, who had changed from his ramen-chef getup back into a white dress shirt and black slacks, knocked softly on the open door. "You wanted to see me, boss?

"Yeah, sit down. How's Beth doing?" Roberts asked.

Wong held a thin manila folder and sat down across from Roberts. "The doctor said it was just a minor gunshot wound. They patched her up and sent her home."

Roberts took a long drag of his cigar and blew a thick wisp of smoke into the air. "Good to hear about Beth. The damned Kamita pilots are talking to the Japanese authorities, and the police are calling the U.S. and Russian embassies, so I think it's only a matter of time before this thing blows up big. I've already got a call from the chief saying that he'll be briefing the White House about Novak. Our orders are now to stop him at all costs, but with that plane gone…"

"Did you ask if they could intercept it?" Wong asked.

"Yeah, but by the time our request gets run up the chain, Novak and Kanda'll already be untouchable. It's only a two-hour flight to Pyongyang, and only an hour to reach their air space. Just my luck…"

Wong leaned back in his chair and crossed his legs, holding the folder in his lap. "We can reveal bits and pieces to the local authorities to keep their appetites in check, but I don't think it'll be necessary to fill them in on the whole thing. Also, we should have someone contact the Chinese government and tell them about this mess. They have influence over the North Koreans."

Roberts shook his head. "That won't do any good; if anything, it'll only encourage the Chinese to try and steal the technology."

"Novak doesn't know that Stockton has a terminal illness, is that correct?" Wong asked.

"As far as we know. And George doesn't think so either, or why else would he be trying to kill him." Roberts blew three smoke rings that hovered in the air in formation.

"And they don't know that we have him?"

"Not unless they saw him at the airfield this morning, but I'm pretty sure they didn't."

"So they will definitely come after him again."

"Probably. It's funny, in a matter of days or hours, Stockton will be dead, and all their problems will be solved without them having to do a single thing."

"Sir, I suggest we keep his death a secret and find a man, preferably another agent, who matches his description.

Perhaps we can bait Novak or the North Koreans to expose themselves. We know they all want Stockton dead because he's still the link that can prove Novak broke international law."

"You mean to let them think Clay is alive so they keep coming after him?"

Wong nodded.

Roberts sucked on his cigar and nodded. "Yeah, I see what you're getting at now. It may be worth a shot. Novak will definitely have someone doing his dirty work, so if we can catch whoever comes after Stockton and make 'em admit they were working for Novak, we can officially go after him."

Wong opened his folder and shuffled through a few papers. "Of course, the best thing would be to get Kanda back. He's obviously being held against his will. If we could somehow pry him away, I'm sure he would sing like a bird, especially if we offered him some sort of immunity."

Roberts straightened himself up in the chair. "Okay, for the time being, let's go with your first plan, and get started on looking for a body-double. We'll keep the real Clay secured at the clinic until, well, until he dies, but no one is to know he died."

"Got it boss," Wong said as he scribbled some notes on his folder.

"Oh yeah, and one more thing," Roberts said. "George and his associates ran tests on Kenji, and the kid has a chance of pulling through."

Wong put away his pen. "I wish there was some way to

help Stockton too. He's not a bad guy."

"Yeah, a bit reckless, but he's got balls, I'll give him that."

Chapter 46

The KamitaJet quickly climbed to its cruising altitude after taking off from Tachikawa Airfield. Novak shifted uneasily in his seat in the main cabin and looked over at Kanda, who sat with his eyes closed in the seat next to him. When he felt the plane level off, he unbuckled his seatbelt and walked into the cockpit, leaving the door open.

"We lost Boris," he said to Sokov in Russian.

"I know. I'm sorry," Sokov replied. His left hand was wrapped in a bloodstained towel, with ice cubes inside.

"Don't be," Novak said. "Boris would have died anyways, and so will Oleg, for that matter. And soon."

"The girl got away."

"No big loss. Yes, she now can identify us, but we'll be safe in Pyongyang. But more important, who were those Americans back there? They had guns, so I assume they were government agents. Has Oleg somehow screwed up and implicated us somehow?"

Sokov shrugged. "I don't know, but he hasn't reported in, so maybe they caught him."

Novak sent his fist crashing into the backrest of the empty co-pilot's chair. "Shit. If that is the case, then we are in a dire predicament. That could mean he didn't dispose of the prototype."

Sokov pointed his thumb over his shoulder. "And what about him?"

Novak looked back in Kanda's direction. "We may still be able to use him as a hostage. We'll keep him around for

now, and then we'll get rid of him when the deal with Pyongyang is done."

Novak took out his satellite phone and punched in
a twelve-digit number on the key pad. He spoke when he
heard someone pick up. "Please put me through to Colonel
Seo. This is Dmitri," he said in English. "I have some bad
news to report, the Americans showed up on our way out…
No, they don't know much, I assure you…The prototype is
being taken care of as we speak…Yes, I see. Thank you."

He hung up and turned to Sokov. "They want us there
right away. They didn't sound happy about the Americans."

Sokov nodded. "We should be there in about an hour
and a half, but we're burning more fuel than normal because
we need to keep our cruising altitude at about ten-thousand
feet."

"Why are we flying so low?"

"There must have been a couple of bullets that penetrat-
ed the fuselage because the cabin can't pressurize. We can't
go any higher because the air is too thin for us to breathe
sufficiently."

"I'll leave the flying to you. Just make sure we get to
Pyongyang," Novak said.

Kanda, sitting in one of two front seats that faced
the cockpit, chuckled as he watched the two men interact
through the cockpit doorway. The main cabin and the cockpit were separated by a short hallway that passed the galley
and flight attendant's quarters, a cramped space the size of a
small closet with a reclining chair and a curtain that could be
drawn for privacy. The bathroom, complete with a shower,

was at the rear of the plane.

Novak turned around and walked into the main cabin. He stood over his guest. "What do you find so amusing, Kanda-san?"

"Face it, minister, it's over. You and I, we will be disgraced forever."

"No. You're wrong. The only glitch is the existence of the prototype, which I'm going to take care of now," Novak tapped on his satellite phone keyboard.

"What are you doing?"

"None of your business, but if you must know, I'm doubling the bounty on your beloved son and getting some serious professionals involved, just in case he's still alive."

Kanda sat up in his chair. "Mr. Deputy Minister. You know as well as I that your clients can't be trusted. I know who they are. They'll throw you into a labor camp as soon as you hand over the technology. So please reconsider my offer. Let Stockton live, take my ten million dollars, and you can disappear anywhere in the world you want."

Novak laughed. "They're getting something only I can deliver, so why would they double-cross me? I am on the cusp of perfecting this new technology for them."

Kanda tilted his head. "What new technology are you talking about?"

Novak put his phone away. "Do you remember poor Boris, who died on the runway?"

"One of your clones equipped with nanotechnology, I assume," Kanda said.

"Not just that, Kanda-san. You don't know this, but

while at Pax-Gen, I was also experimenting with nanobots that could significantly enhance human physical attributes, not just kill diseases."

"Enhance physical attributes? What are you talking about? You had no authority."

"Don't be so naïve, Kanda-san. Do you really think I would not explore the true potential of this wondrous technology? I was really close to the right formula with Boris and Oleg, but they still had some major side effects," Novak said.

"You're trying to create super humans?" Kanda asked.

"That's a nice way of putting it. Bravo, Kanda-san."

"But what you're talking about is the stuff of comic books. I mean it's all fantasy."

Novak grinned, showing a couple of his gold-capped teeth. "No, Kanda-san, it's real, and it's the future. There is no limit to what I can do with nanotechnology."

"You're betraying all humankind," Kanda said. "Man was not meant to play God like this."

Novak burst out in laughter. "I find that comment very amusing coming from you; the man who came to me to try and artificially save your son. People like you disgust me—a hypocrite of the highest order."

Kanda looked Novak hard in the eyes. "You're right. I'm prepared to burn in hell for helping you, but what you're doing, it's wrong, and you're upsetting the balance of nature. And how many of these supermen have you created?"

"Boris and Oleg were the only two. I am about to enter the next stage with better results, as soon as my facilities are ready in Pyongyang."

"All for a few measly bucks. You're despicable."

Novak waved his hand. "You're a small man, Mr. Kanda, and you think like a small man. My research will ultimately ensure the survival of our species, improve the quality of life, and perhaps allow people to live for hundreds of years. There's still much more work to do, but oh, I am so close. Now you know why I wanted those files erased. I can't have anyone else with any knowledge of this technology. It must all be mine and mine only, at least until the rest of the world catches up."

The next twenty minutes of the flight were spent in relative silence as Novak stared into the monitor of his laptop computer, and Kanda sat with his eyes closed in deep meditation. Novak got up to fix himself a drink, when the plane suddenly buckled; the momentary loss in altitude nearly knocked him off his feet.

Sokov threw open the cockpit door from the pilot's seat. "We're not going to make it," he shouted in Russian. "We're going through way too much fuel."

"How far can we make it?" Novak asked Sokov who still manned the controls.

Sokov tapped the fuel readout with his index finger. "Not far. We won't be able to reach the North Korean border."

Novak punched the wall. "Damn it."

He walked over to Kanda and leaned down so his face was even with his own. "Kanda-san, we're going to need another plane. Where do you keep your spares? I know you have several all over Japan."

"Go to hell," Kanda said with a sneer.

Novak took his gun out and pulled the slide back, loading a bullet into the firing chamber. He pointed the muzzle at Kanda's forehead. "I will not ask again."

"Go ahead and shoot. You're going to kill me anyways."

"That's not true, Kanda-san. I wasn't planning on killing you, although the idea does have certain merits. But please don't forget that I know where to find your beautiful wife and boy. You wouldn't want them to have an unfortunate accident, would you?"

Kanda dropped his head. "Our company keeps a press fleet of KamitaJets in a hangar next to our racetrack at Fuji Speedway."

"Viktor, how far to Fuji Speedway?" Novak asked.

Sokov poked and swiped his finger across the Kamita-Jet's highly-advanced touchscreen avionics. "If we reduce our speed even more, we can be there in about forty-five minutes, but it'll be cutting it close."

"Fine, just do it." He reached into his back pocket and pulled out Kanda's cell phone, the one he confiscated back at his home. "I want you to make sure your plane is ready to go when we land. I will dial the facility for you."

Novak checked the phone number to the Kamita Fuji Speedway and dialed it on Kanda's phone.

"What do I tell them?" he asked.

"Have them arrange a plane to be ready in thirty minutes. And also tell them you have another pilot with you, so you won't need a crew. No tricks because I can understand

Japanese, remember. The less the people there know, the better."

"I will tell them you are aviation journalists writing a story on the plane. That way, it would make sense for us to request a press plane without a crew."

"Fine, just hurry up. It's ringing." He handed the phone to Kanda.

As Kanda took the phone and started speaking, Novak could have sworn he saw the old man crack a faint smile.

Chapter 47

Clay wondered if he would ever see Maki again as he watched her walk to the door to leave the examination room. He felt tempted to spring up from the family practice table, hug her from behind, and tell her that he loved her with all his heart, but before he could act, the ring of a cell phone filled the room.

Maki stopped short of the door and pulled her phone from her bag. "*Moshi moshi...Hai...Hai wakarimashita. Jahnorisuto desune...Hai.*"

She ended the call and stood motionless for a brief moment before turning around. Her eyes were open wide, but had a faraway look to them. "You're not going to believe this."

"What?" Clay asked.

"That was the Kamita air hangar at Fuji Speedway. Mr. Kanda just contacted them to get a press plane ready for some foreign journalists he's with. They said he's expected in an hour to switch aircrafts."

Clay nearly fell off the table. "This isn't some kind of weird demented joke, is it? Why would he do that?"

"They said he was having problems with his personal plane, the one he's riding in now."

"Why would the hangar call and tell you?"

"Because all media loans, whether they're automobiles or airplanes, go through the public relations department, which means me. It's company policy. Kanda knew this. We're getting one more chance at this thing."

Clay jumped off the table. "How far is Fuji Speedway from here?"

"About sixty miles away, which in Tokyo traffic, could take two hours, so we won't beat them there by car. We'll need to use our chopper. It's about thirty minutes away, so that'll get us into Fuji in about an hour. I'll call Andrew on the way." Maki gathered her things and headed out the door of the patient's room.

Clay grabbed a container of sublingual pills that Nakajima had left with him and followed Maki out. They went up a flight of stairs to the president's office where Nakajima and Yamamoto crouched over a large table studying MRI scans and X-ray images. The door was open and Maki went straight to Yamamoto.

"Listen to me, Kanda is still in Japan. We know where he is. I need to use your company van," she said.

Yamamoto gasped. "My God. Of course." He walked over to his desk and grabbed a set of keys from one of the drawers. "Here you go. It's all gassed up."

"*Domo arigato,*" she said, snatching the keys from the doctor's hand.

Nakajima looked over at Clay who stood by the doorway. "If you get Kanda back here alive, we'll be ready to perform the transfusion process for you," he said.

"I'll get him here, I promise you that," Clay said as he followed Maki out of the office.

Maki found the Yamamoto Clinic van, a white Mitsubishi Delica converted into an ambulance, parked in the main lot. She jumped into its driver seat, as Clay slid in next to her.

"Shouldn't I drive?" he asked.

Maki shot him a perplexed look. "Please."

She started the diesel engine on the first try and switched on the ambulance's light bar and sirens. With the throttle pedal floored, the vehicle sped out onto the main road, the traffic in front of it parting like the red sea.

"Where did *you* learn how to drive?" Clay asked.

Maki ignored him. Her face was pressed in concentration as she swerved past the cars that were unable to pull to the side of the road in time. Once in the clear, she took out her phone and pressed the Bluetooth button on the van's center console. A familiar voice sounded over the vehicle's speakers.

"Roberts here."

"This is Takano. Kanda is switching planes at Fuji Speedway in an hour. I have Stockton with me, and we're headed to Yokota Airbase. We'll need the helicopter."

"They're coming back? Why?" Roberts asked.

"Something seems to be wrong with their plane."

"Roger that. Our orders now are to stop them at all costs. Do you copy?"

"Yes sir," Maki answered.

"And why the hell is Stockton with you again?"

Maki paused. "Um, he snuck into the van when I wasn't looking. I had no choice but to bring him along." She winked at Clay.

"That little shit. I tell ya, I'm starting to like the idea of him being dead."

"We're on speakerphone, sir," Maki said.

The line went quiet.

"Sir?"

Roberts cleared his throat. "Shouldn't you be back at the hospital resting, young man?"

"I'd rather not spend the last moments of my life in a hospital bed," Clay said. "Please, sir, I can't die like that. I want to be doing everything I can to live."

"You stubborn son of a bitch. Fine, but you'd better obey all my orders to the letter. I'll see you both at Yokota. I'll have the Huey ready to go."

"Roger. We'll be there in twenty," Maki said.

Clay felt a tickle on his upper lip, followed by a sudden burst of pain in his head. It wasn't as strong as the last attack, but when he flipped down the sunshade and looked into the mirror, he could see the distinct lines of the veins in his temple, as well as the lumps that throbbed around them. After wiping his bleeding nose with his shirt, he took out the pill container from his pocket and shook out five pink capsules. He placed all of them under his tongue, letting them dissolve a bit before gulping them down.

Slowly the veins disappeared, and the pain faded away. His nosebleed stopped a few seconds later.

"I'm out of pills. I don't think I have much time left," he said.

Maki looked over at Clay and put her hand over his. "Hang in there."

The ambulance sped onto the Chuo Expressway heading westbound; its sirens blaring. During normal circumstances, the commute from Ueno to the Yokota Airbase, located in the city of Fussa in western Tokyo, would take about an hour, but with the help of the flashing lights, the ambulance covered the thirty-five-mile distance in less than half that time. Maki checked her watch; they had about thirty minutes remaining until Kanda's plane touched down at Fuji.

The Delica stopped at the security gate of the American airbase, home to the 347th Airlift Wing of the United States Air Force. Maki handed her government ID to one of three security men who manned the entrance.

"This is an emergency. Senior Special Agent Roberts is also on his way. We need to get to your helicopter fast," she said.

"He just went through ma'am," said the soldier as he peeked into the car to look at Clay. "He told us to expect you and send you straight in. Please follow that Jeep, it'll take you to the chopper."

"Thank you," Maki said as she took her ID back.

The ambulance followed the beige Jeep, driven by a young African American soldier, through a series of small roads until it reached Yokota's enormous air strip. Clay took in the scene with awe as he saw dozens of military aircraft, mostly cargo planes, including a massive C-130 Hercules and several C-12 Hurons, parked in neat rows on the side of the main strip. The soldier led them to the far side of the airfield where a white Bell UH-1 Iroquois helicopter sat next to an Airbus H120 on a helipad. Roberts stood next to the open door.

Maki pulled the van to a stop next to the Airbus. "Come on, let's go," she said.

"What took you guys so long?" Roberts asked, pointing at his wristwatch.

"We came straight here. How on earth did you beat us?" she asked.

Roberts extended his arm in the direction of a bright yellow Chevrolet Corvette Z06 parked on the other side of the chopper, complete with light bar and sirens. "Not too bad, eh? What do you think Stockton?"

Clay nodded. "Nice. Is the engine stock?"

"Hell yes, it is. Why would I want to mess with perfection?"

"Save your male bonding for later, we need to move," Maki cut in.

"You're right, let's get the hell out of here," Roberts said.

They climbed into the H120 as its main rotors started to spin; Roberts sat up front next to the pilot, Clay and Maki in the back.

They strapped themselves in and put on their headsets. Roberts spoke through the mouthpiece, "This here is Lieutenant Morris, he'll be flying us out to the speedway."

Morris gave his passengers a thumbs-up sign and lifted the white bird into the clear blue sky. It banked left and headed in the direction of the majestic white-capped peak of Mt. Fuji that loomed on the distant horizon.

Chapter 48

There was no piece of pavement deadlier in all of Asia than the banked high-speed corner called "Daiichi" at the Fuji Speedway. It claimed the lives of many race drivers and prompted the racetrack owners to redesign the entire course several times, the most recent coming a few months after Kamita Motors bought the facility from Toyota. No longer part of the race course, the Daiichi corner is now a weed-infested relic of the past that sleeps at the south end of the property. Despite its spotty past, Fuji Speedway was still considered the most scenic racing facility in the world—with the familiar triangular peak of Mt. Fuji serving as an ominous backdrop. It held a firm place in Formula One folklore as it hosted the race that brought James Hunt his world championship over Nikki Lauda, a season of rivalry and comradery that's been chronicled in numerous books, as well as a major Hollywood film.

Although he lived only a few miles away from the historic site, the man in charge of the new airfield at Fuji Speedway, Katsuyuki Suzuki, held no interest in motorsports. Since grade school, he was desperate to escape the monotony of country life, dreaming of traveling to America to open a sushi restaurant in Hollywood where he fantasized about serving famous celebrities. His passion for cooking came from his father, who owned an *izakaya*, or Japanese-style pub, in nearby Fujinomiya, where he'd often help him prepare dishes after he got off school. Although Suzuki didn't attend college, he studied English diligently, acquiring the top certificate at the local language school while training to be an air traffic controller. His other passion was flying, having secured his private pilot license right after graduating high school. He was lucky that Kamita Motors had cleared a section of forest next to Fuji Speedway to install a small runway and hangar because he didn't have to go far to look for a job. After completing his air-traffic qualification tests, he was hired as the manager of the Fuji Speedway Airfield, a position that included being its only air traffic controller.

The air traffic control center at Fuji Speedway was a small, simple room located on the second story of a residential-like building next to the main hangar. It was barely high enough to overlook the far end of the lone runway that stretched out toward Fuji Kokusai Golf Club.

Suzuki sat in his chair, alone in the room like any other day, with his feet kicked up on his desk. He wore the required white Fuji Airfield polo shirt and dark blue slacks, with white tennis shoes. His short straight hair parted down the middle, narrow set eyes, and some razor stubble under his nose earned him the nickname "King Otaku" from some of his old school mates, but he didn't care. The last thing on his mind was attracting the opposite sex, being one of many people in Japan known as *shoshoku-danshi*, which roughly translates to "male-herbivore," a man who prefers not to have intimate relationships.

He had a few minutes to kill before Mr. Kanda's plane came in, so he passed the time reading *Shonen Jump*, Japan's most popular weekly comic magazine. Through the window, a flash of light in the sky caught Suzuki's eye. He got up and took out a pair of binoculars hanging from the wall. He looked out over the horizon and saw a lone jet approaching in the distance. "They're early," he said to himself as he checked his wristwatch and returned to his seat, putting his headset on.

"This is Fuji Speedway, please identity yourself," he said in Japanese.

There was no response.

He repeated his message again, in English, and then again. No response. He wondered whether he should call the home office, but the small jet was almost on top of the lone runway. A moment later, it made a perfect landing on the fresh black tarmac. That was Kanda's plane all right, he could tell by the tail number, but he found it odd that no one answered his call. No harm, no foul, he thought; the plug to the pilot's headset could have been disconnected inadvertently while he was preparing to land, so he left the tower to pick up his guests and drive them to the hangar where their replacement plane waited.

The wounded KamitaJet taxied to the lone hangar located about a hundred yards from the center of the runway. It came to a slow stop in front of the building. As the jet engines wound down, Suzuki got out of his white extended-cab four-door Kamita pickup truck and waited for the plane door to open. When it did, a bald white man stuck his head out from the doorway.

"Welcome to Fuji Speedway," Suzuki said in perfect English.

* * * *

Sokov looked down at the airfield worker and gave him a thumbs-up sign. As he stepped onto the airstair, a faint, unmistakable sound of an approaching helicopter sounded in the distance. He ducked back into the plane and grabbed a pair of binoculars, pointing them in the direction of a speck materializing over the grandstands of the neighboring Fuji Speedway racetrack. Being a former Russian military officer, he recognized the make and model right away.

"There's a helicopter coming, and I think it's the Americans," he said, as he ducked back into the plane's cabin and looked over at Novak.

Novak took out his pistol from the back of his belted pants, pulled the slide back and pointed the muzzle at Kanda's head. "You just signed your death warrant," he said angrily.

Kanda held up his hands. "No. You listened in on my call yourself. There was no way I could have had anything to do with this."

Novak cursed. "Viktor, we need to get the hell out of here. Start the engines back up."

"Sir, we don't have enough fuel to make it very far."

"Land the plane in a nearby field or some empty road. We can steal a car and find a place to lay low until one of our associates can come get us. But we can't stay here."

Sokov pressed the button that automatically closed the airplane door and ran back to the cockpit.

* * * *

About two hundred feet away, the H120 helicopter landed softly on an empty patch of pavement. Roberts, Maki, and Clay stepped out of the bird, where they were greeted by Suzuki who raced over to them in his pickup truck. Roberts carried a large leather shoulder bag over his shoulder.

"Hi Katsu, thank you for the call," Maki said in English, knowing his preference to speak the language whenever possible.

Clay stood behind Maki, and noticed that Roberts had taken a few steps toward the parked plane.

"Shit, they're already here, and it looks like they're getting ready to leave," Roberts said. "Stockton, get in the truck, and stay low, it may get a little hot around here."

Clay opened the door of Suzuki's pickup truck and sat inside.

Suzuki threw up his arms. "What's going on with Kanda-san's plane? Who was that *gaijin* that stuck his head out and then closed the door again?"

Maki grabbed Suzuki by the shoulders. "Katsu, we think Mr. Kanda is being kidnapped. These men with me are part of a secret investigative organization, and they must be allowed to work in private. I must insist you leave here immediately, and do not call the police."

Suzuki stepped back as Maki let him go. "What's going on? I must call this in to the track managers, or it will be my neck. It's highly unusual..."

"Katsu, you need to get out of here now. It's dangerous," Maki said as she once again took a hold of Suzuki's shoulders.

Suzuki flinched at the forceful tone in Maki's voice. Without saying another word, he bowed and ran back toward the air traffic tower.

The plane rolled forward in front of the hangar.

"Should we try to block its path?" Roberts asked.

Maki tossed her Hermes handbag onto the front passenger seat of the truck and took the canvas bag from Roberts' shoulders. After quickly unzipping it, she pulled out a Stoner SR-25 sniper's rifle. "The runway is too wide. The plane would just drive around us." She then moved to the front of the truck and set up the rifle atop the vehicle's hood, pointing its long barrel at the jet plane, which was beginning a wide U-turn.

"Fire when ready," Roberts said.

She let loose a shot. The bullet missed its intended target about two hundred yards away, putting a hole right below the windshield. The popping sound of punctured metal caused Sokov, who was in the pilot's seat, to flinch. "The wind is picking up, and it's swirling," she said as she glanced at a fully extended windsock next to the hangar.

Roberts, who had also taken up position next to Maki, fired off a couple of rounds from his Beretta, but it was difficult to tell if the bullets had even reached the jet.

Clay leaned his head out of the window. "They're going to get away."

Roberts reloaded his gun. "The plane has some mechanical problems so even if it does take off, they won't get far.

We've asked Yokota Air base to track its every move on radar," he said as Maki launched another shot; this one landed just aft of the windshield.

Clay touched his temple; he felt another headache coming on. "I don't have any more time. This next one might be it."

Roberts aimed and fired several rounds, but the plane was now completely out of the Beretta's range. "We'll follow their jet in our helicopter. We won't let them get away."

"No, it'll never be able to keep up. That plane has a top speed like five times that of the chopper," Clay said.

"Our flyboys at Yokota are probably getting their jets ready to intercept it, so don't worry," Roberts said.

The last remark certainly did make Clay worry. If American fighter jets shot down the KamitaJet in midflight, Mr. Kanda would be dead, and he would have no chance at being cured of his disease. And he knew that the CIA wouldn't think twice about shooting it down if it meant keeping Novak from leaving the country. He needed to get on that plane to stop it from taking off, or at least cause a delay to give Maki and Roberts extra time to stop it. If he didn't, he was a dead man. As Clay devised a plan, he noticed that Maki had left her purse on the front passenger seat of the pickup truck. And her attention was still focused on the jet.

Clay discreetly extended his arm between the two front seats and shoved his hand inside Maki's bag. He immediately found what he was looking for; the cold handle of the SIG Sauer slid into his palm. After carefully pulling it out of the bag, he tucked it under his shirt. Then looking over at Roberts and Maki—who both had their gaze fixed intently on the jet—he decided that now was the time to move.

As Maki lined up her next shot, Clay quietly opened the door of the pickup truck and performed a judo roll onto the asphalt. As soon as he sprang up to his feet, he made a mad dash for the jet, not even thinking of looking back. Maki and Roberts saw him at the same time, but by then Clay had already covered a quarter of the distance to the plane.

"Stockton, no," Maki shouted.

But Clay didn't hear a thing, expect the thumping of his own heart.

Without any bullets flying his way, Clay reached the side of the plane unscathed. He jogged along the jet's starboard wing, keeping pace with the aircraft, Maki's gun firmly gripped in his hand. While running, he pointed the muzzle at a metal latch on the fuselage and fired. The bullet punched a hole through the lock, and the door to the luggage compartment swung open. Just as the plane started to speed up, he lifted his body through the narrow opening and crawled into an empty compartment.

Maki fired off a couple of shots at the cockpit, but it was too late. The KamitaJet, its engines now humming loudly, had already started racing down the runway. When it reached a speed of a hundred and twenty miles an hour, its sleek nose tilted skyward and the plane was once again airborne. As he glanced at the departing runway, Clay reached outside for the luggage compartment door and slammed it shut.

Chapter 49

Stockton Clay nearly laughed when he thought about the absurdity of what he had just done: he had snuck into the luggage compartment of a broken airplane that was occupied by people who wanted to kill him. But when he considered that the alternative was dying a painful death by some godawful disease in an empty hospital room, he was comfortable with the decision.

He crouched low to keep his head from hitting the top of the cramped space, shoving the SIG Sauer P226 into his pants pocket and waiting for his eyes to adjust to the darkness…only they didn't. It was pitch black, so he took out his smart phone and used the flashlight app, which provided more than enough light to make his way around. The first thing on his mind was finding a small door on the near wall, about three feet high and four feet wide, which connected the luggage compartment to the bathroom in the plane's main cabin. Clay learned about this door when he performed a walk-around of the jet for his article in Automobile Digest. A Kamita Motors employee made a special effort to point out what the company dubbed the "Luggage Escape" because it was a fairly unique feature for smaller jets. He explained that Mr. Kanda insisted on having a way for passengers inside the aircraft to be able to access their baggage from within the baggage compartment during flight to distinguish the KamitaJet from the competition; therefore, the entire luggage bay was pressurized and heated. Unfortunately for Clay, there was only one light switch, and it was located inside the main cabin.

He felt his way to the far wall, but a sudden jerk from the plane knocked him backwards. The whirring, mechanical and hydraulic sounds of the landing gear being retracted into their housings filled the compartment. The aircraft's ascent was a short one, leveling off a minute or so after takeoff. As Clay continued his search for the hidden door, he ran his fingers up and down the fore wall, which was covered with plastic panels. Then his fingers touched a small piece of cold metal. Eureka. After pulling the small handle out of its cubby and twisting it clockwise, he cautiously pushed open the door and crawled through the undersized doorway.

He was in.

Clay nearly hit his head on the small plastic toilet in the cramped bathroom. As he propped himself up, using the sink as support, he delicately closed the luggage escape door behind him. Then, as he softly pushed open the main bathroom door, the crack from the door gap casting a thin sliver of light down his face, he peeked into the main cabin.

The KamitaJet's cabin was somewhat cramped, with just enough space for six passengers, despite being labeled as a nine-passenger aircraft. There was a couch against one wall, and a table with some chairs next to it on the other. Up front were two larger chairs that faced the front of the plane. Clay knew they were occupied because he could see the tops of two heads sticking up above the backrests. After quietly pushing the bathroom door all the way open, he stepped into the aisle and stopped about five feet from the front row seats. He pointed his gun at the head with the gray hair.

"Turn this plane around," Clay said.

Both men jumped and immediately turned around. Novak's face went from disbelief to anger as he stared at the young man who stood in the aisle pointing a gun to his face. Kanda nearly teared at the sight of him.

"You're alive," Kanda said.

Novak unbuckled his seatbelt and slowly stood up, with both of his arms raised. Clay kept the gun aimed at his head.

"How on earth did you get here?" Novak asked.

"Don't move another muscle. I need you to turn this plane around and return to Tokyo now," Clay said.

Novak smiled, surveying Clay up and down with an amused expression. "So you're the prototype. It's a pleasure to finally meet you."

"If you don't have this plane turned around, I will pull the trigger. So help me God, I will kill you."

"Listen, we can work this out. All I need is for you to disappear for a while. In fact, we can be the ones to hide you. And in return, I will make you rich beyond belief. Not a bad deal, is it?"

Clay looked over at Kanda who quietly watched the proceedings. The old man's eyes were fixed intensely on his son.

"Sorry, no deal," Clay said.

Novak's face turned red. He thrust his index finger towards Clay. "You would be dead a long time ago if it weren't for me. You should thank me for the years of life that I gave you."

Clay's body trembled with rage. With his face molded into a scowl that creased the outer edges of his nose, he tightened his grip on the gun. It would feel good to shoot him in the face, he thought, but after taking a deep breath, he calmed his nerves. "Don't try me. I have nothing to lose, you know."

Novak took a step towards Clay. "You're irrelevant. Go ahead, if you think you have the guts."

All right smart ass. Clay pointed the gun at Novak's leg and started to squeeze the trigger when an intense pain shot through his temples and spread throughout his entire body. *Shit, not now.* He clenched his jaws tight as a killer headache ripped through his skull. His hand on the gun shook uncontrollably, and he felt blood seeping out of both nostrils, dripping down his chin and onto the floor.

Novak watched with a bemused look. "What's wrong with you? You're sick, aren't you?"

"You can think whatever you want. I'm going to…" Clay's sentence was cut short by another sharp wave of pain in his temples that caused his body to sway left to right; he fought the urge to crumple to the floor.

Novak jumped forward; his hands going straight for the gun and his shoulders smashing into Clay's chest. Clay took the body hit and recovered his balance, gritting his teeth to shut the headache out. But by then, Novak had gotten both hands on the SIG and was trying to yank it away. Clay was not going to let go so easily.

The two men pulled on the weapon, as their bodies spun in one direction and then the other, bouncing off the chairs like a pinball. Novak's own firearm fell from his waist in the tussle, dropping on the carpeted cabin floor. Clay was astonished by the incredible strength of the older man, and he felt his own strength begin to drain as the nanobots started to take over his body.

Novak cracked a devious smile as he slowly-but-surely established control of the scuffle and forced the muzzle of the gun toward Clay's face. Clay remembered one of the first judo techniques he learned in college and hoped it would work in real combat. He swept the bottom of his foot into the side of Novak's left ankle simultaneously pulling the left side of his body downward. The technique known as *deashi-barai*, or foot sweep, worked like a charm. Novak fell onto his back, but he didn't loosen his grip on the pistol, pulling Clay down on top of him to the cabin floor. The two men rolled, trying desperately to gain an advantageous position.

A gunshot sounded.

An instant hot sensation seared through Clay's leg, causing the entire right side of his body to go numb. He knew he had been shot because he actually felt the slug pass through his thigh. The pain from the gunshot temporarily canceled out his headache; it felt as if someone took a blow torch to his leg. He screamed in agony.

Sokov pushed open the cockpit door and looked back from the pilot's seat. He said something in Russian and then saw Clay writhing on the floor, holding his bleeding leg.

Novak stood over Clay with the SIG in his hand. "Nothing to worry about, Viktor. I have everything under control, just keep flying the plane," he said in English, so Clay would understand.

"Okay," Sokov said, and closed the cockpit door behind him.

Novak turned his attention back to Clay. "Now, my pesky little friend, do you have any idea how much trouble you have saved me by sneaking on board this plane? And it seems you have what Dr. Sato called Andor's Disease, don't you? Which means your days were numbered anyways. If I would have only known. Well, none of it matters now. Good-bye, my failed experiment."

Clay got up on his knees and instinctively held his hands up. He knew that assuming the universal posture for surrender would accomplish nothing now, but it felt like the right thing to do. Despite the sad fact that his life was about to end, he felt at peace knowing that he did everything he could to stay alive. It just wasn't meant to be, he conceded, and he closed his eyes, waiting for the bullet that would end his life.

He flinched as he heard the loud pop of the gunshot fill the cabin, but oddly, he felt no pain, and he was still alert. In fact, as far as he could tell, he was still on his knees with his hands up. He slowly opened his eyes and saw Novak, standing in front of him, motionless, his eyes looking off into the distance. He teetered for a moment and then fell to the floor's plush carpeting, his head turned to the side and a red puddle forming around his expressionless face.

Kanda kneeled behind Novak in the aisle, holding the Tokarev that had dropped from Novak's belt during the scuffle. He held onto the weapon tightly, pointing it at the space Novak had occupied only seconds before. By the look on his ashen face, it was obvious that he had never shot another human being.

Clay slowly rose to his feet and limped towards his father. With every step, his thigh muscles felt as if they were going to explode, but he was thankful though that his headache was gone, and his bloody nose had stopped, at least for the time being. As he kneeled next to Kanda, he softly pulled the gun from his hands, but the older man didn't let it go. Kanda, his mouth slightly agape and his body trembling, looked at Clay.

"Isao," Kanda said.

"I'm not Isao. My name is Stockton Clay. Can you please give me the gun?"

Kanda let go of the Tokarev. "I am so sorry for what you have gone through. It's all my fault, and I swear that I will make it up to you."

"It's all right. We'll talk about it later. First we need to get this plane back to Tokyo."

"I don't know how to fly. What do you propose we do?" Kanda asked.

"I have no idea, but let me see if we can force the pilot to land it for us," Clay said holding up the Tokarev.

As he straightened, he felt a presence immediately behind him.

"Stockton, behind you," Kanda shouted, but the warning came too late. Before Clay could turn around, something hard and heavy came crashing down on his upper back.

Chapter 50

The force of the blow felt like it came from a sledge-hammer. It just missed the base of Clay's neck; still, it was forceful enough to snap his head back and bend his body over. Luckily, he was able to catch himself on the armrest and swing his body around, hoping to get the pistol around in time to shoot who he knew to be the pilot.

Sokov stood at the ready, his left hand still wrapped in a blood-stained towel. He crouched in a wrestler's stance and intercepted Clay's arm with a fierce cross-body open-hand strike, sending the gun flying through the air. The burley Russian followed it up with a hard right fist to Clay's midsection, knocking every cubic ounce of air out of his body. Clay fell to one knee holding his stomach, with his body doubled over. The blow had temporarily sapped all the strength from Clay's body.

Sokov casually walked to where the Tokarev had landed and picked it up. He winced as he struggled to pull the slide back with his wounded left hand. "You are like a cockroach, you know that? What happened to Oleg?" he asked.

Clay's breathing slowly returned to normal, and he rose to his feet; one hand clutching his stomach. "We gave him an oil change at one-thousand feet. Your buddy is dead as a door nail."

"If he is dead, then he is dead. No big deal. He was going to die soon anyways. You will now join him." Sokov pointed the pistol at Clay's head.

Clay raised his arms and noticed Kanda quietly crawling behind Sokov. Kanda's face was set in determination, looking like that of a Kabuki mask. Whether it was a rapport shared between father and son, Clay wasn't sure, but he felt like he knew what his old man was planning. He needed to stall Sokov.

Clay turned his attention back to his adversary. "Listen, your boss is dead. I could help you make a deal. You're in this for the money, right?"

Sokov raised an eyebrow. "I'm listening."

"The CIA would offer you plenty of cash if you were to let us live. Not to mention the money Kamita Motors would give you for bringing back their president unharmed. Come on, do the smart thing here."

Sokov laughed. "Do you think I'm stupid. The CIA would lock me up before I could get off this plane. And besides, I can sell this technology on the open market and get paid more than your CIA can offer. I've already been secretly dealing with a few organizations who've asked me to steal the files from the Minister's computer. So thank you for your offer, but I must decline. I will keep the gun though. *Dasvidan...*"

Before Sokov could complete his goodbye, Kanda threw himself onto the Russian's back and dug his fingernails into his face. The gun went off, but the shot went high and into the plane's ceiling. As Kanda buried his fingers into Sokov's eye sockets, the Russian screamed, but quickly countered by grabbing Kanda's wrists and throwing him off his back.

Kanda landed with a thud on the carpeted floor.

"You bastard!" Sokov said, as he wiped the blood from

the fresh fingernail marks off his face.

Sokov pointed the gun at Kanda and pulled the trigger.

Kanda grunted as the bullet entered his side, just under his ribcage.

Trying his best to ignore the burning pain in his thigh, Clay sprang towards Sokov with all his might, hurling his body into the Russian's side. He considered going after the SIG that was still in Novak's hand, but decided against it because it would take too long to pry it from the dead man's grip. As Sokov turned around, Clay grabbed the Tokarev and slammed his fist into the bloody towel wrapped around Sokov's left hand, causing him to yelp and send the gun flying down the aisle. As Clay turned to go after it, Sokov slid his right arm around Clay's neck, his left arm over the top of his head, putting him into a tight sleeper choke hold.

The Russian squeezed his forearms together, applying pressure to the sides of Clay's neck, gradually cutting the blood flow to the brain. Immediately, Clay felt consciousness slipping away as Kanda twitched on the carpeted floor. In an act of desperation, Clay grabbed Sokov's thick forearm and pulled down to loosen the choke, but it didn't budge. Sokov kicked at Clay's feet, trying to take him to the ground, but Clay stayed standing, knowing that if he were taken down, he was a goner. If this were a judo match, he would have just tapped on his opponent's body to signal that he was giving up, but there was no tapping out in this contest. It was life or death.

Clay's vision started to go white, but an idea came to him. He lifted his right knee as high as it would go and brought his heel down onto Sokov's foot, crushing his big toe. The Russian let out a scream and loosened his hold on Clay's neck for a split second. It was all the time that he needed. Clay slipped one hand under his opponent's right arm, grabbing it tight, and stepped into his favorite judo throw, *ippon-seoinage,* or shoulder throw.

He bent his knees deep, dropping his torso as low as he could without going all the way down. The pain in his thigh burned like hell, but it wasn't going to stop him. Keeping his back pressed tightly against Sokov's chest and stomach, Clay pulled hard and bent forward. The Russian's body went airborne as it rode onto Clay's back. One final pull and Sokov went flying over his shoulder like a sack of potatoes, crashing onto the cabin floor.

Clay kept a hold of one of Sokov's arms and applied an armbar, or *juji-gatame*, a popular judo submission used in mixed martial arts. Clay lay on his back at a perpendicular angle to Sokov, while he held his opponent's right wrist with both hands, trapping his right arm between his knees. One of Clay's legs rested across the Russian's chest, the other across his face. Sokov was already grimacing from the pressure exerted on his elbow, but Clay wasn't done yet. As he arched his back, he put even more pressure on the joint, and then yanked his hands down, forcing the elbow to bend in the wrong direction. The arm gave out a loud pop, followed by an ear-piercing scream from Sokov. Clay released his grip, got up, and ran to where the Tokarev lay while Sokov squirmed on the floor, holding his dislocated elbow.

"You son of a bitch," the Russian shouted. "You broke

my arm." He slowly got up on his knees, his eyes burning red.

"Don't you dare move," Clay said, pointing the gun at Sokov's chest.

Sokov ignored the warning and jumped forward, prompting Clay to aim low and squeeze the trigger. The bullet entered the Russian's thigh, making a loud snapping sound on impact, causing him to scream and crumble to the floor. From the sound of it, and because the slug didn't come out the other side, Clay was sure the bullet snapped his femur bone.

"Go ahead, you punk. Finish the job," Sokov said as he lay on his stomach, drool dripping from his mouth and blood seeping through his pants.

Keeping his eyes and gun fixed on Sokov, Clay shuffled backwards to Kanda. He kneeled down and propped the old man up, holding Kanda's head in his hands. "Are you all right?" he asked.

Kanda winced, his face pale. "I don't think so."

"Well you better be because if you die, I die." Clay helped Kanda into the nearest seat. "Keep applying pressure to the wound, it'll slow the bleeding."

"What about him?" Kanda asked, pointing to Sokov, who was face down on the floor.

"His arm and leg are broken, and he'll probably pass out soon from the loss of blood, so I don't think he'll be much trouble anymore."

"We should just finish him," Kanda said.

"I'm not a murderer. And like I said, he won't be any

trouble to us now."

Kanda grabbed Clay's shoulders and looked at him with tears streaming from in his eyes. "Let me look at you. I'm so sorry for what has happened. I didn't know until recently of your existence. Novak and Sato kept this information from me. I'm so sorry."

Clay released himself from Kanda's grip. "I still have a million questions for you, but right now, we have more pressing issues to deal with."

"Yes, you're right. So now who's going to land this plane?" Kanda asked, wiping the tears from his face.

"Well, I suppose I'll have to."

"You know how to fly?"

"Not exactly, but I'll figure it out."

Kanda shot him a confused look.

Clay fastened the seatbelt around Kanda's waist, pulled it tight and made his way to the cockpit.

Chapter 51

Stockton Clay entered the cockpit of the KamitaJet and stared wide-eyed at the sight in front of him. While the average automobile possessed a dozen or so controls, the large touchscreen panels that graced this jet plane seemed to access a million different functions. He was somewhat familiar with the cockpit of the KamitaJet from playing it on his flight simulation program at home, but he never imagined in his wildest dreams that he would ever take the controls of a real version of the aircraft. The even hum of the jet engines filled the cabin, as he sat down in the pilot's chair and surveyed his surroundings. The general design of the KamitaJet's cockpit was similar to those of luxury sports automobiles: sticking out in front of him was the yoke that looked like a Formula One steering wheel; the Electronic Flight Instrument System, or EFIS, and the Engine Monitoring System on the co-pilot's side dominated the main panel, with the navigation display monitor set in between them, and on top of the displays were a row of switches and knobs.

The base of the center console housed the throttle levers, as well as a couple of touch-pad screens and a dozen more knobs and switches. Clay looked out the front windshield and saw only blue sky. The plane seemed like it was flying steadily, which meant that it was on automatic pilot. The fuel warning light was already flashing, so he quickly got to work, strapping himself in and putting the headset on. Reaching for the button on the console, he switched on the radio.

"Hello, can anyone hear me. This is KamitaJet 025, we're very low on fuel, and we need to make an emergency landing."

He waited, but heard only static. No response.

He repeated the message, and added at the end, "Mayday. Mayday."

A voice crackled in the earpiece. "This is Fuji Speedway Airfield. I'm the traffic controller, Katsuyuki Suzuki. I hear you. I don't know who you are or why people were shooting at you, but I've called the police, just so you know."

"Roger that, but I'm pretty much out of fuel and requesting an emergency landing," Clay said as he closed his eyes and took long controlled breaths. He could feel his heart beating rapidly.

"Please be prepared to turn yourself in as soon as you land," Suzuki said.

"That's fine. I don't have time to explain, but I'm not the bad guy. I've been able to take over the plane, and I need help now to get it down."

"I see. Takano-san and the other man flew off in the helicopter, presumably after you. I'm going to clear them out of the way. Hold on."

Clay heard a click and then static. As he softly ran his hands over the handles of the control wheel, he checked the plane's altitude, speed, and heading.

Another click in his earpiece signaled Suzuki's return. "You're clear to land. The wind is strong, thirty knots from zero-three-zero...I mean blowing northeast, so come around over the golf course."

"I've never flown a real plane before, so I'm gonna need a little help," Clay said.

There was no response from the other end.

"Hello, Fuji? Can you hear me?" Clay repeated.

The pitch in Suzuki's voice was an octave higher than before. "What do you mean you've never flown a plane before? Do you have any experience with aircrafts at all?"

"Does three hundred hours on X-Pilot count?"

Another pause. "*Maji*?" Suzuki said, an informal way of saying "Are you serious?" in Japanese.

Although Clay didn't understand the word, he got a gist of its meaning. "Sorry man, but it's all I got."

"Well, lots of experience on a flight simulation program is better than nothing. I learned a lot about flying myself on X-Pilot before I got my license. Did you ever fly this type of plane on your computer?"

"Yes, more than a few times. I think I know where all the key controls are."

"Good. Almost everything is the same as on X-Pilot, but the main difference is you'll feel the gs and turbulence. So when you do, don't freak out, okay?"

"Roger."

"How low on fuel are you?" Suzuki asked.

Clay looked at both fuel gauges, the digital needles were near zero. "Pretty much empty. The fuel-warning light's been on for a while."

"Please turn off the auto pilot," Suzuki said.

"We're not going to land using the auto pilot?"

"You would have to program an entirely new set of variables to compensate for the plane's current condition and the strong wind, and there's no time for that. And I'll need you on the controls in case you do run out of fuel in mid-air."

"Roger," Clay said as he switched the plane to manual control. Immediately, he felt the yoke become heavier, as the plane slightly tilted to one side.

"Turn right zero-four-zero and slowly push the yoke forward, then hold it steady when the descent rate shows seven hundred feet per minute—you can find this info in the lower left-hand corner of the display in front of you," Suzuki said.

Clay did what he was told and banked the plane right until he could see that the artificial horizon on the screen showed that he had achieved the ideal thirty-degree banked turn—something he had learned from his many hours on the flight sim—before leveling off on the zero-four-zero heading. The nose dipped downward. His tightening stomach confirmed the drop in altitude.

"You are doing great. Keep your speed and rate of descent steady."

"Shouldn't I lower the landing gear now?" Clay asked.

"Negative. We'll wait. We want to keep the plane as clean as possible; it'll save fuel."

"I don't see anything out the windows yet."

"Stay calm. You're almost home. The runway should become visible soon," Suzuki said.

Clay stretched his neck and looked down the front of the plane's nose. Suzuki was right, the runway was visible, but it looked like a white and gray speck on the vast forested landscape below. "Yes, I can see it, but I don't think I can do this."

"Yes, you can. It's just like X-Pilot, no different. Now lower the landing gears."

Clay activated the landing gear control. He heard the mechanical sounds of the contraptions activate. "Okay, they're down..."

Before he could finish his sentence, the plane shook violently as it hit a small pocket of bad air. Then the hum of the engines died down as the plane's nose dipped. The engines went totally silent, and the main monitors flashed bright red warning signs, accompanied by a loud beep.

"Oh shit. I just lost the engines. We're dropping fast."

"At your current rate of speed, you'll be able to glide for a few hundred yards. Move the flaps down to the "approach" setting—this will help the wing create a little more lift while scrubbing off some speed and getting you to the ideal glide angle. Do you read? You're going to make a dead-stick landing."

"I'm not going to make it."

"Get the goddam flaps down and keep the nose steady," Suzuki said.

Clay furiously worked the flaps and pushed on the yoke. He felt a tickle under his nose, and knew blood was dripping down the front of his face. Oddly, he didn't experience any sort of headache, but he did feel a "pop" in his right temple, as if someone with thick fingers had just flicked him there extra hard. From the warm sensation on his cheek and jaw, he knew blood was running down the side of his face, probably from a popped vessel. The disease had finally reached its final stages, but he hardly gave it a second thought, as his mind was focused on the quickly approaching runway.

The plane dropped like a falling brick, making Clay feel he was in a freefall. The ground was nearly in his face and closing.

"I'm coming in too fast. I'm going in," Clay said.

"Pull up. Pull up." Suzuki shouted.

The KamitaJet slammed into the ground, belly first, just short of the runway, kicking up brown dirt a hundred feet into the air. Clay's vision was instantly blocked by rocks and dirt hitting the windshield, but miraculously, the Lexan glass held. The sound at impact was like a bomb detonating right next to his ear, as he instinctively curled into a ball, his arms and legs tucked in, his eyes shut tight, and the safety belt straps digging into his skin. The plane bounced once and when it came down again, the landing gears snapped like twigs, sending the dislodged tires flying in different directions across the airport. One of the broken landing-gear struts dug into the soft dirt, spinning the plane sideways and causing it to temporarily slide onto the asphalt before resuming its uncontrolled skid onto the dirt shoulder. The seatbelts ate into Clay's flesh as his body was thrown about in the seat. The jet's left wing caught the metal restraining fence next to the runway and lifted the opposite side of the aircraft straight up into the air. The plane hovered on its side, seeming as if it were deciding whether to go all the way over and land on its roof or return to an upright position. It chose the latter, as its underbody crashed back onto the dirt, snapping the wing completely in half. The yoke came loose and hit Clay's chest like a freight truck, as a panel from the ceiling came down and caught the side of his head.

A thick cloud of dust gradually settled around the downed KamitaJet that sat motionless a hundred yards from the runway with half of its fuselage in a neighboring rice field. Through the cracked windshield, Clay thought he saw farm workers rushing out of a nearby shack to see the aftermath of what was probably their first live plane crash. He heard a helicopter landing close by, and then everything went black.

Chapter 52

Clay saw the white light. It was bright and burned his eyes. He was expecting it to suck him into heaven—for he didn't think he did anything so bad as to be cast into hell, at least he hoped not—but nothing happened. As the focus gradually returned to his vision, he realized that the white glow originated from a row of fluorescent lights hanging from the ceiling of a small hospital room. Was he still alive? But he couldn't be. Even if by some miracle, the plane crash didn't kill him, the disease—which he was fairly certain had entered its final stage—would have. So, what the hell was he doing on a soft bed in a brightly lit hospital room?

He tried to get up, but couldn't, so he looked down to see if his arms were strapped to the bed, in the same way doctors secured mentally-ill patients, but there were no restraints of any kind; he was simply too weak to move. His right arm was hooked up to an I.V. drip, and there was an electronic monitor on a metal stand next to it that registered his vitals, beeping every second. To his side was a vase full of violets on a wooden nightstand. A single folding chair sat unoccupied across the bed.

The door to his room creaked as it opened. It was a nurse—in fact, it was the same woman who tended to him inside the Yamamoto Private Clinic hours before. She held a metal clipboard in one hand and didn't even look over at him as she walked to the vital signs patient monitor to check his status. Satisfied by what she saw, she scribbled some numbers down on a sheet of paper on the clipboard.

"Where am I?" Clay said in a crackling voice. His mouth and throat suddenly felt bone dry.

The nurse looked over at him with a surprised look. "You're not supposed to wake up for another three hours."

"Can you tell me where I am?"

"You are back in the Yamamoto Clinic, in one of our private recovery rooms. Please wait, I will call the doctor. He has asked to see you as soon as you awoke." She left the room as quickly as she entered, leaving the door ajar. At least she wasn't playing with her smart phone, Clay thought.

A few seconds later, George Nakajima walked in, wearing a white lab coat and a stethoscope around his neck. He held the same metal clipboard. "I must say, you are one tough customer. How are you feeling?" he asked as he studied Clay's vitals through his thick glasses.

"I don't know. What happened?"

"Roberts and Maki brought you here by helicopter right after pulling you out of the wrecked plane. You suffered some minor injuries from the crash—a broken wrist and fractured ribs, not to mention a gunshot wound to your leg. More important, your disease was in its final stage, but we were able to treat it just in the nick of time," Nakajima said.

Clay gradually felt his strength returning, and he slowly propped himself up against the metal headboard of the bed. He touched his head, which he noticed was heavily bandaged. His right wrist was in a light cast. "What do you mean you were able to treat it?" he asked.

"Stockton, we performed the transfusion. It was a success."

"So what are you saying, George? Am I going to live?"

Nakajima grinned from ear to ear. "Yes, Stockton. We successfully introduced Kanda-san's cells into your system, and the nanobots are leaving your healthy cells alone. You made it, Stockton. You made it."

The words hit Clay like a hard slap to the face. His eyes watered. "Where's Maki?" he asked.

Nakajima pointed over his shoulder with his thumb. "She's in the waiting room, sleeping. It's three in the morning now, and she hasn't left the building since they brought you in."

"How long have I been out?"

"A day. Well, actually, a day and a half."

"And Mr. Kanda, how's he?"

Nakajima's face suddenly turned grave. "He's in the room down the hall, but he's in very bad shape. He lost a lot of blood from a gunshot wound, and he has massive organ injuries. But I want you to know that even in his weakened state, he wanted us to go through with the transfusion to save your life."

"Can't my nanobots help him?"

"It's too late for that, I'm afraid. He's past the point of no return, and we can't extract enough bots from you anyways."

"Can I see him?"

Nakajima rubbed his jaw. "I don't know about that. You're in no shape to get out of bed, and he's still unconscious. And even if he was awake, he wouldn't have the energy to speak."

Clay winced in pain as he twisted his body on the bed so his feet dangled to the floor. "Take me to him, George. Please."

Nakajima put his hands on his hips and looked disapprovingly at Clay. He then relaxed his shoulders and grabbed Clay's arm, helping him off the bed. "You are a determined son of a bitch, you know that?"

After Clay slid off the bed, he leaned on the doctor, taking one slow step after another out of the room. Pain shot through his wounded leg when he put the slightest bit of pressure on it, and he had trouble taking deep breaths—his lungs felt as though they were going to explode every time he inhaled. The lights to the narrow, clean hallway were lit, but not a sound was to be heard except for Nakajima's soft footsteps and Clay's slippers sliding on the linoleum floor. Nakajima led him to a room two doors down and entered without knocking. The lights were dimmed, and Clay could see a vital signs monitor, which beeped every few seconds, next to a slightly inclined bed where Kanda lay. Clay dropped onto a stool next to the bed, grunting from the sharp pain in his midsection.

"Where is everyone?" Clay asked.

"Agent Roberts has placed a strict moratorium on visitations. Only Mrs. Kanda and their son have been allowed to come, and they're resting upstairs in a guest facility," Nakajima said. "Be careful you don't aggravate your injuries. I'll be back in a few minutes. If he comes to, shout for me. I'll be down the hall, so I'll be able to hear you." He left the room, leaving the door halfway open.

Clay couldn't make out Kanda's entire face because of a breathing tube hooked up to his nose, but he didn't see much by way of resemblance to the old man.

"I don't even know what I should say to you," he said.

Clay noticed Kanda's index finger twitch. He stared at the hand, wondering if it was some kind of unconscious reflex or just his imagination.

"Stockton," Kanda said in a low hoarse voice. The old man gazed at him through half open eyes.

Clay nearly fell off the stool. "Whoa shit, you're awake. I'll call George right away,"

"No, please. Don't call anyone. I want to be with you, just you," Kanda said, raising his hand ever so slightly off the bed.

Clay sensed a deep earnestness in Kanda's tone and sat back in his chair. "Thank you for agreeing to help me with the transfusion."

Kanda spoke between short laboring breaths. "Of course. I would do anything to save my son. I am so sorry this happened. I hope that you can forgive me someday."

Clay bit his lip. "I know you did it to save my life, so I don't blame you. I'm appreciative. But the fact that I will never know my real mother really makes me sad."

"Victoria was the loveliest creature on Earth. So beautiful, so warm. She was passionate about life, and she had the kind of aura that lit up a room when she entered. I see a lot of her in your eyes, Stockton. It's time I went to your mother and asked for her forgiveness for what I have done," Kanda said.

Clay softly put his hand on Kanda's. "Don't talk like that. You're going to make it through this."

Kanda's face relaxed, as the corner of his mouth curled into a smile. "Thank you, Stockton. I am so lucky to have had you for a son. I only wish I got to see you grow up. Knowing that you are alive has truly made my life worthwhile, and thank you for helping Kenji." He gasped for air and coughed.

"Hang on, pops, I'm going to get George," Clay said.

"Goodbye, Stockton," he said as he closed his eyes and exhaled for the last time.

"Hey, don't..." Clay looked down at Kanda's face and noticed a tear had dropped from the corner of the old man's eye. The reading on the EKG monitor flat-lined, and the incessant beeping stopped, replaced by an even hum.

Clay sat motionless for several minutes, gazing at his father's face, and then wiped his own teary eyes. He didn't look up when someone stepped into the room.

"I was monitoring his condition remotely from down the hall. I'm sorry Stockton," Nakajima said as he walked up and put his hand on Clay's shoulder. He then checked Kanda's pulse and examined each pupil. Once he visually confirmed that he was no longer alive, he covered his face with a square piece of white cloth and noted the time of death on a clipboard hanging from the edge of the bed.

"I think he died in peace. And you guys were able to cure Kenji?" Clay asked.

"Yes, but it's you who truly saved him, Stockton. The nanotechnology is working."

"That's great. I'm so glad he's going to be all right."

Nakajima glanced at his wristwatch. "Would you like for me to get Ms. Takano? I'm sure she would be very glad to see you."

Clay thought about it for a moment and shook his head. "Nah, let her sleep. I'd like to be alone right now."

"Understood. Now let's get you back to your room, and I must notify Mrs. Kanda."

"Thanks, George," Clay said as he stood up slowly and leaned on Nakajima's shoulder.

Once they reached Clay's bed, Nakajima tucked him in like a father tucked in his son. "Get some rest," he said, before leaving the room.

As Clay dropped his head down on the soft pillow, his thoughts quickly turned to Maki. He wanted to see her badly, but was still wary about revealing his true feelings for her. The mere thought of rejection made his heart ache. But now that he was going to live, what should he do? The answer was simple, he would tell her at the first opportunity; he intended to keep the promise he made to himself that he wasn't going to return to the old Stockton Clay, the one who lived life in a shell.

He felt a tinge of excitement as he looked forward to what the next few weeks, the next few years, would bring. Nothing would ever be the same as before, of that he was sure, and he looked forward to the moment he returned to his home in America with a fresh perspective on life, reborn and ready to live life for all it was worth. He felt grateful to Kanda. Now, more than ever, he didn't want to waste this life that had been given to him. As he contemplated his future, his eyelids grew heavy. He searched for the switch to dim the lights, but before he could locate it, he was fast asleep.

Chapter 53

Clay sat up in his bed when Andrew Roberts came into his hospital room, holding a large, thick cell phone, a model he had never seen before. He was dressed in his usual loose blue suit, with the top button of his dress shirt undone. His curly red hair bounced with each step.

"How you feelin'?" Roberts asked.

Clay touched the thick bandage wrap that covered his ribs under his hospital gown. "Pretty sore."

Roberts took a seat in a chair next to the bed. "I gotta tell ya, I don't think in all my years in the Company have I seen a looser cannon than you. Still, you saved us a lot of trouble, and created some too, but all in all, I gotta commend your bravery. If you ever get tired of being an automotive writer, let's talk."

Clay laughed, and winced at the pain it caused. "I don't know if I could do what you do for a living."

Roberts handed him the cell phone. "This is a secure phone for you to call your parents. You do remember what Wong told you earlier, yeah? About what you can and can't say."

Clay nodded. "I think so. Let's see, don't mention anything about nanotechnology, cures to cancer, nothing about the CIA; nothing about the Russians…"

Roberts broke in. "Right, right. I'll be sitting here anyways. Hit the green button, the number has already been inputted, and we know that at least one of your parents is home."

Clay flashed Roberts a suspicious look, took the phone, and pressed the button.

JoAnne Clay picked up on the third ring. "Hello?" she said.

"It's me, mom."

"Stockton! We were so worried because we haven't heard from you. So how did the interview go? Did you get the job?"

Clay eyed Roberts, who sat watching him intently. "Mom, it wasn't exactly for an interview. Is Dad there?"

"No, he just took the truck to the shop. I keep telling him to buy a new one, but he says that the one he wants is way overpriced. Sometimes, he's too frugal for his own good, that man."

Clay laughed, and grimaced as he put his hand to his ribs. "Mom, please listen. I just found out who my real father is."

There was a long pause, followed by a soft response just over a whisper. "What?"

"His name was Tetsuro Kanda, the president of Kamita Motors. That's why I'm here in Japan. He found out about me and flew me out here to meet me. I'm sorry I didn't tell you right away."

JoAnne said nothing, so Stockton continued.

"But I didn't get to meet him. He died in a plane crash a few days ago. It should've been on the news. I was waiting for him in a hotel when it happened." Stockton felt a tinge of guilt for lying.

Roberts nodded and gave him a thumbs-up sign.

"Your father and I haven't been watching any television lately. We had no idea," JoAnne finally said.

"Mr. Kanda was assisting the police with some kind of investigation, so they asked to keep my relationship with him quiet for now, so don't tell anyone except Dad, okay?"

Clay could hear his mother gasp. "Are you all right?"

"Yes, I'm fine. Listen I need to go…"

JoAnne cut him off. "Do you know who gave birth to you?"

Clay was taken aback by the directness in his mom's voice.

"No. It seemed I was the result of a fling a long time ago, and Mr. Kanda's assistant, the person who reached out to me, told me she could not be located. Sorry mom, I guess I didn't come from royal blood, but I did come from a powerful tycoon. I'll tell you more when I get home okay?"

Clay heard the distinct sound of his mother sobbing through the earpiece.

"Mom, don't cry. It's a good thing, really. I finally know my roots. And you know that nothing will change between you, me, and dad. I will always be your son."

"I know, Stockton. I just really miss you, and I want you to come home."

"I'm flying back in a couple of days. I love you. And tell Dad I love him too. I can't wait to see you guys." Clay wiped the tears welling in his eyes before they had a chance to fall. He pushed the end call button and handed the phone back to Roberts.

"They seem like great people," Roberts said.

"Yeah, they're the best."

Roberts stood up. "Right, and you can tell them when you get back that your injuries were suffered when you took one of their cars for a test run. Me or someone else will be in touch if there's any more we need to add to our story. If I don't see you again, take care buddy." He thrust his right hand out towards Clay.

Clay took it and gripped it hard. Roberts gave him a wink and headed for the door.

"Andrew," Clay called out.

Roberts did a one-eighty. "Yo."

"Thanks for everything."

"You're giving me too much credit. Who you need to thank are George and Maki. They're the ones who had your back the whole time," he said, and he walked out of the room.

Chapter 54

Dressed in a light blue patient's gown, Stockton Clay limped into the shower stall and turned on both hot and cold knobs to full. He sat on the shower seat and removed his waterproof bandage around his thigh. Six days had passed since the plane crash, and the bullet wound was healing quickly; he could now get around without a wheelchair or crutches. His bad wrist and cracked ribs made climbing out of bed a chore, but those injuries were also getting better by the day. The warm water felt good as it caressed his stiff body. After soaking under the strong shower spray for fifteen minutes, he toweled off, brushed his teeth, and contemplated what he would wear for his return to the world. The television was set to CNN where Clay watched the news of Kanda's death in an "accidental plane crash" over and over the past few days. One part of him felt sad from losing the man responsible for his existence, but another felt pride, knowing that his father was heralded by so many as one of the most successful businessmen in the world. He hoped that some of those talents trickled down to him.

Clay had just finished putting on his T-shirt and jeans when he heard a soft knock on the door.

"Come in," he said.

Maki Takano entered, wearing a black kimono and her hair done up in a small bun. She wore light makeup that made her alabaster skin glow pink around the cheeks, and accentuated her ruby red lips and large hazel eyes. There was something to be said about a woman in a kimono, how it exuded a quiet sexiness that could drive men crazy—he now knew why geishas were so popular in Japan. She held a brown garment bag in her arms.

Clay hadn't seen her since she visited him after the plane crash. "Aren't you a sight for sore eyes. I was wondering where you've been."

Maki hung the bag on a metal hook behind the door. "I'm sorry Stockton, but it's been incredibly busy the last few days. We're cleaning up, so all of us have been working around the clock to close up our operation. All it takes is one curious journalist, and everything can go public. We need to be thorough. Andrew flew back to Langley yesterday to brief the DD."

"I understand," Clay said. "Are you dressed up for Mr. Kanda's funeral?"

"Yes, I do hate wearing these things. They really restrict your movement. Have you been able to speak with your parents?"

Clay sat down on his bed. "Yeah, Andrew set it up for me the other day."

"Just so you know, Andrew sent Russell Whitaker to visit your parents yesterday to ask them to keep the information about you and Kanda-san secret because of an ongoing investigation into Kamita Motors. They were very cooperative and didn't ask too many questions."

"It wasn't necessary. My parents wouldn't have said anything."

"Your dad understood right away, but Russell did say that your mother kept saying she didn't trust him or the CIA."

Clay smiled as he pictured his mom harassing Agent Whitaker. He envisioned her standing in front of him, with her hands on her hips, preaching about how unethical some of their methods were. "Yeah, my mom worries a lot. But you can trust her; deep down, she loves our country."

Maki studied Clay's wardrobe with a frown on her face. "You weren't thinking of wearing that to the memorial service, were you?"

Clay looked down at his white T-shirt and jeans. "It's all I have."

"I figured as much, so I brought you some clothes. They're yours to keep, compliments of the U.S. government. And I spoke with Nena. She said you're on the guest list, so just tell them your name at the reception desk. Oh, and just so you know, we told her that you're Mr. Kanda's son, and that he only found out about you recently, which is actually true."

Clay looked at the black bag. "Thanks for the clothes, but I was hoping that we could go to Kanda-san's funeral together."

Maki sat down in the chair in front of him. "We can't be seen together in Japan for a while, Stockton. We need to keep a low profile for a bit longer. So far, we've been lucky that the real story hasn't leaked to the media. Thank goodness that the Japanese police agreed to cooperate with us."

"What about the air traffic controller?" Clay asked. "He saw everything."

"We had no choice but to reveal my involvement with the CIA to Katsu Suzuki, but he promised to keep quiet. So, the plan for me is to report to work at Kamita Motors for another month and then turn in my two weeks' notice. But we will meet again, I promise you that, and probably sooner than you expect."

"Maki, you're the most amazing person I have ever met," Clay said in a confident, even tone. "My life would not be complete without you."

There, he said it, and he couldn't believe how naturally it came out. His heart beat faster and his palms began to sweat. He nervously rubbed his hands together as he looked all about the room, everywhere but in Maki's direction.

Maki's pink cheeks became a shade darker. She stood up and held Clay's face with both hands. She closed her eyes and softly kissed him on the lips. "You're so sweet. And my real name isn't Maki."

Clay sat motionless, his face and body numb. Maki turned and headed for the door. "Wait," he said when he snapped out of his trance. "Maki Takano's not your real name?"

She shook her head. "Of course not. You wouldn't expect an undercover agent to use her real name, would you?"

"Can I ask what it is?"

She walked back to where Clay sat and leaned forward, placing her lips next to his left ear. She whispered, "My real name is Rina Akiyama. But keep it a secret."

"Rina Akiyama…I like it," Clay said.

"See you around." She gave him a wink and stepped out of the room.

For a good minute, Clay sat there with his eyes fixated

on the shut door. He was certain that he would never in his life find a more captivating and beautiful woman, and he hoped in his heart of hearts that she meant what she said about meeting again. While he was sad to see her go, he was excited about the kiss, the first one he had scored in a very long time, and he was ecstatic that he was able to reveal how he felt about her. The pressure was now off.

Clay stepped off the bed and limped over to the garment bag hanging against the door. He unzipped it and pulled out a brand new black slim-fit Calvin Klein suit, a white dress shirt, and black tie. A pair of shiny black wingtip shoes was stored in a separate pocket. He ran his hand over the smooth, cool material of the wool jacket. He changed as quickly as he could, but found it difficult to slide the necktie under his shirt collar because of the soreness in his neck and bad wrist, so he decided to ditch it. He checked himself out in a full-length mirror on the bathroom wall; the suit fit him like a glove. He hardly recognized himself, but he liked the way he looked: his hair slicked back still wet from the shower, a three-day old beard providing just the right amount of ruggedness to his face.

A loud knock on the door interrupted his thoughts.

"Come in," he said, hoping that it was Maki. To his disappointment, a lean Japanese man, with short straight hair, wearing a casual green button-down shirt and khaki slacks, entered.

"Are you Stockton Clay?" the man asked in a slight Japanese accent.

Clay recognized the face and voice, but couldn't place

them immediately. "Yes. I am. I'm sorry, I can't remember…..

"It's me. I'm the air traffic controller that helped you land the plane. Well, sort of land it, anyways. My name is Katsuyuki Suzuki."

It came back to him now. This was the man who met him at the airfield, and his voice was unmistakably the one that shouted instructions to him in his earpiece. Clay owed him his life. He stepped up to Suzuki and gave him a big hug. "Thank you, Mr. Suzuki. I'm so glad you came."

Suzuki kept his arms to his sides. "No, I only did my job. It was you who was extraordinary."

"Rubbish," Clay said, letting go of the smaller man. "Did you come all the way from Fuji just to visit me?"

"Well, yes and no. I'm on my way to New York tomorrow, so I thought I would stop by and meet you face to face. Ms. Takano told me you were here, but don't worry, I didn't tell anyone I was coming."

"Yes. I'm still not sure what happened. Doctors said I have a little amnesia." Clay made the last part up, not knowing how much the CIA had told Suzuki.

"I'm so glad you survived that crash."

"Are you going to New York for vacation?" Clay asked.

Suzuki shook his head. "No, I quit my job at the airport, and I am going to help my friend's restaurant in New York."

"What? You're quitting your job? Why? You're like the best air traffic controller in the world."

Suzuki grinned. "After our incredible experience, how can I ever top that? It would all be downhill. The best of luck to you, Clay-san," he said. "I will never forget you."

"You too."

Suzuki bowed deeply and saw himself out of the room. Clay wanted to talk to him more, perhaps ask him for his contact information, so they could keep in touch. But he decided to just let him go; if they were meant to meet again, he knew Fate had a funny way of making it happen. And he was counting on Fate to help bring him together again with Maki.

Chapter 55

Hundreds of people crowded the entrance to the Shimbashi Enbujo Playhouse in Tokyo to pay their final respects to one of the most influential Japanese industrialists of their generation. The guest list was a who's who in the automotive world, as many company executives and some politicians traveled from abroad to attend the memorial service. While many public funerals were held in shrines, no temple in Tokyo could handle the number of guests expected at Kanda's service, so the city opted to use the playhouse. Most of the people wore dark suits and dresses, while a few donned hakamas and kimonos, the traditional Japanese attire for formal gatherings. Clay's taxi pulled up to the entrance of the facility, stopping alongside an NHK news van.

The playhouse itself was a large rectangular building made of red brick. It took up an entire block—seating capacity was fifteen hundred people—with the front entrance facing the main street. Dozens of black stretch limousines were parked all around the area.

Clay took his time getting out of the car, being careful not to put too much weight on his sore leg. He limped over to a long wooden table where he signed his name in an open booklet before cuing in a long line that entered the playhouse. Nena and Kenji stood at the front entrance, greeting every guest who walked by to pay their respects to the widow and only son.

Nena wore a black dress and held a white silk handkerchief damp with tears, while Kenji, wearing a black suit, stood alongside her holding her hand. When Clay reached the two, he bowed to the widow, as the people in front of him in line had done. Nena leaned forward and whispered, "Thank you for coming. Maki told me who you really are, and I'm so sorry for all that you have been through. Tetsu would have been happy that you came."

"Thank you," was all Clay could think of saying. He stepped over to Kenji, to whom he flashed a friendly wink. Kenji smiled back.

Clay followed the crowd into the playhouse, where most of the invited guests had already taken their seats. There was a grand stage up front, which usually hosted the latest musical or play, covered with white chrysanthemums. A poster-sized framed photo of Tetsuro Kanda, wearing a suit and tie and a wide smile on his face, hung from the ceiling. To either side were dozens of flower stands and large banners with kanji characters.

Clay found a row of empty seats near the back of the playhouse and made his way towards the middle of the row, where he flipped down a red cushioned seat bottom and sat down. On the armrest was a small translation device with the option of English, Spanish, French, Chinese, and Russian, connected to a cheap headphone, which Clay put on. As soon as he did so, a middle-aged Japanese man, with salt-and-pepper hair, dressed in a navy suit, and a small round gold pin stuck to his lapel, walked up to him.

"Is this seat taken?" he asked in English.

"No, please," answered Clay, gesturing with his hand that the seat was unoccupied.

The man sat down next to Clay, reached into his jacket pocket and pulled out a business card. "Are you Mister Stockton Clay?" he asked.

Clay eyed the man suspiciously, studying his face carefully. "I'm sorry, who are you?" he asked.

"My name is Kunio Seki. I am the attorney who represents Mr. Kanda and his family. We request your presence this afternoon at two o'clock at our offices in Ginza. Mrs. Kanda and her son will also be present," he said.

Clay took the business card. "What's all this about?" he asked.

"We will disclose everything at our meeting."

"I'm not in any trouble, am I?" Clay asked.

Seki laughed. "No, Mr. Clay, most certainly not. You're…"

The lawyer's words were cut off by light violin music that signaled the start of the ceremony.

Clay looked at the photo of Kanda and couldn't help but see how happy he looked in it. Under the photo were large kanji letters. He leaned over to Seki and whispered, "What does that say under his photo?"

"That's his name. Kanda is a somewhat common surname in Japan, but those characters can also be pronounced Kamita. Kanda-san's grandfather thought 'Kamita' had a nicer international ring to it so that's what he named his company," Seki said.

"I didn't know that. Do they mean anything?"

"I suppose the direct translation is 'God's Field.'"

Clay thought about the irony of it all for a moment.

The lights went down in the arena and a Shinto priest appeared from a side entrance. He sat on the floor in front of the stage and began chanting. The entire ceremony lasted about an hour and a half, with a few dignitaries, including the mayor of Tokyo, taking turns onstage to say a few things about the man being remembered. Clay listened carefully to each word uttered about his father, and couldn't help but feel a wave of pride.

After the service, Seki stood up and straightened his suit. "I will see you in a few hours at my office. There's a limousine outside for you. The driver will be holding a placard with my firm's name on it. Tell him who you are, and he will take you wherever you want to go and bring you to my offices in time for our meeting. He'll also drive you back to the hospital afterwards. He speaks good English."

"Okay. Thank you," Clay said.

"See you later." The lawyer bowed and made his way out of the building.

Clay searched the arena for Maki, but he couldn't locate her among the hundreds of people in attendance. He took his time leaving the facility, scanning the playhouse for her familiar face, but she was nowhere to be seen. When he stepped outside, he immediately found the man holding a sign that read "Seki and Associates, Attorneys at Law."

"I'm Stockton Clay. Mr. Seki told me you're giving me a lift."

The driver tipped his hat and bowed curtly. "Yes, sir. Where can I take you?"

Clay checked his G-Shock watch. "Can we just drive

around the city before heading to the meeting?" he asked.

"Of course, sir." The driver opened the rear door of the black Kamita Presidente and stepped to the side.

"Oh, and can we stop at a Yoshinoya? I'm famished."

"Of course, sir. Mr. Seki said to treat you to anything you like, so if you'd like, we can stop for something a bit, um, fancier."

"No, Yoshinoya is fine." Clay stepped into the rear seat. The driver took his position and pulled the sedan away from the sidewalk. Through the window, he spotted Maki along the side of the playhouse, bowing to various important-looking people.

"Can you stop the car?" Clay asked.

"Yes sir," the driver said as he scanned the street for a place to park.

"You know what, never mind," Clay said.

"Are you sure, sir?"

"Yeah, I'm sure." Clay remembered Maki mentioning that they should not be seen together in public. The last thing he wanted to do was cause trouble for her.

The car turned the corner and sped onto the main thoroughfare. Clay watched the glorious skyscrapers and crowds of pedestrians on the sidewalks blur by. He was smack dab in the middle of one of the most populated cities in the civilized world, yet to him, without Maki at his side, it felt like the emptiest place on earth.

Chapter 56

The black Kamita limousine stopped in front of one of many high-rise buildings in the Ginza ward, known as the Beverly Hills of Tokyo and also home to Kamita Motors' global headquarters. Clay marveled at the number of luxury shops and fancy restaurants that lined the streets.

The tops of the tallest buildings were covered by low gray clouds as a light rain fell on the city. Clay exited the limousine and pulled his jacket over his head, as he limped over to the thirty-story Nakasone Building in the first district, a few miles away from Kamita's main offices.

He took the elevator to the top level, where Kunio Seki's law offices occupied the entire floor. A twenty-something woman with medium-length dyed brown hair and wearing a neat black suit, welcomed Clay with a smile. She escorted him through a short hallway that ended with large double doors. The place had an old-school feel to it, with dark brown wood covering the doors and the floor, and expensive looking oil paintings lined the hallways. The receptionist pushed open the double doors without knocking and gestured for him to enter. Seki's office was enormous, with classic Western-style furniture and a large window that looked out toward the Sumida River.

The senior partner of one of the most prestigious law firms in Japan sat regally behind a high mahogany desk, speaking with Nena Larsson-Kanda while Kenji looked on from a seat next to hers. Nena was still dressed in her black dress, and Kenji sported his pint-size black suit.

"Ah, Mr. Clay. Please have a seat," Seki said in perfect English.

Clay sat down in the chair next to Nena and waved. "Hello again," he said.

Nena replied with a curt nod of her head. Seeing her up close, Clay thought she appeared emotionally exhausted, with discolored bags under her eyes and makeup that was slightly smudged in places—telling signs that she had spent the past few days mostly crying and without much sleep.

"I know your time is valuable, so I will get straight to the point," Seki addressed all three of his guests. "I've called you here today to go over Mr. Kanda's will. You three are the sole beneficiaries."

Clay perked up in his chair. The thought of inheriting Kanda's money had never occurred to him. "There must be some mistake. I don't know how I could be part of this conversation," he said.

"While you were unconscious, Mr. Kanda called me from the hospital and, at his insistence, we redrafted his will. This was several hours before he passed away," Seki explained.

Nena placed her hand on Clay's arm. "Stockton, Tetsu and Maki told me that you are his son, and how he didn't know of your existence until recently. Please hear Mr. Seki out."

"Um, yeah, sure," Clay answered.

Seki opened a folder on his desk and read from a single piece of paper. "Mr. Kanda has sold all of his interests in Kamita Motors to the shareholders, so none of you have any rights or association with the company from this day on. After the sale of his shares and the subsequent liquidation of his assets, his personal wealth came to three-hundred-million, two-hundred-and-four-thousand and sixty-three U.S. dollars. He leaves eighty percent of this sum to Nena Larsson-Kanda and Kenji Kanda, the latter who will take possession of seventy-five percent of that total when he turns twenty-five years old. The remaining twenty percent of the total will go to Mr. Stockton Clay immediately."

The lawyer closed the folder on his desk.

After a brief pause, Clay cupped his non-bandaged hand to his ear. "I'm sorry. What did you just say? How much did you say was left to me?"

"Twenty percent," Seki replied.

"How, how much does that come to?"

"That would be sixty million, four-thousand-and-eighty-one dollars, U.S.," Seki answered. "And minus about twenty percent for the tax man."

Clay stopped breathing. With his eyes wide open, he stared at Seki. "I'm sorry. You're telling me that I have sixty million dollars, minus the tax, that I can do whatever I want with?"

"It's your money, so yes," the attorney responded.

Clay's jaw dropped. He looked around the room, half-expecting one of them to say, "Fooled you," but no one did. He turned to Nena. "Is all of this all right with you, Mrs. Kanda? I mean, this is way more than I'll ever need, and I don't think I deserve even a penny."

Nena replaced her hand on his forearm. "Of course, it's

all right. It's what Tetsu wanted. He left Kenji and me with more than we can ever spend, so please respect his wishes. He wanted you to have it."

"Are you okay with all this Kenji?" Clay asked.

"Uh-huh. Mommy said you were my big brother, so we should all share," Kenji said.

Clay smiled. "Thanks. You and Mommy are so nice. And so was our daddy."

"I want him to come back," Kenji said, putting his forearms across his face. The act of strength he had been putting on since the death of his father, probably for his mother's sake, suddenly snapped. He cried out loud.

"Me too, Kenji," Clay mumbled. "I wish he would come back too."

Nena wiped fresh tears from her eyes with her handkerchief. "Kenji, we promised each other we wouldn't cry in front of people."

Seki clapped his hands once. "I'm sorry, but I have another appointment soon, so, if you have no more questions, let's call this meeting to an end. One of my associates will be in touch with both of you regarding the dispersal of the funds and all the vital documents." He stood up and shook Nena's hand, followed by Clay's, and he lifted Kenji up and hugged him tight. The lawyer escorted the three millionaires to the front door.

"If you need any assistance with anything, please don't hesitate to call," he said.

The receptionist guided them down the hall and bowed as they walked into the elevator.

Once outside, Clay noticed that the rain had turned into a light drizzle. His black Kamita sedan was parked across the street. "May I take you to wherever it is you're going? Mr. Seki has provided me with a driver for the day."

"No, that won't be necessary. We have our own car here," Nena said, waving her hand to a waiting driver in a beige Presidente down the street.

"Then at least let me see you off," Clay said.

The Kamita luxury sedan pulled to a stop next to them. Clay promptly pulled open the rear door and stepped to the side.

Before getting in, Nena turned to Clay. "I want you to know, despite all that you've had to go through, that my husband was a good man. He had a great heart, and he wanted only to do good."

"Yes, I know," Clay said. "Hey Kenji, you better promise to come visit me in America, okay?"

Kenji climbed into the rear seats. "Can we play catch?"

"Absolutely. Hey, high five." Clay extended his uninjured arm toward Kenji with his palm out. Kenji looked at it for a moment and then slapped it as hard as he could, a big smile forming on his face.

"Yeah. That-a-boy," Clay said.

"Thank you for everything, Stockton, and please give my regards to Maki," Nena said as she ducked into the car.

"If I see her, I will."

Clay closed the door for her. As the car pulled away from the curb, the rear window lowered, and Kenji stuck his head out.

"Bye, Stockton," he shouted waving his hand.

Clay smiled and waved back. As he watched the car's taillights join a sea of others on the main road, the vehicle splashed its way down the wet pavement. He then limped back to his own car, where he spent the entire commute back to the hospital, and on the ensuing airplane trip back home to Los Angeles, wondering what he was going to do with his newfound fortune. Topping his wish list was a new truck for his dad, a Rolex watch for his mother, the latest flight simulator for himself, and something special for Maki and George.

Chapter 57

Jeremy Simmons showed the letter inviting Automobile Digest to cover the annual running of the Dakar Rally to Peter Lee, who sat in one of the Barcelona chairs on the other side of the desk.

"What do you think, Peter?" he asked.

The Dakar Rally was one of the most grueling and dangerous off-road races in the world. Formerly known as the Paris-to-Dakar Rally, a six-thousand-mile contest that ran through a dozen countries and the heart of the Sahara Desert, it was known throughout the world as the ultimate test of man and machine. The venue moved temporarily to South America because of political unrest in northwest Africa, but it recently returned to its original home two years prior.

"No thanks," Lee replied. "It's a bit too extreme for me. Don't they camp out in tents for like three weeks?"

Simmons nodded. "Yeah, a bit too intense for me too. I always say, eating at a local fast-food joint is as adventurous as I'm willing to get..."

Lee laughed out loud, making an odd snorting sound. "Good one, Jeremy."

Simmons tossed the invitation in the wastebasket. "So what else is on your mind, Peter?"

Lee leaned on the armrest of his chair. "Has there been any word on Stockton yet? He still hasn't come by and cleaned his office out, and it's been two months already."

"I've had Lorraine call his cell phone every day, but she says he doesn't pick up. It's like he dropped off the face of the earth. If he doesn't come and get his stuff by the end of the day, I'll have someone in HR get it out for him."

"Thank you," Lee said. "Now if you'll excuse me, I have to finish my story on the new Ferrari. I hope you like it."

Simmons gave him a wink. "I'm sure I will. Good ol' Peter."

As Lee stepped out of the office, the inter-office phone on Simmons' desk flashed. He looked down at the caller ID, and it showed "Robert Kelly," the publisher and editorial director of Automobile Digest. He pressed the answer button.

"Simmons here. What can I do for you, boss?"

"I have a major announcement to make. Get your entire staff, and I mean everyone, and have them assemble in the conference room. I'm calling all heads of departments," Kelly said excitedly.

"Now?"

"Yes, now." Kelly hung up.

Simmons put his elbow on his desk and rubbed his clean-shaven face. He didn't know what to make of the impromptu meeting. He hoped he wasn't going to get chewed out again; the big boss had constantly been on Simmons' case to increase the views of the Automobile Digest website because they were falling behind their competitors. "The owners are not happy, Jeremy. They want to sell our publication, which would be good for us, but they're having a hard time finding bidders," Kelly reminded him almost on a daily basis.

Simmons got up from his leather chair and stepped out of his office to where his secretary, Lorraine, typed away on her computer.

"Can you please call everyone who's in today and have them meet in the conference room immediately? It seems our esteemed publisher has a big announcement."

Lorraine put her pen in her mouth and bit down. "Maybe I should start putting my resume together."

"Yeah, wouldn't hurt," Simmons said. He then made his way down the hall to the conference room.

The conference room of the Automobile Digest offices also served as the company's main library. In the middle of the room was a large mahogany table with a dozen chairs placed around it. The walls were lined with bookshelves filled with nearly every important automotive book ever published. Simmons walked into the empty room and took his customary seat at the front of the table.

Within five minutes, every chair at the table was taken and a dozen late-arriving staffers stood against the bookshelves. The air rustled with hushed conversation, as Simmons could hear the gathered crowd conjecturing on what was about to go down. Some warned that half the staff was going to be laid off, while others predicted that the Automobile Digest headquarters were moving out of state. The room went instantly quiet when a chubby man with white wavy hair, dressed in a loose dark brown suit, walked in. Robert Kelly looked like a cartoon character, standing only five-feet-five with puffy cheeks that were pink from either too much sun or too much drink, and wearing gold-rimmed glasses.

Kelly leaned over to Simmons. "Is everyone here?"

Simmons nodded. "Yeah, I think so."

Kelly faced the crowd and spoke loudly. "I've asked you all here today because I have a major announcement. As most of you know, Automobile Digest has been for sale for some time now, but our owners, Consumer Publishing Corporation, never received a good offer. That is until yesterday. At ten o'clock this morning, Consumer Publishing finalized a deal to sell Automobile Digest to a private individual who I am confident will right our ship and take us where we need to go. He has expressed that he will do whatever necessary to keep this publication alive and flourishing for a long time to come."

The employees looked at each other with surprise. Many smiled, relieved their jobs were safe, at least for now.

Simmons raised his hand. "And who may I ask is this pious savior?" he asked.

Kelly pointed to the back of the room to a man leaning against the edge of a bookshelf in the far corner. No one had noticed him enter through the back door during Kelly's speech. He was dressed in a navy Armani sports jacket over a faded gray Space Invaders T-shirt and slim-cut jeans. His hair was slicked back and he wore a two-day-old beard.

Craig, the mail boy, raised the bill of his Nike golf cap and squinted, trying to get a better look at the man's face. "Stockton?"

Simmons' eyes opened wide when he saw that it was indeed Stockton Clay.

"Hey, he doesn't belong here. I fired…"

Kelly cut him off. "Be quiet, Jeremy."

"But he…" Simmons' words drifted off.

Kelly turned his attention back to Clay. "Would you like to say a few words, Stockton?"

The room went silent as all eyes were fixed on Clay, who walked slowly to the front of the room. He stood tall and faced the crowd.

"Hi. It's good to see you all again," he said.

No one said a word.

"Um, let's see. Where do I start? I've had a really amazing past couple of months. There were lots of revelations about my life, and the whole experience was pretty spiritual. I discovered that I had a rather wealthy father, who recently passed away and left me a sizeable amount of money. This wasn't money I actually earned, so I struggled to decide what to do with it. What I didn't want to do was waste it away by spending it carelessly, you know, like partying every day without any goal in life, as tempting as that sounded."

A few people in the back laughed.

Clay continued. "So I decided to invest some of this money towards what I believe in, and I believe in this magazine. I still think it has the potential to be the best automotive publication in the country. We have the talent here to make that happen, so I want you to join me on this journey to recovery."

Simmons shifted in his seat and rubbed his temple. Then he looked over at Lee, who watched Clay speak with wide eyes. Simmons liked Lee, and he didn't regret giving him preferential treatment—the kid certainly earned that privilege through the various gifts, including dozens of bottles of expensive wine, provided by his generous father—but now that Simmons' own job was on the line, he decided that it would be best if he distanced himself away from good ol' Peter. He heard someone begin to clap, and the entire room soon followed suit.

"What should we call you now? Is it *Mr. Clay*?" Craig asked.

Clay smiled. "Don't you dare. Stockton is fine. But I must say that I will be getting together with Mr. Kelly next week to discuss strategy, but let me assure you that everyone's jobs are safe. Thank you, and I look forward to working with you."

Kelly turned to Clay and shook his hand. "Call me Bob." He then turned to his audience. "Now everyone back to work."

Simmons was the first to stand up and greet Clay, being that he was the closest. "It's good to see you, Stockton."

Lee quickly approached them and stood next to Clay. "Yes. I'm so glad to see you are well. I love your vision for the future," he said.

Clay shot both of them a hard look. "You're really glad to see me? I don't know if I believe that."

"No really," Lee said.

"Although I said everyone is staying on, I do plan to shuffle duties around, so please be prepared to present your cases if you would like to stay in your current positions."

Simmons was about to reply when the Automobile Digest staffers crowded around the new owner. Craig stepped up front and center, with his puffy cheeks rosy with excitement and wearing a big smile on his face. He was dressed in his usual polo shirt and Bermuda shorts. "Dude, what the hell man?"

Clay put his hand on Craig's shoulder. "It's a long story. I'll tell you about it over a beer."

Tiffany Velazquez forced her way to the front, pushing Craig and Lee out of her way. She fixed her dress and touched the end of her long brown hair. "Hi Stockton. I hardly recognized you. You look great, I mean really great. I'm looking forward to working *very* closely with you."

Clay laughed, as he didn't know how exactly to respond to her. He was saved by a light vibration in his pocket. "Gimme a second," he said to the others as he took out his smart phone.

Simmons grabbed Clay's arm. "Listen, Stockton, I think we should talk. There are a few things we need to discuss."

Clay peeled Simmons' hand off as he looked down at the phone screen. "Yes, we'll talk, but not now. I have to leave immediately."

Simmons didn't like being treated as an afterthought by a man who was more than fifteen years his junior, but he had little choice, but to go along. "Please call me when you can," he said.

Clay turned to the others. "I'll be speaking to you all very soon, so keep up the good work," he said as he gently pushed his way through the small crowd and made a beeline for the stairwell.

Simmons followed the crowd to the front window that overlooked the main street in front of the office building.

Parked along the sidewalk was a white Kamita Presidente. A young man with wavy hair, wearing a white T-shirt, black jeans, and designer sunglasses, stood beside it.

As the small crowd waited for Clay to appear outside, Ray Hymson, the senior editor of the magazine, put his hands against the glass and shouted, "Hey, that's Marco Senna."

Simmons looked closely, and it was indeed Marco Senna, the winner of the first two Grand Prix races of the season in the new Kamita Formula One racecar and the son of the late, great Ayrton Senna.

Then, it was Craig's turn to shout when a stunning Asian woman, dressed in a tight knee-length blue dress and matching high heels, stepped out of the back of the car. She smiled as she saw Clay come out of the building.

"What the hell is going on?" Craig said.

Chapter 58

Clay greeted Maki with a big smile as he approached the Presidente. She looked as radiant as ever, with her black hair blowing across her face and ruby red lips pressed into a hypnotizing smile. It wasn't until he reached the car when he realized who her chauffer was.

"Marco Senna, what the hell are you doing here?" Clay asked the young man standing next to the car.

"Ms. Takano said she needed a driver, so I volunteered. I'm in town for testing, and I have the day off," Senna said.

"Wow, that's great. By the way, congratulations on your win last week. What an amazing drive, and in all that rain."

Marco tilted his head.

Clay then turned his attention back to Maki, who wrapped her arms around his neck and squeezed.

"I've been looking so forward to seeing you," she said softly into his ear.

"Me too. But I thought you said you were coming next week."

Maki stepped into the rear seat of the car. "I wanted to surprise you, so I moved our lunch date up. Is there a problem?"

"No problem at all." Clay looked up and noticed his workmates staring down at him from the second-story window of the office building. He gave them a quick wave and slid into the car next to Maki.

Marco shut the door for them and jumped into the driver's seat.

As Marco drove away from the curb, Clay leaned close to Maki. "You know that you just hired the world's most expensive chauffer."

"The perks of being a Kamita employee. Today is my last day," she said.

Clay asked in a soft voice: "By the way, does he know about, you know?"

"No, not yet. Do you think we should tell him?"

Clay shook his head. "Nah, why turn his life upside down. Let him live as Marco Senna. He doesn't need all that baggage…hell, no one does. And the blonde hair's a nice touch."

"I agree," Maki said as she slid her arm under Clay's.

Clay's heart raced. Her skin felt milky smooth and cool on his. He struggled to decide what to do next. He didn't want to be too aggressive, yet at the same time, he didn't want to miss an opportunity. "It's a really nice day for a…"

Maki cut him off with a hard kiss to his lips. Clay's entire body froze. When she pulled her face away slowly, he sat there with his eyes wide open and lips still puckered.

"That was the single most unbelievable thing ever," he said.

"For me too, Stockton."

Clay's face turned beet red. He thought he felt a nose bleed coming on, but for different reasons than before.

"So, where are we going to lunch?" he asked.

Maki giggled. "Maui."

There was a brief pause. "Maui, like in Hawaii, Maui?"

"Do you know of any other?"

"You mean right now? You and me? To Hawaii?"

"Is there a problem?"

Clay shook his head. "No, no problem at all."

Maki squeezed his arm tighter. "Step on it Marco, we don't want to be late for our flight."

"Yes ma'am," Marco said as he pressed his foot down on the accelerator.

Clay held Maki close and kissed the top of her head. He looked out the side window and saw the blue ocean in the distance. He finally felt like he found his place in this world; it was a warm feeling that could only be realized by a sense of belonging. It was good to be home, he thought. It was good to finally be home.

Epilogue

Matt Crawford was enjoying what would probably be his last night as the owner of the Yankee Bar. He had asked a real estate agent to list the property for sale earlier that day. He poured himself a small glass of Suntory Scotch whiskey while sitting behind the counter. Three men in military uniforms—two African Americans and one Latino—sat across from him knocking back bottles of beer and ribbing each other with off-color language.

"Man, I tell ya, I can't wait to get back home next week. I haven't seen my wife in seven months," the bigger of the two African American men said. He wore a brown leather jacket with a Petty Officer Second Class patch on the sleeve.

The Latino man, who was much smaller with cropped brown hair, wearing a similar jacket with the same patch, waved him off. "Damn, you're lucky, McIvy. I'm stuck here through the holidays."

"Hey, I did my turn on the last Trans-Pac tour, Rodriguez. And besides, I was promoted three months before you," Chris McIvy retorted.

Crawford slid another glass of whiskey in front of the other African American man seated at the edge. "That one's on me, Kenny."

Senior Chief Petty Officer Kenny Jones, who looked to be in his late twenties, but was in fact in his early forties, smiled and raised the glass before knocking it back in one gulp. He let out a satisfying "Ahhh."

McIvy protested. "Hey Matt, where's ours?"

"Yeah," added Stuart Rodriguez.

"You need to earn those, marines," Crawford said.

Jones slapped his open hand on the bar counter. "Damn right. Me and Matt were in Iraq together when you boys were barely born."

Crawford raised his glass of whiskey in the air. "Here's to the United States Marines, and the United States of America. Semper Fidelis."

The three servicemen raised their respective glasses in unison. "Here here," they said before downing their drinks.

A light snow fell from the night sky outside, as the four men swapped stories about war and their personal lives for three hours until Jones checked his watch and got up. "Matt, we need to move out. Last train back to Yokohama is leaving soon. Give me the check, will ya?"

Crawford walked over to the register, touched a few icons on the tablet screen and presented Jones with the bill. "Guys, I'm shutting the bar down," he said.

"What? Why?" McIvy asked. "I love this place."

"Yeah, me too," Rodriguez said. "I look forward to drinking here every time I pass by."

"What's wrong, Matt?" Jones asked as he placed a small stack of one-thousand-yen notes on the counter.

Crawford picked up the cash. "It's getting harder to make ends meet, and with Rebecca going into high school next year, I really need to think about her future, you know, how to pay for her college and all. The monthly check from Uncle Sam just isn't enough."

"What will you do?" Jones asked.

"Probably go back home to Nebraska and live with my parents. Rebecca doesn't want to leave, and neither do I, but we got no choice. I'll help out with my uncle's construction business or something."

Jones shook Crawford's hand and pulled him in for a hug. "I got your back wherever you end up. You know that, man."

"Yeah, I know. Thanks for coming in guys."

Crawford silently watched the three active-duty service men head out the door. He gave them a quick salute, before collecting the empty beer bottles off the bar counter. As he wiped down the countertop, he recalled the first time he and his wife, who was still pregnant with their only child, stepped into the place. It was originally an office building, and they spent most of their savings converting it into their dream bar. Although the business barely made enough to meet the mortgage payments, it was home—the only home his daughter knew. It served as their fortress during the long months of his wife's illness, and he couldn't help but feel that he would be letting a part of her go by moving out of the place.

His thoughts were interrupted by the creaking sound of the front door opening.

"We're closed, sorry," he said as he looked up and noticed that the customer was a middle-aged Japanese man, dressed in an expensive-looking overcoat and wearing a felt fedora hat sprinkled with snow. "*Sumimasen, mou omise wa shimattemasu,*" Crawford said with a thick Western accent.

The Japanese man took off his hat and dusted the snow off his coat, revealing his neatly cropped black-and-pepper hair and shiny wool suit. He sat down on a corner stool. "My name is Kunio Seki. May I have one drink, please," he said in perfect English.

Crawford scratched his head. "Okay, sure, one drink, but I really need to close up. What will it be?"

"A Jim Beam whiskey."

Crawford poured a serving of Jim Beam into a small shot glass and placed it in front of Seki. "Here you go."

"Thank you. Here is payment for the drink," Seki said as he reached into his coat and pulled out a blank white envelope, which he placed on the counter.

"What the hell is this?" Crawford asked.

"Please open it."

Crawford picked it up and tore one side of it open. He pulled out a white piece of paper, and in the process, another piece of paper fell out and dropped onto the counter top. His eyes grew wide when he saw that it was a cashier's check, made out to him for one million U.S. dollars.

"What the hell is this, some kind of joke?"

"No joke. Please read the letter," Seki said.

Crawford unfolded the white piece of paper and read its hand-written contents:

Matt,

How are you? Do you remember me? It's Stockton Clay, the guy who crashed at your pad several months ago. I never paid for my drinks or for my unintended one-night stay, and I promised you that I would. Here is my payment. It may seem like a little much, but if it weren't for you, I would not be where I am today. Please accept this as a token of my ap-

preciation. Knowing you, you probably wouldn't accept it, so I made it a cashier's check and thought it better if someone else handed it to you. He is a lawyer who I've asked to help me handle some of my affairs in Japan. If you don't want to cash the check, that's up to you, but as you know with cashier's checks, the money has already been drawn out of my account, so ripping it up would be like throwing away a million dollars. So please don't do that. And tell your daughter I said hello. If I am back in Japan, I will pay you a visit, but let's go a bit easier on the whiskey next time.

Your good friend,

Stockton Clay

Crawford stared at the piece of paper, his mouth open.

"Is this for real?" he asked.

Seki stood up and placed his hat on top of his head. "I was hired to simply deliver the envelope. Good night, Mr. Crawford." He stood up and walked out of the Yankee Bar as quickly and mysteriously as he had come in.

Crawford put down the letter and stared at the check. He grabbed the whiskey that Seki had left untouched and raised it in the air. "Here's to you, Stockton. Cheers," he said, raising the glass in the air. He swigged the fire water down and wiped his mouth with his forearm. It was the tastiest shot of whiskey he had ever had.

* * * *

From across the way, Stockton Clay, dressed in a Burberry overcoat and scarf, watched Kunio Seki exit the bar.

The street was dark, lit only by a dim light that hung from a nearby telephone pole that illuminated the swirling snow falling from the sky.

Seki gave a curt nod to Clay, touching the brim of his hat, before heading towards the train station. Clay answered the gesture with a nod and turned his attention back to the Yankee Bar. Through the large front window, he watched as Crawford raised his glass of whiskey in the air as if he were making a toast with a make-believe friend.

Clay smiled, pulled up the collar of his coat, and walked to a waiting car down the street, leaving behind his footprints in the fresh fallen snow.

Acknowledgements

It was almost surreal on how certain events came together when I was working on this book, from the pilot who happened to sit next to me on a commercial flight just as I was researching how to land a plane (I grilled him for three hours) to my good friend Ben Hsu, formerly of the National Human Genome Research Institute, who turned me onto the amazing potential of nanotechnology.

My deep appreciation also goes to Jim Hall, my reliable proofreader, and Michael Gin, my friend and business manager. Of course, I can't forget to thank my family, which gave me the time and freedom to spend many hours at home pounding away on my computer keyboard, and my former boss at *Road & Track,* Thos L. Bryant, who patiently-yet-sternly helped craft my writing skills from the day I graduated college.

There are many others who have helped me directly and indirectly over the years, and without their support and guidance, my journey to this point would not have been possible.

Author Bio

As the first Asian-American writer at one of the Big Three American automotive publications (*Car and Driver, Motor Trend, Road & Track*), Sam Mitani faced plenty of scrutiny and challenges as he established himself as one of the foremost American authorities on Japanese cars. In addition to being the International Editor of *Road & Track* in its heyday, he has been published in magazines in Singapore, Malaysia, Hong Kong and Japan, and in his spare time, authored a couple of travel books on Southeast Asia.

Satisfied with his accomplishments in the magazine industry, which paved the way for Asian-American automotive writers, Mitani has since taken on a new challenge: breaking into the highly-restricted fiction market. His expertise in martial arts and numerous adventures around the world—including participating in the treacherous Dakar Rally and setting a speed record at the Bonneville Salt Flats going 204 mph—have provided him with a rich source of experiences to tap for his creative writing projects.